Praise for the *Out of Uniform* series

"I'm so glad I discovered this series."
— Mandi Schreiner, *USA TODAY*

"I love this erotic series by Elle Kennedy. Featuring Navy SEAL heroes and the women who tame them ..."
— *Smexy Books*

"...a delight to read...funny yet natural. I think Elle Kennedy books should have a tagline that says something like 'She gives good dialogue'."
— *Dear Author*

"Each story I pick up by Kennedy has me falling further and further in love with her writing. She has quickly become one of my favorite go-to authors for a sexy good time!"
— *Book Pushers*

"You can always count on Elle Kennedy to bring the sexy times. There are plenty of steamy scenes and the romantic build up starts early on and just keeps on building."
— *Fiction Vixen*

Also available from Elle Kennedy

Out of Uniform
Hot & Bothered
Hot & Heavy

Off-Campus
The Deal
The Mistake
The Score
The Goal

Outlaws
Claimed
Addicted
Ruled

***

A full list of Elle's print titles is available on her website
www.ellekennedy.com

Hot & Heavy

Out of Uniform

Elle Kennedy

Copyright

Author's Note

I am SO excited to be re-releasing the *Out of Uniform* series! For those of you who haven't read it before, this was one of my earlier series, and it also happens to be one of my favorites, probably because this is when I realized how much I love writing bromances!

Seriously. The boy banter in these books still cracks me up to this day. You see more and more of it as the series progresses, and by the later books there are entire chapters of crazy conversations between my sexy, silly SEALs.

For new readers, you should know that a) you don't have to read the stories in order, though characters from previous books do show up in every installment. And b) the first six stories are novellas (20-35,000 words), while the last four are full-length novels (80,000+ words).

I decided to release the novellas as two books featuring three stories each (*Hot & Bothered, Hot & Heavy*) making the total books in the series SIX rather than the original ten.

***IMPORTANT: These books have NOT changed, except for some minor editing and proofreading. There are grammatical differences and some (minor) deleted/added lines here and there, but for the most part, there is *no new content*. If you've previously purchased and read *Heat It Up, Heat of the Night* and *The Heat is On*, then you won't be getting anything new with *Hot & Heavy*, aside from a gorgeous new cover!

So, I hope you enjoy the new cover, the better grammar, and the hot, dirty-talking SEALs who to this day hold such a big place in my heart!

Love,

Elle

Heat It Up

An Out of Uniform Novella

Elle Kennedy

Prologue

IT WAS HOT AS HELL. THE TEMPERATURE WAS ALREADY IN THE 90S AND steadily rising. Sweat stained the front of Thomas Becker's camo T-shirt. Not even the gust of air hitting the chopper could cool him down, and the other men inside seemed to be experiencing the same discomfort.

"I hate South America," Carson Scott remarked, raising his voice to be heard over the sound of wind and rotors.

"It'll get cooler when we're in the jungle," John Garrett said with a shrug, wiping beads of sweat from his forehead with the back of his hand.

Carson sighed. "I hate the jungle, too. Monkeys freak me out."

Next to him, Ryan Evans, the youngest and rowdiest member of the team, hooted. "Does Holly know what a wimp you are?"

"Nah, I bet he tells her a bunch of stories when he gets home," Matt O'Connor chimed in. "Painting himself as the hero in each one."

"Oh, I'm definitely Holly's hero," Carson shot back, wiggling his eyebrows. "She's always the damsel in distress when we role-play. Except for that one time when I got to be the weary, injured traveler and she was the virgin nurse who tenderly nurtured me back to health."

The men in the chopper laughed. Becker cracked a smile, but it didn't quite reach his eyes. Not that he didn't like the other guys or find them entertaining, but the four of them had worked together for years. He was the new guy. Well, technically, he was their new superior. As the senior lieutenant, he now headed up this SEAL platoon, but for the past five years, he'd led a team out on the east coast.

He'd moved to California six months ago, after his wife — now *ex-wife* — landed a modeling campaign that required she relocate to the west coast. Alice's career was everything to her, and like a good husband, he wanted to support his wife. Two months later, he was signing divorce papers. Rather than go back east, he'd decided to stick around for a while.

He'd been assigned to Team Fifteen, whose members were legendary around the base. Not just for their impressive mission success records, but for their success with the ladies. Players, other SEALs called them.

Garrett was married now, and Carson had been in a long-term relationship for a couple years, but the others, especially Ryan and Matt, apparently kept the reputation alive by prowling the club scene and hooking up with warm, willing females.

Becker didn't get the lifestyle. He was only thirty-two, but he'd been in a committed relationship since he was eighteen years old. Sure, that relationship had died a fiery death four months ago, but even now, divorced and single, he couldn't picture himself doing the casual sex thing.

Lately, he hardly thought about sex at all. He much preferred going out on missions, even in scorching-hot parts of the world like Colombia. At least when he was stealing through the jungle he didn't have to be reminded of Alice.

Looking down at the map in his hands, he studied the area they were going to be dropped at. It was at least half a day's hike from their target, but they couldn't land any closer to the rebel camp without alerting the enemy.

"That's where she's being held?" Matt said, leaning in closer for a better look.

Becker nodded, then pointed to a ridge on the map. "I say we separate there. Split up, approach from two directions."

The other men offered their opinions, but it didn't take long to formulate an extraction plan. Elizabeth Harrison had been a hostage of the rebels for three days now, and during that time the SEALs were able to get satellite images of the camp, detailed notes about the terrain, as well as the locations of the twenty or so armed guards.

Becker wondered how Elizabeth was holding up. It had been seriously shitty luck on her part, being captured during an assignment in the neighboring village. She was a photographer in the wrong place at the wrong time, but she was lucky that the government gave a damn about her. A lot of people up on the chain of command were anxious to see the American journalist brought to safety.

Which put a lot of pressure on Becker and his team to make sure they got her out safe and sound. Fortunately, Becker was damn good at his job.

As he rolled up the map and tucked it in the pocket of his camo pants, he gave each man on the chopper a stern look that had them squirming in their seats.

Then he clapped his hands together and said, "All right, boys. Elizabeth Harrison needs rescuing. Let's not keep her waiting."

Chapter One

JANE HARRISON LINGERED IN THE DOORWAY, UNABLE TO TAKE HER EYES off the man across the large workout room. As far as faces went, his was nothing extraordinary. No Brad Pitt or anything. Average features, eyes an unremarkable shade of brown, a dark buzz cut. Handsome, sure, but nobody who would make you freeze in the middle of a busy street with your tongue hanging out.

Yet, that's exactly what she was doing, wasn't it? Half-drooling as she stared at him. It was the body. She'd never seen anyone so ripped, so masculine. He was about six feet or so, with broad shoulders, a chest that looked rock-hard, and a trim waist that led to a taut backside.

He wore a light blue T-shirt, and his biceps flexed and bulged each time he lifted one of the weights in his hands. A tall, brown-haired woman stood next to him, frowning, and even from across the room, Jane heard the woman tell him to take it easy. But this wasn't the kind of man who took anything easy. Intensity rolled off him in waves.

She'd planned on approaching him here, in the brightly lit gym at the physical therapy center, but she hesitated by the door. Liz hadn't mentioned how commanding this man was. Or what a great body he had. Then again, Liz was probably too busy getting shot at to notice what her rescuer looked like.

Jane watched as the therapist finally took the weights from Thomas Becker and set them down on the rack. The brunette looked annoyed. Probably because her patient seemed determined to push his physical limits when four weeks ago he'd taken a bullet to the arm.

"See you on Friday," the physical therapist said.

Thomas Becker just nodded, then headed for the door.

As he got closer, Jane drew in her breath. Okay, she had to quit focusing on his body and remember why she'd come here. This man had saved her sister's life. She was here to interview him, not fuck him.

"Mr. Becker?" she said when he reached the door.

He glanced at her, forehead wrinkling. "Who's asking?"

"My name is Jane Harrison. You were in charge of the rescue mission for—"

"Elizabeth," he finished. "She okay?"

"She's great. Thanks to you and your team." His serious expression unnerved her. He hadn't even smiled in greeting. "Liz is my sister."

"Oh. Okay."

Jane faltered for a moment, not sure what to say next. It was obvious Thomas Becker didn't have much interest in talking to her—his brown-eyed gaze kept darting toward the elevator at the end of the hall.

"Do you have a moment?" she asked.

"Not really," he admitted. "I have an appointment in twenty minutes."

"I'll walk out with you, then." She took a step down the corridor, and he followed her, his strides a million times longer than hers.

He didn't do the gentlemanly thing and try to match her gait, just barreled down the hall, while she struggled to keep up in her three-inch heels. She still wore the short black business suit and heels she'd donned for her morning meeting with her editor at *Today's World*, the magazine she worked for, and the outfit hadn't been designed for chasing after a very tall, very hot Navy SEAL.

"So, I came here to ask you a favor," she said as she hurried after him.

"Yeah, what's that?"

They reached the elevator, which triggered a spark of panic in her gut. She usually avoided elevators like the plague, but she wasn't about to ask this man to go down ten flights of stairs after he'd gotten shot rescuing her sister. As he reached to punch the *down* button, she noticed how large his hands were. He had long fingers, oddly graceful considering the size of his hands, but covered with just enough calluses to give him that manly, rough edge.

"I'm a journalist, and I'd like to write a story about my sister's rescue. Since you were in charge of the operation in Colombia, I was hoping to interview you."

Thomas Becker studied her for a long moment, his gaze sweeping up and down, side to side. She felt it the second those brown eyes rested on the cleavage spilling out of the camisole under her suit jacket, because her nipples tightened and poked against her bra. She could tell he was assessing her. Not in a sexual way, since his eyes remained expressionless, but like he was figuring out whether to take her seriously or not.

Evidently he decided *not* was the answer to his internal question, because he offered a brusque shake of the head and said, "Sorry, not interested." The elevator doors opened, punctuating his stiff response.

Without glancing back, he stepped into the car.

Jane stood frozen in place for a moment. Insulted. A tad pissed. Then she bounded into the elevator after him, hoping he couldn't see the hot flush on her cheeks. Why was this guy so rude? Liz had said he'd been extremely warm and gentle as he'd lifted her into the helicopter. So either Liz was wrong and Becker was an asshole or, as usual, Jane's Playboy Bunny body had caused yet another man to reach an unfair conclusion about her.

Sometimes she hated the way she looked. And to this day, she still wondered if her mom had engaged in a torrid affair with some Irish stud in order to produce a daughter like Jane Harrison. Because really, how else could she explain how different she looked compared to everyone else in her family?

Her parents, sister, and younger brother were skinny as twigs, with sandy-blond hair and dark brown eyes.

Jane, on the other hand, had a head of shocking red hair that nobody ever believed was natural, blue eyes that were far too big for her face, and a centerfold body. Her sister was willowy and graceful, a few inches short of six feet, like everyone else in the family. Jane? She was a paltry five-six, with huge boobs, a small waist, and curvy frame—all guaranteed to make sure most people lumped her in the airhead, sex kitten category without a second's thought.

Well, she was no airhead. A bit of a wild child, sure. Definitely at one with her sexuality. But stupid? Nope. And she was a damn good journalist, with a big brain in her head to match those big breasts.

Setting her jaw, she fixed Thomas Becker with a steely look and said, "Why not?"

He blinked, looking startled that she was in the elevator with him. "Huh?"

"Why aren't you interested in doing the interview?" She crossed her arms. "I can assure you, *Today's World* is a very prestigious magazine, and I'm very good at what I do. I could paint you as an All-American hero, a regular GI Joe."

The corners of his mouth twitched. "It sounds very tempting, Ms. Harrison—"

"Jane," she cut in.

"Jane," he amended. "But I'm still not interested in having an article written about me."

"It won't be just about you. Look, Mr. Becker—"

"Just Becker, or Beck."

"Okay, *Becker*. It'll revolve around Elizabeth and her experience. I'd just like some quotes from you about the rescue itself, how you planned it, the strategy, maybe a picture."

His features hardened. "No."

Frustration bubbled in her stomach. "Will you at least give me a reason why you're so determined not to do it?"

He glanced at the flashing numbers over the doors, his stiff shoulders telling her he couldn't wait to get out of this elevator. Wonderful. Now he was dying to get away from her.

Glancing at her again, he released a sigh. "I don't like being in the spotlight, okay? And I definitely don't like having my picture flashed around." He rolled his eyes. "For someone who considers herself a good journalist, I'd think you'd understand why that is."

She bristled. "Why a man who saved a woman's life doesn't want some good old praise? No, I don't understand."

"I'm a SEAL. My job requires keeping a low profile, getting in and out of places before people even realize I'm there. How well do you think I'd do if everyone knew my face?"

Jane paused. Fine. So he made a good point. "Okay," she said thoughtfully. "I get that. But there are ways around it, you know. We don't have to print a picture, and we can change your name in the article. What's your next argument?"

A flash of amusement filled his eyes. "Has anyone ever told you you're very persistent?"

"Yep. Goes with my line of work."

The elevator slowly ground to a stop. Jane glanced up and noticed they hadn't reached the lobby, but had stopped on the third floor. She waited for the doors to open to let in a passenger, but nothing happened.

Wrinkling her forehead, she glanced at Becker. "Why did we stop?"

"I have no idea." He moved toward the panel and punched in the lobby button again.

A shrill ringing suddenly blared in the elevator, startling her so badly she nearly fell over backwards. "What the hell?" she shouted over the noise.

Becker studied the panel then jammed his finger against the intercom button. The ringing died immediately, replaced by the sound of static. Becker leaned into the speaker. "Hello, anyone there?"

A moment later, a voice responded. "Hi there, folks, what seems to be the problem?"

"The elevator stopped on the third floor. It might be stuck."

"All right, just stay put. Let me see what the trouble is."

"Stay put?" Jane echoed as the static crackled and disappeared. "Where the hell else would we go?" Her suit jacket suddenly felt way too tight, her skin super hot.

Becker shrugged. "He's probably scared we'll try to climb out the ceiling panel and rappel down the cables."

His attempt at humor fell flat, mostly because Jane was barely listening to him. She glanced wildly around the car, measuring it in her mind. Five by five, she guessed. Maybe a couple of feet more. Oh God.

"You okay?"

Her head jerked up. "What? Yeah. Sure. I'm great. I'm wonderful." Her eyes ping-ponged around the tiny space. "Why isn't he answering us?" she burst out.

Becker came to her side, concern in his eyes. "Hey. *Hey.*" He touched her arm. "Don't worry, okay? I'm sure they'll have it up and running in a few minutes. Fifteen, max."

Sweat bloomed on her forehead. "Fifteen minutes? We can't survive in this teeny little box for that long! What if we run out of air? What if—" She quit talking, her heart pounding so fast she feared it might stop.

"I take it you're not good with small spaces," Becker said with a sigh.

She sucked in some oxygen. "It's a problem," she admitted.

"How the hell did you get to the eleventh floor, then? You didn't ride the elevator up?"

She shook her head, pressing her hands to her sides because they were beginning to sweat. And shake. "I took the stairs."

"You climbed *ten* flights of stairs to—"

He was interrupted by the sound of static. Jane's entire body flooded with relief as a voice filled the car.

"Folks, you still there?"

"Oh, for fuck's sake, where else would we go?" she muttered.

Looking like he was smothering a smile, Becker moved back to the intercom. "Still here."

"It seems we're experiencing some technical difficulties," the man said apologetically. "The repairman is on his way over to take a look."

Jane's heart took off like a terrified horse in a thunderstorm. *Oh shit.*

"Shouldn't take too long to get you folks out of there," the man—no, the *devil*—added. "Half hour, hour tops."

Jane promptly dropped to the ground and stuck her head between her knees. She sucked in shallow breaths, knowing she was making a fool of herself, but unable to stop the fear spiraling inside her.

"Okay, thanks. Keep us updated, please," Becker said into the intercom. Then he was by her side, on his knees beside her. "Jane. Jane, look at me."

Miserably, she raised her head, ashamed of the tears prickling her eyelids.

"Just breathe, okay? Breathe with me."

She opened her mouth, but when she tried to inhale, her throat tightened. "There's no air," she wheezed. "No. Air."

She grew light-headed, her cheeks so hot she knew they must look like two enormous apples. And her heart...oh God, she really was going to have a heart attack. In this miniscule elevator car with no air and walls that were closing in on her and—

A pair of strong arms wrapped around her and suddenly she found herself in Thomas Becker's lap. His hands cupped her scorching cheeks, those brown eyes blazing with intensity. "Jane, *look at me.* You're okay. We're okay. We'll get out of here in no time, all right? And there is plenty of air, so you really need to stop hyperventilating before you pass out."

Pass out? She was more worried about her heart bursting right out of her chest. As panic spiraled through her, she buried her face against Thomas Becker's sturdy chest and started to cry.

Chapter Two

FUCKING WONDERFUL. NOT ONLY WAS HE GOING TO BE LATE FOR HIS appointment with the realtor, but now he had to contend with the panicky, crying sexpot in his arms.

With a sigh, Becker awkwardly patted Jane Harrison's back, attempting to offer reassurance. But all he got in return were a few more muffled sobs and a growing erection.

The hard-on couldn't be helped. The woman in his lap was smoking hot, with high, full tits, shapely legs that were bare beneath that short skirt of hers, and a firm ass that felt pretty damn good against his thighs. And she smelled incredible, like honey and lavender and a flowery perfume that made his groin ache. He couldn't resist pressing his face to the wild mane of red hair spilling down her back and inhaling her sweet shampoo as the soft tresses tickled his nose. Then he forced himself to pull back, because one, it was inappropriate to smell a woman's hair while she was crying in his arms, and two, because he really, *really* didn't need this headache right now.

His shoulder was fucking throbbing, the bullet wound still in its early healing stages, and he knew he'd overdone it in the physical therapy session today. But hell, he needed to get back in fighting shape, and fast. He was going stir crazy in his hotel room, dying to get back to work, and if it meant pushing himself to his physical limits, so be it.

"Jane," he said firmly. "Look at me."

When she didn't lift her head, he did it for her, grasping her chin with both hands and tilting it. He found himself staring into a pair of big blue eyes awash with tears.

"There's plenty of air, okay?" he said in the same calm, reassuring voice he used when dealing with hostages he'd rescued. "We're going to be fine."

She didn't respond. He could see her pulse throbbing in her slender neck, a sign that her panic hadn't diffused, despite his words.

He brushed away her tears with his thumb. "I get you're scared, but there's no reason to be, all right? We could survive in here for days. You won't pass out, you won't have a heart attack, and you won't stop breathing."

She blinked, sending another tear down her unbelievably smooth cheek, which he couldn't resist caressing. "You promise?" she finally murmured.

"I promise."

A flicker of relief filled her gaze. "Do you…would you mind holding me a bit longer?"

Becker suppressed a groan. Did he mind? Hell, yes, because any moment now, she was going to snap out of her panic-induced haze and notice the massive erection pressing against her thigh. But since he wasn't an asshole, he couldn't very well push her out of his arms when she was still so shaken up.

"I don't mind." Damn, his voice came out thick, hoarse.

"Thank you."

They sat there for a few moments in silence, Becker painfully aware of the woman in his arms. She was all curves, a glaring contrast to his ex-wife, who'd been far too thin for his liking. He'd always urged Alice to gain a few pounds, add some curves to her stick-straight figure, but Alice was all about her image. She'd been modeling since she was eighteen years old, the same age Becker had been when he married her. They'd managed to make it work for fourteen years, shocking really, considering their hectic schedules. With Alice working on becoming a supermodel and Becker traveling the world with the Navy, it was a wonder they'd been able to stay married for that long.

Becker resisted a groan. Shit, he really needed to quit thinking about the divorce. It'd been finalized months ago, and yet here he was, constantly obsessing about his ex-wife. Maybe he needed to take a page out of his teammates' books and indulge in some random, no-strings sex.

Actually, scratch that. Sex was definitely something he shouldn't be thinking about either. Not now, anyway.

The woman in his lap shifted, letting out a wobbly breath that broke through the silence. "Okay, this isn't working," she choked out. "Maybe you can try to distract me? Talk to me about something."

Becker fought a wave of discomfort. Wonderful. If there was one thing he sucked at, it was talking. Especially to women.

"Please," she added, obviously seeing the reluctance in his eyes.

"Talk about what?" he asked, caving in.

"Anything. Tell me about the bullet wound in your arm, your favorite movie, your pet peeves. I don't care." Another shaky breath.

"Um, okay." He paused. "Well, bullet wounds fucking hurt."

Her lips quirked, and Becker was startled by the little spark of pleasure he got from knowing he'd made her smile. "What does it feel like? Is it like a knife wound? Because I know what *that* feels like."

"When the hell did you get a knife wound?"

"College. I was a reporter for the school paper and I went to interview this meth addict for a piece I was doing. Only he was super high and thought I was a narc." She offered a small shrug, as if to say *no biggie*.

Despite himself, Becker grinned. "Remember earlier how I said you were persistent? Well, correction — you're nuts."

"It was an important story. Getting knifed added some color to the piece." Her blue eyes twinkled. "So, the bullet…?"

"Right. Well, to be honest, I didn't even feel it at first. Adrenaline running too high, you know. I was too focused on getting your sister into the chop—" He narrowed his eyes. "All this is off the record, right?"

Jane made a face. "Unfortunately. But I still think you should let me interview you."

"Not interested."

"Fine." She gave a little pout, which brought another smile to his lips. "At least finish the story."

"Yes, ma'am. So, like I said, didn't feel a thing at first, not until I climbed into the chopper. Then the pain hit me like a streak of lightning. Arm started throbbing, head spinning from the loss of blood. Felt like someone stuck a live wire straight into my bone."

"Is that the first time you've been shot?"

"First time I've had a bullet in me, yeah. I've been grazed a few times, knifed, slashed by a machete once…" His voice drifted, and he smiled at the horror in her eyes. "Part of the job."

"I could never do it," Jane said frankly. "A job where I'm constantly getting injured? No thank you. I'd way rather interview people in the comfort of their homes."

He shot her a curious glance. "What kind of stories do you write?"

"Whatever I get assigned. Last issue I had a piece about insider trading, the one before that was a story about human trafficking."

"And now you're working on a story about your sister?"

She nodded, then released a long breath. To his relief, this one didn't sound shaky. She was calming down. "I was so worried about her, Becker. When her office called and told us she'd gone off the radar, I thought she was dead." Jane swallowed. "I always tell her not to take such risky assignments, but she never listens."

He arched a brow. "Would you ever turn down a story because someone told you there might be some risk?"

The corner of her mouth curved. "No. I guess it runs in the family, huh? Pigheadedness is probably the only thing I have in common with them."

"You don't get along with your family?"

"No, I do. I love them to death. But sometimes I feel like the odd man out, you know? My mom, Dad, Liz, my brother Ken—they're all so similar. Look alike, think alike. Hell, they all chose the same career. Photographers, all of them!" She shook her head, looking baffled. "Journalism is a related field, I guess, but I know squat about photography. We have dinner together every Wednesday night, and the four of them drone on and on about new techniques they're using or what not, and I just sit there, twiddling my thumbs." She halted suddenly, her cheeks reddening. "Sorry, I don't mean to complain. You're probably bored by my rambling, huh?"

Actually, he was the farthest thing from bored. Becker couldn't remember the last time he'd enjoyed listening to a woman talk. And he knew exactly what Jane was saying. How many times had he sat at the dinner table listening to Alice go on and on about her headshots and runway walk and the latest fashion trends only for her to get all huffy when he had nothing to contribute to the conversation? Too many.

"I don't mind the rambling," he admitted. "I find you interesting."

She smiled again. "Thank you."

Fuck, he liked that. Thank you. Alice had never been able to take compliments, always feigning humbleness while in reality she loved hearing how wonderful she was.

He swept his gaze over Jane's beautiful face, and then, before he could stop himself, lightly ran his hand over her hip.

Her lips parted slightly, a flicker of heat in her eyes.

Becker's hand instantly stilled. Shit, what was he doing? The air between them sizzled, while the heat from her curvy body seared into him and made his pulse race. Okay. Wow. This was the first woman he'd been attracted to since the divorce, and the notion unnerved him.

Clearing his throat, he struggled to snuff out the flame of desire burning in his body. "So, did you always want to be a journalist?"

"Yeah. Ever since I was a kid. I used to write articles about everyone in the neighborhood." She grinned. "I was convinced Mr. Jervais from across the street was up to no good, so I'd spy on him and then write about what I saw."

"What *did* you see?"

"Well, he took out the garbage a lot, so I decided he was getting rid of dismembered body parts. And he spent a lot of time in his garage, which was obviously where he killed his victims."

Becker laughed. "Poor man. I hope you didn't show him any of the stories."

"No, my parents made me shred them. They said even ten-year-olds could be arrested for slander and harassment."

"And ten years later, you're still at it, huh?"

"That would make me twenty. I'm twenty-eight, thank you very much. But I appreciate the compliment. And yes, I'm still at it. I'm going to win a Pulitzer someday, you know."

The flash of ambition he saw in her eyes brought a wave of uneasiness. He'd seen that look far too many times in his ex-wife's eyes.

"And what about a husband and kids? Do you see that in your future too, or just the Pulitzer?" he asked.

She shrugged. "Sure, I want those things, but there's no rush. I want to focus on my career right now, make a name for myself. There'll be time for all the rest."

Becker stifled a snort. *There's no rush. There's time.* Alice had spouted that bull for fourteen years of marriage, before finally dropping the bomb that she *never* planned on starting a family.

A spark of bitterness ignited in his gut, but he forced himself not to reveal his thoughts on the subject to Jane. He seriously needed to stop comparing her to his ex. He didn't even know this woman. He had no right judging her choices and goals. So what if they weren't aligned with his? Wasn't like he was going to marry the girl.

"I do make plenty of time for sex, though," she added with a small grin.

His hard-on returned with full-force, straining against his zipper.

No doubt Jane felt it straining against *her* too, because her eyes widened slightly. "Oh my," she murmured.

Becker rolled his eyes. "That's what happens when you say the word *sex* while you're sitting in a man's lap, sweetheart."

She gave him an impish look. "Do you want me to say it again?"

"Seeing as we're trapped here in this elevator, I can't really stop you from saying anything, can I?"

He instantly knew he'd said the wrong thing, because Jane's blue eyes flickered with terror. She glanced around the small space, as if remembering where they were and why there were there. Her throat worked as she swallowed repeatedly. Beck could practically hear her pulse began to race. Shit. Why on earth had he reminded her they were *trapped* in an elevator?

"Jane—" he started.

"How long has it been?" she cut him off. "Didn't he say a half hour? It feels like ages since—"

"Jane—"

She shifted in his lap, hand fumbling toward her purse. "My phone has the time on it. I need to see—"

"Jane—"

"—how long we've been here. Do you feel hot too or is it just me? And it is getting hard to breathe, because I really can't—"

Becker pressed his lips to hers. He hadn't planned on kissing her, but it was the only way to shut her up, to distract her before she hurled herself headfirst off another panic cliff.

Only, the second his mouth touched hers, he forgot all about why he'd kissed her in the first place. Instead, all he could think about was... well, kissing her. Kissing the holy hell out of her.

So he did.

Chapter Three

JANE LET OUT A STARTLED SQUEAK, WHICH QUICKLY TRANSFORMED INTO a whimper as Becker's tongue slid deftly into her mouth. Oh, sweet Jesus, this man could kiss. You wouldn't think it based on his stiff, serious demeanor, but clearly all the intensity he kept bottled up came pouring out when he kissed.

Her surroundings completely faded as she lost herself in the kiss. His mouth was firm and warm, his tongue lazy as it danced with hers. Jane's entire body went soft, muscles turning to jelly. She ran her fingers over Becker's buzz cut, his short spiky hair tickling her palms. He responded by sliding one hand to her waist, while angling her head with the other in order to deepen the kiss.

She moaned into his mouth, unable to stop herself from rubbing against the bulge in his jeans. An answering moan sounded deep in his throat. His fingers tightened over her hip.

"We should stop," he ground out, breaking the kiss.

"Probably," she agreed with a faint smile.

They stared at each other for a long moment. Becker's brown eyes glimmered with heat. Jane's pulse thudded in her throat.

And then they were kissing again, and the word *stop* was blown away by a gust of mutual attraction.

This was *crazy*. She'd had one-night-stands before, but always with men she'd known for more than twenty minutes, damn it. And never in an *elevator*. Yet Jane couldn't stop the rush of desire swirling through her body. She placed her palms against Becker's rock-hard chest, moaning at the feel of his defined pecs and the thump of his heart under her fingers. His hands were equally busy, unbuttoning her jacket, slipping under the lacy white camisole beneath it. He stroked the bare skin of her belly, then moved his hands north and cupped her breasts.

"Christ," he choked out, squeezing her breasts over her bra. "I could probably come just from fondling these."

She let out a soft laugh. "And I could probably come just by doing *this*." She rubbed herself against his crotch again to illustrate her point.

Becker groaned. "You realize this is a really bad idea, right?"

"Oh, it's a terrible idea." She shrugged out of her jacket and peeled the camisole off her chest.

Becker sucked in a breath, those intense dark eyes narrowing at the sight of her lacy black bra. Slowly, he took off his own shirt. His chest was absolutely spectacular, broad and rippled, with a dusting of brown hair leading down to his waistband. The tender spot between her legs began to throb, making her move restlessly against him.

"Are you turned on, Jane?" he asked hoarsely.

"Yes." Her voice came out in a hiss.

"Yeah? Let's see how turned on you are." A big hand reached between her legs to stroke the damp crotch of her panties. He groaned. "Christ, feel how wet you are." His gaze locked with hers. "You really want to do this?"

"Yes," she said again.

"Fuck. So do I."

The next thing she knew, he shoved aside the strip of material covering her core and pushed one long finger deep inside her.

Jane gasped in shock and delight, and then started rocking against his probing finger. Why did it feel this good? It wasn't like she'd never been fingered before. Yet...this...this felt different. Better. So insanely amazing she almost shuddered in orgasm from the feel of his finger sliding in and out of her pussy.

Suddenly frantic, she fumbled with his zipper, whimpering when it stuck halfway. With a chuckle, Becker used his free hand to unzip his jeans. Jane's mouth watered at the sight of the long, erect cock that sprang out of his pants. No boxers. She should've known this man went commando. It suited him to a T, considering the commanding aura he radiated.

Her fingers trembled as she wrapped them around his cock. "You're enormous," she murmured, marveling at his thickness, his length.

Becker's eyes smoldered as she stroked his shaft. He continued teasing her pussy while she worked his cock, until the air around them grew thick with need and all pretense of foreplay was swallowed up in the haze.

Jane yelped when Becker removed his finger and planted both his palms under her ass. He met her eyes again, his features creased with raw lust, then lifted her onto his cock and pushed her down on it.

A mindless moan slipped from her lips. He was lodged inside her, stretching her pussy, filling every inch of her.

"You're so fucking tight," he breathed out. "Am I hurting you? Should we stop?"

"No." Her breath came out in sharp gasps. "God, no. Don't even think about stopping."

To punctuate the remark, she pressed her mouth to his and started to move. She rode him fast and furious, her knees knocking against his powerful thighs. Becker gave a desperate groan and dug his fingers into her waist, moving his hips with hurried thrusts, drilling upwards as she pushed herself onto his cock.

"That's it, Jane, fuck me," he muttered. "Harder, baby, milk me dry."

His harsh words sent a thrill soaring up her spine. She'd never had sex like this before. So raw and dirty and completely uninhibited. She gripped his bare shoulders, holding on for dear life as she did what he asked, fucking him faster, harder. The first ripples of orgasm fluttered in her belly, gathering in strength, and then Becker tugged on the cups of her bra, dipped his head to suckle on one hard nipple, and her climax ripped through her. Pleasure exploded in her body, vibrating in her clit, throbbing in her breasts.

She cried out, pushing her nipple deeper into Becker's mouth as she came, riding out the orgasm as he sucked hard and groaned against her skin. He didn't take long to reach his climax either. Within seconds, she felt his cock pulse and jerk inside her, and he released her breast to let out a husky groan.

Jane pressed her lips to his neck, licking his damp, salty skin as he continued to shudder. When the waves of pleasure finally ebbed, they stared at each other again, and she was pretty sure the wonder and bewilderment she saw in his eyes matched her own.

What the hell had just happened? She'd had sex with a total stranger, yet not only had it been the best damn sex of her life, it hadn't felt the slightest bit sleazy.

It felt…perfect.

A ragged breath slid out of Becker's mouth. "Well." He swallowed. "So…uh…"

Jane couldn't help a smile. "Well. So. Uh. My thoughts exactly."

The corner of his mouth lifted. "That was…unexpected."

"Yep," she agreed.

Becker slowly lifted her off his still-erect cock. Then he cursed loudly. "Aw fuck. *Fuck.* We didn't use a condom."

Surprise jolted through her. Sure enough, hot come was sliding down her thighs, blatant evidence of the fact that she'd just had unprotected sex for the first time in her life. "Oh shit." She searched his gaze. "I'm on the pill and disease-free. Please tell me you are too."

"I'm clean," he said quietly. "Had my most recent physical last month and all the tests came back negative."

Relief coursed through her, but the uncomfortable subject pretty much killed the mood. And reminded her that they were still in the elevator. An elevator, which, now that she thought about it, probably had a camera pointed right at them.

The thought triggered a sharp laugh. "Damn."

Becker arched a brow. "I think it's too late for second thoughts," he said dryly.

"No, it's not that. I just realized there might be a camera in here."

"Shit, I didn't think about that."

With a sigh, Jane reached for her purse. "Well, if there is one, then the person manning it just got one hot show."

Becker gave a wry smile. "Yup."

She pulled out a travel pack of tissues and quickly cleaned herself up, while Becker put on his shirt, zipped up his jeans and got to his feet. He was just reaching for the intercom button when the lights flickered. The numbers on the elevator pad lit up all at once, and then a low hum filled the car. A moment later, they started to move.

Jane quickly rearranged her panties and whipped on her camisole. She was sliding her arms into the sleeves of her jacket when the doors dinged open to reveal the brightly lit lobby of the medical center. A man in a brown jumpsuit waited there, an apologetic but slightly amused look on his face.

"We're very sorry for the delay," he said instantly. "I hope it wasn't too much of an, um, inconvenience."

The stutter, as well as the way he studiously avoided their eyes, told Jane that the likelihood of a camera being in the elevator was pretty darn high.

Jane flushed. "No inconvenience."

"Thanks for taking care of the problem so quickly," Becker added.

The man apologized again, then hurried off, leaving Jane and Becker alone in the lobby.

She felt awkward as she looked at him. "So...I know the interview is out of the question, but..." she took a breath, "...how about dinner?"

His face went expressionless, but not before she saw the hesitation in his eyes.

A spark of anger lit her belly. Seriously? They'd just had sex in an elevator and now he was just going to blow her off?

"I don't know if that's a good idea." Remorse seeped into his features. "What happened just now...things may have gotten a little out of hand. Don't get me wrong, it was incredible, but it doesn't change where my head is at right now."

"And where is that?"

"Recovering from a divorce," he said frankly.

"Oh."

He dragged a hand through his short hair, then let it dangle to his side. "I'm in no place for a relationship. Hell, I don't think I'm even ready to date."

A part of her wanted to kick him for giving her the best sex ever and then refusing to do it again. But there was genuine regret in his eyes. She could tell he wasn't lying. He seemed sincerely messed up over his divorce, and she wasn't about to act like a heartless shrew by demanding he go out with her.

"I understand," she finally said. Shifting on her feet, she readjusted the strap of her purse and managed a smile. "At least you're one step closer to dating, huh?"

He offered a rueful smile in response. "I guess so."

A short silence fell. Jane cleared her throat and took an awkward step away from him. "Okay. So, I should be heading back to my hotel. I need to rethink this article now that you've so rudely denied my interview request."

"I'm sorry about that too. But I'm not interested in being in the spotlight. You get that, right?"

"Unfortunately, yes." She sighed.

Becker shoved his hands in the pockets of his jeans. He cleared his throat too. "Um…I should go. I've got to call my realtor and apologize for missing our meeting."

"Okay."

Another silence, this time broken by the sound of their footsteps as they headed for the glass doors at the building's entrance. When they walked outside, the warm breeze slid under Jane's tousled hair and cooled the nape of her neck. Disappointment mingled with the desire still coursing through her blood. Damn it. She didn't want to say goodbye to him yet. How could she, after their explosive hookup in the elevator?

But Becker had goodbye written all over his face. He glanced at her for a moment, and she could swear she saw another flash of hesitation. But then those intense brown eyes went all shuttered again and, in a quiet voice, he said, "I'll see you around, Jane."

"See you around, Becker," she echoed.

He offered a final nod and then he was gone, disappearing into the afternoon crowd bustling down the sidewalk.

Jane watched him walk away. Disappointed. Turned on. A little bit pissed.

After a few long moments, she forced herself to snap out of this silly trance of longing, and headed for her car.

"You can't change his mind?" Maureen Willis asked, her dissatisfaction emanating from the other end of the line.

Jane sighed and shifted the cell phone to her other ear. She was stretched out in a lounge chair on Coronado Beach, enjoying the late afternoon sun on her skin and the sight of the calm ocean. She wished the magazine had sprung for one of those gorgeous cottages sitting a hundred yards away, but she wasn't unhappy about her suite. The Hotel del Coronado was one of the most beautiful hotels she'd ever stayed in. She was already dreading having to get into her car and drive back to LA next week.

"I can't change his mind," she told her editor. "He was pretty adamant. He doesn't want to be interviewed."

"That's a damn shame." Maureen's voice grew wistful. "I'm looking at those photos your sister sent over, and the one of Thomas Becker by the helicopter is seriously sexy."

Jane knew precisely which picture Maureen was referring to. He was standing by the helicopter after they'd landed at the Navy base. The sun was just beginning to set, his big muscular body looked amazing, and his head was turned to the side, revealing his handsome profile. Jane had stared at the photo several times last night, and each time she saw his face, she remembered what they'd done in the elevator.

And wished they could do it again.

"I could just run the photo anyway," Maureen said, sounding thoughtful. "We'll mention his name in the caption, say he was the head of the rescue mission."

"You can't," Jane answered firmly. "He doesn't want his picture in the article. He said he prefers to keep a low profile, and he definitely won't sign a photo release. Don't worry, though, I'm working on the first draft, using my interview with Liz, and it's pretty good. I don't think we even need Thomas Becker."

"What about the other members of the team? Can you speak with them?"

"I could try, but I was hoping to get the one who led the rescue." Jane chewed on the inside of her cheek. "I think Liz's firsthand account will be enough, Maureen. It'll be an emotional piece, trust me."

"Fine," her editor said. "Try to talk to the other men if you think you need to, otherwise email me the story by the end of the week. You may as well stay there since the hotel is already paid for, so enjoy the vacation."

"Will do."

Jane ended the call and tossed the phone into her green oversized beach bag. She leaned back in the chair, causing the big straw hat on her head to shift. She hated the damn hat, but if she didn't shade her face, she sunburned like crazy. She'd slathered sunblock all over her body too, but already she could see her skin turning pink. Time to get out of the sun, she decided with a sigh.

She started to gather up her things, tossing the romance novel she'd been reading into her bag, picking up her towel and fanning the sand out of it. She'd just slung the bag over her shoulder when a familiar voice sounded from behind.

"Jane?"

She whirled around.

Thomas Becker stood a few feet away, looking as perplexed as she felt. He wore a pair of long khaki shorts and a pristine white T-shirt that molded to his chest, and he looked so sexy she wanted to rip off her bikini and throw herself into his powerful arms.

"What are you doing here?" she asked in surprise.

"I'm staying in one of the cottages until I find a house." He gestured to the beachfront suites she'd been admiring earlier. "Are you staying at this hotel?"

She nodded. "I'm here 'til Sunday, then I'm driving back to LA."

Becker shoved his hands in his front pockets and walked toward her. "How's the article going?"

"Good." She grinned. "My editor is a tad upset that we won't be able to print your handsome face, though."

He grimaced. "You're doing the public a favor. No one wants to see my face."

Jane rolled her eyes. "Don't tell me you think you're unattractive, because that's just silly. You're a hottie, and you know it."

His mouth twitched. "I'm a hottie, huh?"

"Yep. Deal with it."

There was a short pause, and their gazes locked again. A streak of awareness sizzled between them like lightning.

Jeez, what was up with this chemistry? Jane couldn't figure it out. She'd dated other men, slept with other men, yet being around Becker made her body burn in a way it never had before. There was a relentless throbbing between her legs, which deepened when she swept her eyes over his chest.

"Are you undressing me with your eyes?" he asked gruffly.

"Yes."

A smile crossed his face. "You really are the bluntest woman I've ever met, you know that?" He let out a quick breath. "Are you hungry?"

She blinked. "Hungry?"

"You know, requiring nourishment," he said dryly. "I was about to head back to my cottage and order some room service. Want to join me?"

He was inviting her to dinner? After he'd told her he wasn't interested in dating? She wanted to ask him what changed, but then realized this wasn't the time to look a gift horse in the mouth. Because this was definitely a gift she'd been given. Another chance to get naked with Thomas Becker? Oh, yeah.

She looked up at him from under the brim of her tacky hat and said, "I would love to."

BECKER SPENT THE WALK BACK TO THE COTTAGE WONDERING WHAT THE hell was wrong with him. Why had he invited Jane Harrison over for dinner? He'd meant every word he'd said to her yesterday when they'd parted ways. He didn't want a relationship. He didn't want to date.

And he especially didn't want either of those things with a woman who reminded him way too much of Alice.

But the second he'd laid eyes on her on the beach, he'd thought of nothing but being with her again. She looked so fucking sexy in a bright pink bikini that clashed with her shocking red hair. And that grandma straw hat, which should have looked wrong on a woman as wildly attractive as Jane, but, well, the hat was pretty damn sexy too.

What was the matter with him? Why was he so drawn to this woman? He'd only spent an hour with her yesterday, ten minutes of that with his cock shoved inside her. But that was all the time he'd needed to know that, while they were explosive in the sex department, she wasn't his type. At least not anymore.

He wasn't into bold, ambitious women any longer. He wanted someone…wholesome. A woman he could start a family with, who'd have dinner waiting for him when he got home, who wouldn't argue with him about every goddamn thing. Fine, so it was old-fashioned of him to long for a Suzie Homemaker, but after the fourteen years he'd spent with Alice, he wanted old-fashioned. He wanted *safe*.

Jane Harrison was not safe.

Oh no, everything about her screamed danger, from her pouty red lips to those mouthwatering tits to the sass that came out of her sexy mouth.

Stifling a groan, he strode into his cottage, his gaze immediately landing on the phone sitting on the coffee table of the elegant living area. Jane had gone back to her room to change, so he still had time to fix this. To tell her he'd decided he wanted to be alone.

Only problem was he didn't want to be alone.

He wanted to be with Jane.

The groan he'd been holding slipped out. He kicked off his flip-flops and stared at the doorway leading into the bedroom. Before he could stop himself, he imagined Jane lying on the king-size bed, her naked body stretched across the silk sheets, her red hair fanned over the stark white pillow. His cock instantly hardened.

Damn it, why did he want this woman so badly?

Turning away from the bedroom, he sank down on the leather couch situated in front of the electric fireplace and switched on the flat-screen TV mounted on the wall. He channel surfed for a while, but his attention was elsewhere. His gaze kept moving to the front door, anticipating Jane's arrival.

By the time she finally sauntered up to his door a half hour later, his entire body was tense, every muscle taut with barely restrained desire.

He opened the door before she could even knock, causing her to grin and raise her delicate reddish-brown eyebrows. "Have you been waiting by the door this entire time?"

"No," he lied.

Jane's strappy sandals clicked against the floor as she walked into the cottage. Her blue-eyed gaze swept around the room, from the living area to the kitchen and dining room, to the bedroom door. Then she turned to look at him, her eyes narrowed. "Are you a drug dealer?"

"What?"

"You can't possibly afford this place on a SEAL's salary. I know, I researched it," she said frankly.

Becker couldn't help a laugh. He should've been insulted, both by the fact that she was asking if he was a drug dealer and also because she was inquiring about the finances of a stranger, but somehow it seemed completely normal coming from Jane.

"I'm not a drug dealer," he assured her. "And since you're so curious, I can afford this suite because I come from a wealthy family. Ever heard of BCI?"

She wrinkled her forehead. "The pharmaceutical company?"

"Yeah." He shrugged. "My family is the B in BCI."

Jane looked impressed. "Can you buy me something outrageously expensive?" she demanded, a mischievous smile curving her lips. "You know, so that I can tell everyone the B in BCI is my sugar daddy?"

He barked out another laugh. "I really hope you're kidding."

"Of course I am," she said as she dropped her purse on the arm of the couch. "I don't need outrageous gifts." Her voice suddenly grew husky. "Everything I want is standing right in front of me."

A jolt of arousal sizzled straight down to his dick. He knew exactly how she felt, because everything *he* wanted was standing in front of *him*. She'd changed out of the sexy bikini into an even sexier knee-length sundress that clung to her curvy frame. The vibrant yellow dress looked amazing with her red hair, and the way the material swirled over her legs sent another spark of heat to his groin.

"Are we going to keep ignoring it?" she asked.

He swallowed. "Ignore what?"

"The fact that we want to rip each other's clothes off." She took a purposeful step toward him. "Tell me the truth — have you ever felt anything like this before?"

"No," he admitted.

He could swear he saw a flicker of vulnerability on her face. "Me neither." Whatever he'd seen in her gaze was burned up in the seductive fire that filled her eyes. "I don't quite understand it, but I know I don't want to fight it."

"What about dinner?" he said roughly.

"I'm thinking we satisfy the other hunger first." She tilted her head to look at him, making him realize just how petite she was. "What do you think?"

He stared at her mouth, his throat becoming dry. He could just say no. Tell this hot little seductress that he had no interest in being seduced.

But that would be a lie.

"I think," Becker said in a measured tone, "that you really need to take that dress off."

Chapter Four

THERE. HE'D SAID THE WORDS, AND THERE WAS NO TURNING BACK NOW. Becker couldn't tear his eyes off Jane as she slowly reached for the straps of her dress. She slid one over her shoulder, then arched a brow. "You're sure?"

He licked his dry lips. "Yes."

With a satisfied smile, she pushed the straps down, tugged on her bodice, and peeled the dress down her body. The bright yellow material pooled at her feet, leaving her in a sheer white bra and a pair of skimpy panties between her tanned thighs.

Shit, she was gorgeous. With her hair cascading over her bare shoulders and her endless supply of curves, she looked good enough to eat. The thought made his cock jerk against his fly. Fuck, he wanted to eat her. He hadn't gotten the chance to taste her in the elevator, and he was dying to lick her up.

"Take off the bra and panties," he said gruffly.

Jane did as he asked. When she stood completely naked in front of him, he took a moment to feast his eyes on her. Her skin had a pinkish hue to it, as if she'd stayed out in the sun too long. Her cherry-red nipples were rigid, demanding attention. But it was the thin stripe of red curls at the juncture of her thighs that called out to him. She was a natural redhead. That was hot.

Licking his lips again, he pointed to couch and said, "Lie down and spread your legs wide for me. I want to taste that sweet pussy of yours."

Her blue eyes flashed with excitement. Without a word, she moved to the couch, sank down on the cushions, and spread her legs just as he'd requested.

Becker's pulse drummed in his ears as he got down on his knees. Her pussy was slick with arousal, her clit swollen and in need of his tongue. Rearranging the enormous bulge in his pants, he dipped his head to take his first taste. It was as sweet as he'd imagined, the feminine scent of her flooding his senses and making him dizzy with need.

He dragged his tongue over her, flicked it against her clit, then licked down her wet slit toward her opening. Jane gasped when he plunged his tongue inside her. "You like that?" he muttered, pulling back.

"Yes…God, yes."

He fucked her with his tongue again, enjoying the breathy moans that slipped out of her mouth, loving the way she pressed her hands on his head, pulling him closer. He wasn't new at going down on women, but licking Jane was a mind-blowing experience. His cock throbbed as he teased her pussy, licking, suckling her clit, nipping at her inner thighs. She pulsed under his tongue, her thighs clenched and released. She was getting close. He captured her clit between his lips and sucked on it like a piece of candy. Jane exploded.

Wetness coated his mouth, his lips, his chin as he kept working her pussy with his tongue, drawing every last drop of pleasure from her body.

When he finally lifted his head, Jane was trembling like crazy. Her eyes were glazed, her tits heaving from the aftershocks of release.

"You are way too good at that," she squeezed out.

Smiling, Becker rose to his feet, already reaching for his T-shirt. He pulled it over his head and threw it aside, then tackled his jeans and boxers. Naked, he bent down and lifted her into his arms.

Jane yelped. "Where are we going?"

"Bed." One word. It was all he was capable of formulating. Lust had taken over, and he could barely see straight as he carried Jane into the bedroom and deposited her on the king-size bed.

She propped herself up on her elbows, a small smile curving her mouth. Her gaze rested on his cock, which was harder than ever and giving her a full salute. "Is that for me?" she asked, the smile widening.

"All for you," he confirmed.

She scooted to the edge of the bed where he stood and reached for his dick, her warm hands encircling it. Becker's breath hitched. She teased the sensitive underside with her fingers and then leaned forward to lick the drop of precome at his tip. Becker groaned.

"You like that?" she asked, mimicking his earlier taunt.

"I'd like it more if you wrapped your lips around my cock," he ground out.

She did exactly that, her soft laughter vibrating along his shaft. Heat enveloped his cock, and his balls tightened as Jane's hot, wet mouth moved over him. She sucked him as if her only goal in life was to get him off, swirling her tongue over his tip, then taking him so deep in her mouth he was practically down her throat.

"Fuck. Yes," he hissed out. "Just like that, baby."

Jane was making sexy little sounds in the back of her throat as she sucked on his cock. She was loving it, and damn, so was he. The hot suction of her mouth felt like heaven, and when she cupped his balls with one hand and squeezed, not so gently, he nearly shot his load.

With a groan, he pried his dick out of her eager mouth, eliciting a disappointed pout from Jane's sexy swollen lips. "I wasn't done," she complained.

He grabbed the condom he'd left on the end table and put it on. "I would've been, if you kept sucking me like that." He pushed her onto the mattress so she was flat on her back, and climbed on top of her. "And I'd rather come inside you."

Before she could reply, he slid his cock into her to the hilt. Jane let out a cry of delight, then wrapped her arms around him and stroked the sides of his arms. He winced as she made contact with the puckered bullet wound.

She immediately dropped her hand, her blue eyes filling with concern. "Oh, God, are you okay? I keep forgetting you got shot!"

He smiled faintly. "I keep forgetting too. Whenever you're around, all I seem able to do is *this*." He pumped into her, emphasizing his point.

"We can stop. If your arm hurts, we *should* stop."

"My arm doesn't hurt." He bent down and sank his teeth into her shoulder, then licked away the sting. "My cock, on the other hand, will hurt something fierce if I don't come soon."

Jane shoved her hands on the back of his head and pulled him down for a kiss. "Well, we can't have that." She swept her tongue over his bottom lip before biting it, sending a jolt of pleasure to his groin. "Come on, Beck, let's see what you've got."

Chuckling, he grabbed her hands and shoved them over her head, locking her wrists together. Then he thrust into her, hard, fast, meeting the seductive challenge she'd tossed out and making demands of his own. "You first," he muttered as his hips pounded into her. "Come for me, Jane. I want to feel you coming all over my dick."

She gasped from each sharp thrust, each dirty word. Her inner muscles squeezed his cock.

"Fuck, that's it, baby, I feel that pussy throbbing, you're close, aren't you?"

"Yes." She arched her back, taking him in deeper, and then another *yes* slipped from her mouth, this one thick with desire.

Ecstasy flashed across her face as the orgasm ripped through her. Becker barely had time to enjoy watching her come apart, because pleasure seized his balls and then his own orgasm sizzled down his spine. He came hard, shoving his tongue in Jane's mouth. He continued pounding into her, desperate, erratic thrusts that made Jane writhe beneath him. Their groans mingled together. He felt Jane's heartbeat hammering in her chest, matching the frantic beats of his own heart.

When they finally grew still, their breathing steady, their bodies still joined, Jane released a soft laugh. Planting a kiss to his jaw, she moved her lips to his ear and whispered, "Okay, let's have dinner now."

Becker just laughed.

"I'm here for eight more days," Jane said, setting down her fork.

Their dinner was spread out on the table, the aroma of chicken and rice filling the air. Becker had ordered a bottle of wine too, and they'd already consumed half of it. Jane was feeling a little tipsy, which was probably the reason she'd decided to vocalize her thoughts. She hadn't wanted to push him, but she couldn't stop herself from making this proposal.

Becker popped a piece of chicken in his mouth, chewing slowly. "And?"

"And I think it would be a complete injustice if I spent the next eight days not getting fucked by you."

He coughed, then shook his head and shot her a grin. "I'm trying to figure out if I'm ever going to get used to how blunt you are."

She grinned back, oddly pleased that he didn't seem to mind her painfully honest nature. She'd always been this way, speaking her mind, often blurting out things she probably shouldn't. Other men had seemed put off by it, especially when her honesty revealed something they didn't want to hear. But Becker actually seemed to appreciate it.

"I'm serious," she said as she reached for a glass of wine. "I think we've stumbled onto something good here. Look me in the eye and tell me you don't want to see me naked again."

She stared at him. He stared back.

After a moment, his brown eyes grew resigned. "I want to see you naked again."

Pleasure jolted through her. "Good. So let's do naked things for another week."

Becker laughed, but his expression didn't stay amused for long. "I wasn't kidding the other day," he told her. "I'm getting over a divorce."

"How long were you married?"

He instantly became guarded. "Why do you ask?"

"Because this divorce is obviously our only obstacle, so we might as well tackle it. That way we can get back to bed."

Becker's lips twitched.

"So, how long?"

"Fourteen years."

Jane couldn't hide her surprise. Wow. Fourteen years? She couldn't imagine spending that much time with a person. Her longest relationship had barely lasted three months. "You must have married young," she remarked.

"We were eighteen."

"High-school sweethearts?"

He nodded.

"Let me guess," she said dryly. "Football quarterback, head cheerleader, passionate romance for four years, got married because you couldn't live without each other and wanted to face the exciting new world together?"

"Almost." He shrugged. "Football quarterback, head cheerleader, passionate romance for four years, got married because I knocked her up."

"Seriously?"

"Yeah." Sadness crossed his face. "She got pregnant, decided to keep the baby, so we got married. She miscarried three months later."

"And you decided to stay married?"

"We wanted to make it work." Another shrug. "And we did, for a long time. Alice and I were always pretty independent people. She did her modeling thing, I did the military thing, and the marriage kept us grounded."

"So what happened?"

"Her modeling thing became more important than the marriage," he said simply.

Jane took another sip of wine, thoughtful as the cool liquid slid down her throat. "She's a model, huh?" Somehow that surprised her, that this quiet, intense man had been married to a model.

"Alice Dawes," he supplied.

"The Mystique perfume chick?" When Becker nodded, Jane couldn't fight the tug of insecurity in her gut. Jeez. Only yesterday she'd flipped through a magazine and admired the perfume spokesmodel. Alice Dawes was drop-dead gorgeous. Long, silky blonde hair, pale silver eyes, a tall, willowy body. Just looking at the woman's picture had made Jane feel frumpy and dwarfish in comparison.

"Wow," she finally said, reaching for her wine again. She drained the glass, wondering why she suddenly felt so inferior. One, she and Thomas Becker weren't seriously involved. And two, he'd divorced his wife, so obviously Alice Dawes wasn't that awesome.

Becker pushed away his plate, smiling ruefully. "What, you find out my ex-wife is a model and now you've changed your mind about all those naked things you wanted to do?"

"I haven't changed my mind." She hesitated. "You still haven't told me if you're even interested."

He met her eyes. "I am interested. But I'm also realistic. I don't want a relationship."

"I'm only here for another week. That's not a relationship."

"Then what is it?"

"A fling."

Becker looked uncertain. "I...uh, I'm not a fling kind of guy."

Rolling her eyes, Jane pushed back her chair and stood up. She rounded the table and, before he could object, lowered herself into Becker's lap. He wore only a pair of boxers, and the second she straddled his powerful thighs, his cock went stiff, poking against her thigh.

Jane raised her eyebrows. "I think every man is capable of being a fling man, Beck. And I think your dick agrees with me."

His dark eyes went even darker, burning with arousal. Although she'd put her dress back on before dinner, she wasn't wearing any panties, and it would be so very easy to move the material of her dress aside and slide down onto his big, erect dick. But she fought the temptation. They didn't have a condom handy, and besides, the second his distracting erection filled her pussy, she knew she would lose the capacity for speech.

"My cock isn't very reliable," Becker said, resting one hand on her thigh. "He likes you way too much." Sweeping his tongue over his lower lip, he stroked her bare knee.

"And what about you?" she asked softly.

He leaned forward to nuzzle her neck. He pressed his lips to her skin, kissing his way down her throat. His voice was muffled as he said, "I like you too."

A shiver of pleasure danced up her spine. "Then fling with me. I promise, I won't make any demands. I already told you what I want."

He lifted his head, meeting her gaze. "A week of sex. Is that what you want, Jane?"

She nodded.

The reluctance on his face was beginning to chip away. She could see his resolve crumbling. The lust creeping into his eyes and pushing all the hesitation away. Deciding he needed one final push, Jane reached between them and curled her fingers over his cock. She squeezed gently, then moved down to cup his heavy balls. He moaned.

"Come on, *Thomas*, you know you can't say no," she murmured. "You don't *want* to say no. So just say yes."

She continued playing with him, stroking, squeezing, until he released a strangled groan and said, "*Yes*."

Chapter Five

FOUR DAYS LATER, BECKER WAS STILL TRYING TO FIGURE OUT IF AGREEING to Jane's proposition was the best decision of his life, or the worst. What *wasn't* up for debate was the fact that this was the best sex of his life.

How he'd gone for thirty-two years without experiencing sex like this was a mystery. All Jane had to do was take off her clothes and he turned into an animal. He'd fucked her every which way for the last four days. Indoors, outdoors, on every piece of furniture, on the floor, in the shower, from behind. And no matter how many times he came inside that tight, hot pussy of hers, he never seemed to be sated.

But what bothered him more was how seamlessly she'd insinuated herself into his life. Well, insinuated was probably the wrong word. That implied she'd been the one to seek out a bigger role, when it was him who'd told her to move her stuff into his cottage, him who'd convinced her to stay for breakfast every morning instead of heading back to her room to write. Since he was still on leave thanks to the bullet wound, he had absolutely nothing to do other than look for a place to live, yet instead of meeting with the realtor, he'd been spending all his time with Jane.

For a man who didn't want a relationship, his actions of the last few days troubled the hell out of him.

Those same actions evidently confused Jane, because as they pulled out of the hotel parking lot on Thursday afternoon, she turned to him with a deep frown. "I don't get it. Are we dating?"

Her no-nonsense tone made him smile. He'd never met anyone like Jane. Sex-goddess looks aside, she was smart as hell, unfailingly honest, and way too perceptive for his peace of mind.

"We're flinging, remember?" he said, heading toward the bridge that separated Coronado from San Diego, their destination.

"People who fling do not go to play mini-golf." Jane shot him a sideways glance, looking flabbergasted. "Why are we going to play mini-golf?"

"You mentioned you liked to play, so I figured it was a nice way to spend the afternoon," he pointed out.

"It is, but I still don't get why you suggested it." She shook her head, which caused strands of wavy red hair to fall into her eyes. She blew them away in frustration. "You told me you didn't want a relationship. The stuff we've been doing? That's relationship stuff, Becker. Dinner on the boardwalk, Netflix marathons, *mini-golf*—that is *not* a fling."

He sighed. "I know."

"So what is this?"

Discomfort crept up his chest and settled into a lump in the back of his throat. That was precisely what he'd been asking himself for the last couple of days. Since when had this turned into more than just sex? It was Jane's fault, for being so damn likable. He'd never really connected with many people. In high school, even though he'd been on the football team and part of the popular crowd, he hadn't had many close friends. During SEAL training, where most of the men bonded, he'd kept to himself. Even now, he was part of a close-knit team and he never saw the other guys off the base.

But Jane...he connected with her. She made him laugh. And she turned him on like no other woman ever had, not even his ex-wife.

He thought of what she'd just asked him. What was this? Fucked if he knew.

"I don't know," he admitted, keeping his gaze glued to the road.

"Okay." She paused. "This conversation is pointless, anyway. I leave in a few days, so even if we are dating, we won't be for much longer."

The jolt of unhappiness that suddenly raced through him was disconcerting. He'd forgotten she would be leaving on Sunday. But they'd agreed from the beginning that this was a short-term thing. There was really no reason why the thought of her walking out of his life made his chest feel so tight.

He didn't reply, and neither of them said much as he drove to the mini-golf course Jane had found the address for online. They'd been lying in bed, recovering from their respective orgasms when he'd brought up the idea, though he still wasn't sure why he'd suggested they spend the afternoon playing mini-golf. Jane was right — this was relationship stuff. He'd agreed to a casual fling, some fun in bed. So why was he suddenly so eager to have fun with Jane *out* of bed?

He pulled into the gravel lot and killed the engine of his SUV. He and Jane got out, and she immediately plopped a pair of sunglasses on the bridge of her freckled nose. The sun shone overhead in a cloudless sky, a warm breeze brushing across Becker's bare arms. He slipped on his own sunglasses, aviator-style ones that Jane had teased him about, declaring they belonged in a cheesy action movie. But he liked his shades, and he ignored her giggle as he put them on. What he couldn't ignore was the way her blue halter dress molded to her curves.

Dresses. That's all the woman ever wore. Cute little sundresses, halter ones, the long green one made from that filmy, see-through material. It drove Becker crazy each time she came out of the bedroom in another one of those fuck-me dresses. It drove him even crazier knowing that, half the time, she didn't wear panties. She wore them today, though. He'd seen her sliding into a flimsy black thong before they left the cottage, and his mouth went dry, hands tingling with the urge to reach under the hem of her dress and pry that thong off her firm ass.

"You're thinking about sex," Jane said, jarring him from his thoughts.

He shot her a sheepish smile. "Yep."

"Well, stop. I won't be able to kick your ass on the course if I'm distracted."

Becker moved closer and wrapped his arms around her slender waist. "Maybe I want to distract you. Maybe it's part of my dastardly plan to kick *your* ass in golf."

Jane stood up on her tiptoes and brushed her lips over his. She gave a mischievous grin. "In your dreams, Thomas. I'm *very* good at this game."

"CRAP, YOU WEREN'T KIDDING," BECKER SAID TEN MINUTES LATER, AFTER Jane had sunk her third consecutive hole-in-one.

She demurely held her putter to her side, enjoying the look of awe in his eyes. She might be the least athletic person on the planet, but she'd always been pretty damn good at mini-golf. "When I was a teenager I dated a guy who worked on a putt-putt course," she confessed. "We used to sneak onto the course after he finished his shift."

"Please don't tell me you lost your virginity on a piece of green felt in front of a fake earthquake scene."

She shot him a solemn look. "I did."

Becker let out a sigh. "Seriously?"

Jane grinned. "No. I lost my virginity in the backseat of a Ford pick-up, which is probably just as bad."

They crossed a little bridge that hovered over a pretty pond with fake yellow and blue fish. The path leading to the next hole wound around a papier maché mountain, which made no sense since the last hole had looked like a beach. Obviously this course had no discernible theme. As they headed around the bend, the sound of male voices drifted toward them. Jane couldn't help but laugh as she listened.

"What the hell are you saying? There's no way to know which tunnel to tap the fucking ball into," someone said, sounding aggravated.

"Trust me, Ry, it's the third one," a second voice argued.

"He's trying to sabotage you, Ry," a third voice said. "He's out for blood."

Next to her, Becker tensed up. She glanced over. "What's wrong?"

"Those voices sound way too familiar," he said with a heavy breath.

They rounded the corner, and Jane was hit by a dose of testosterone, her eyes taking in the sight of four ridiculously sexy men. And then the sight of four jaws dropping in unison when she and Becker stepped into view.

"Lieutenant?" the one with sandy-blond hair demanded. "What are you doing here?"

Becker lifted his putter. "What does it look like?"

The one they'd called Ry looked utterly delighted. "See, I told you guys he has a secret life we don't know about." Ry's playful blue eyes landed on Jane. He let out a soft whistle. "And it's obviously even better than I imagined. Are you going to introduce us, Lieutenant?"

Becker made the introductions, but it was hard to focus on names when each man Becker introduced her to was sexier than the last. The blond one was Carson, who looked like he belonged on the cover of *GQ*. Will had dark, almost black, eyes and a head of messy dark hair that fell onto his forehead. Ry was Ryan, who was possibly one of the cutest guys Jane had ever met, with his brown hair, blue eyes, and gleaming biceps revealed by the sleeveless basketball jersey he wore. The last one was Matt, who boasted a shaved head and green eyes that twinkled as he reached out to shake Jane's hand.

All four men, who Becker introduced as members of his SEAL team, stared at her appreciatively. And stared at Becker as if he'd just arrived from another planet. It didn't take a genius to figure out that Becker wasn't Mr. Social. Judging from the surprise in his team's eyes, this was probably the first time they'd seen him somewhere other than the base.

"So how did you two kids meet?" Carson asked curiously, looking from her to Becker.

Jane shrugged. "In an elevator."

The other men raised their brows. "In an elevator?" Carson echoed.

"Yep. We got stuck." She didn't look at Becker, scared that if she did, her expression would reveal exactly what they'd done *while* stuck. She forced the blush from her cheeks and glanced at the SEALs. "Actually, you guys all know my sister."

Ryan's eyes lit up. "She has a sister," he said to Matt.

"You saved her life," Jane added, rolling her eyes.

"Jane's sister is Elizabeth Harrison," Becker supplied quietly.

The mention of Liz's name had the men going somber. "How's she doing?" Carson asked with concern.

"She's fine," Jane answered. "Completely recovered from her near-death experience. I'm writing a piece about it for the magazine I work for." She suddenly remembered her editor's suggestion. "Maybe one of you guys can give me an interview. Becker here has politely declined."

"I'll do it," both Ryan and Matt said immediately.

Carson grinned at the other two. "She said interview, not sex."

The sound of children's voices came from the other side of the bridge. Becker rested a hand on Jane's waist and turned to the other men. "Let's keep moving before this hole turns into a parking lot."

The six of them played the hole quickly. Well, technically, the five of them. Jane noticed Will, the intense one with black eyes, didn't take a turn. Instead, he jotted down the other men's scores and announced them when they reached the next hole.

"Okay, so as of now, O'Connor's taken the lead, Carson is at a close second, and Evans over here…" Will smirked at Ryan, "…is six over par."

Becker glanced over at Will. "You came all the way here just to keep score?"

Will's expression grew sullen.

"He's not allowed to play," Carson explained in a grave voice.

Jane looked from Carson to Will. "Why not?"

"Well, it all traces back to the putter-in-the-clown's-mouth incident," Carson said.

"Which is what?"

He grinned. "Exactly what it sounds like. He threw his putter in the clown's mouth. It was insanely childish."

"Screw off," Will grumbled at the man. He then fixed those dark eyes on Jane. "It really isn't as bad as it sounds. Carson over-exaggerates."

She choked down a laugh. "I'm sure he does."

The next five holes went by far too fast for Jane's liking. Although Becker didn't say much to the other men, she liked them immensely. Carson's sarcasm was endearing, Will's brooding made her laugh, and the two young ones were unbelievably entertaining. Ryan and Matt flirted up a storm with her, complimenting her, quizzing her about how serious she and Becker were, which elicited a frown from her date. But she knew Becker wasn't angered by their behavior. He seemed to be fighting back laughter the entire time, as if Evans and O'Connor, as he addressed them, were harmless little siblings he didn't take seriously.

After they finished the last hole, Jane took her bows as she was declared the official winner. Becker and Will headed over to the booth to return everyone's putters and balls, leaving Jane alone with Carson, Ryan and Matt, who all eyed her with extreme curiosity.

"What's he like?" Carson asked, lowering his voice despite the fact that Becker was completely out of earshot.

"Seriously," Ryan chimed in. "We've been trying to get a handle on the Lieutenant for a while now. He's barely spoken two words since he joined the team."

Jane felt her cheeks grow warm. What was Becker like? *Intense*, she wanted to say. She thought about the way he moved inside her body and added *passionate* to the list. *Thoughtful,* because he made her breakfast.

But as she opened her mouth to respond, the only word she really wanted to say was *mine.*

She had no clue where it came from, this weird idea that Becker belonged to her. That she even wanted him to belong to her. All she knew was that, in the last five days, she'd started to really like Thomas Becker. They were almost polar opposites. He was cautious and serious, she was wild and outspoken. He considered each word carefully before speaking, she just blurted out whatever entered her mind. But sex... that's where they were completely in sync.

"He's sweet," she finally said.

That got her three pairs of wide eyes.

"Sweet?" Carson echoed. "No way."

Ryan nodded in agreement. "No way is Lieutenant Becker sweet. He's prickly as hell."

Jane laughed. "Yeah, he's prickly. But he's also…"

"Sweet," Matt supplied, looking like he was holding back laughter.

"*Yes,*" she insisted.

"Whatever you say," Carson answered with a careless shrug.

"So, about that interview," Ryan suddenly said. His blue eyes swept over her face, the corner of his mouth quirking. "When and where?"

"You'll really do it? I thought you were joking before."

"No, I'll answer a few questions. But only if you don't publish my name. Our commanding officer is pretty anal about that shit. He doesn't like the team getting any publicity."

"No names," she assured him. Deep down, she wished Becker could have agreed this readily to the interview, but she respected his decision. She wasn't one of those overbearing journalists who stalked potential sources.

"You're here until Sunday?" Ryan asked.

"Yeah. Maybe we can meet up tomorrow?"

"Sure," he said easily. He stuck his hand in the back pocket of his red surf shorts and pulled out a cell phone. "Put your number in here and I'll call you tomorrow to figure out a time."

Jane took the phone and entered her contact info. As she handed it back, Ryan's hand brushed hers and a spark of heat went off in her belly. She stared at his long, callused fingers, then met his gaze, which was playful with just the slightest glimmer of sensuality. Lord, this man probably had no problems getting women in bed. One touch, one heated look, and even she, who'd been having the best sex of her life for the past week, was tempted to get naked with him.

She took her hand back, just as footsteps sounded from behind. She turned and greeted Becker with a smile, but he didn't return it. His dark eyes were expressionless, but she saw a muscle jump in his jaw. Was he pissed at her? Angry that they'd ended up spending the afternoon with his teammates rather than by themselves?

"Ready to go?" he said roughly.

"Sure." She turned to the other men. "It was nice meeting all of you."

Carson, Will, and Matt nodded in agreement, shooting her charming grins. Ryan grinned too, adding, "I'll call you tomorrow to set up the interview."

They said their goodbyes, and then she and Becker were walking back to his SUV. He still had that distant look on his face, and he didn't say a word until they were well away from the golf course. "They liked you."

Jane smiled. "I liked them too." She hesitated. "How come you don't spend more time with them?"

"Different interests," Becker said with a shrug. He flicked the right turn signal and changed lanes. "Evans and O'Connor are out every night, chasing women and partying. Can you honestly see me doing that?"

"No. But what about Carson? Or Will? Will totally seemed like your man-soulmate."

Becker barked out a laugh. "Yeah, I like Will. He's married, lives with his wife in a small town about an hour or two from here. So he's not around much, from what I hear. And Carson lives with his girlfriend and spends most of his time with her."

"He said they do this mini-golf thing once a month," Jane pointed out. "Maybe you should go with them next time."

"Maybe."

Becker fell silent again. They drove over the bridge into Coronado, in the direction of the hotel, but it wasn't until they reached the parking lot that he spoke again.

"You were attracted to him."

Jane's head jerked up. "Huh?"

"Ryan. You were attracted to him."

She was unsure how to respond, especially since she couldn't figure out where he was going with this or how he even felt about it. He was completely pokerfaced, his tone calm.

"I saw your face when he touched your hand," Becker added when she still didn't answer.

"I reacted to him, yeah," she said frankly. "He's a good-looking guy. They all are."

"But you only reacted to Evans."

Becker shut off the engine and unbuckled his seatbelt, but made no move to get out of the car. Jane undid her own seatbelt and studied him carefully. "Where is this coming from? And what is it you want me to say? Yes, there was a spark of attraction when he touched me."

Becker searched her eyes, a deep line creasing his forehead. "If I wasn't there, if you'd met him on your own, would you fuck him?"

She couldn't help but laugh. "After a five-minute encounter? I'm not *that* bold. Maybe if he bought me dinner first." She tilted her head to the side. "I'm not sure why we're talking about this. I don't plan on fucking anyone but you, Beck." She reached for the door handle. "In fact, let's get out of the car and find us a bed. I think I need to show you who I *really* want to be with."

Chapter Six

BECKER FOUGHT A STRANGE WAVE OF ANGER AS HE FOLLOWED JANE into the bedroom of his cottage. She was already reaching for the tie around her neck that held her halter dress in place. She lifted her wavy hair and undid the knot beneath it, letting the dress slip down to the floor. Now she wore a bikini-style bra and the sexy thong he'd watched her put on earlier. He wanted nothing more than to step toward her and run his fingers over every inch of her body, but for some reason he remained rooted in place.

And for some reason, he couldn't stop picturing another man's fingers on Jane's body. Another man's fingers pinching her nipples. Sliding into her pussy. The thought made him curl his hands into fists. Jealousy streaked through him, so strong that his entire body went stiff as a rod. He still remembered the pink flush of Jane's cheeks as Evans touched her hand, the seductive little smile she'd shot him. At that moment, Becker had wanted to throttle the younger man, and the volatile reaction had caught him off guard.

So what if Jane was attracted to another man? She was only here for three more days. They would both go their separate ways then, and unless Jane took a vow of celibacy, she would probably find another man after she and Becker said goodbye. Maybe not right away, but eventually she'd be fucking someone else. Someone who wasn't him.

His blood began to burn again.

"What is the matter with you?" Jane asked, rolling her eyes. She stood half-naked in front of him, while he was fully dressed and loitering in the bedroom doorway. "Please don't tell me you're still thinking about Ryan and me."

"I…" He cleared his throat, then opened his mouth to continue, but the words that came out were ones he'd been trying not to think about since he'd witnessed the sparks between Jane and Evans. "I was actually considering inviting him back here with us."

Jane's eyes widened. "What? Why?"

"So he could fuck you." His voice thickened. "So *we* could fuck you."

Her breasts rose as she sucked in a sharp breath. "Why would you want to do that?"

"Because…because it would get you out of my system," he burst out.

Painful understanding dawned on her face. "You want to see me with another man. You want to think of me as promiscuous, don't you?" Her tone softened. "That way you could hate me. And if you hate me, then you wouldn't have to like me so much, right?"

He didn't answer, his throat suddenly going dry. Damn her. Why was she so fucking perceptive? She'd completely called him out. Figured him out. And she was right. When he'd seen the arousal in her eyes while she'd been standing with Ryan, the jealousy had come fast and fierce. Jealousy he shouldn't be feeling over a woman he'd known for only a week. Sex for eight days, that's all he'd wanted out of this. But he'd gotten much more. *Too* much more.

"Well, you know what?" Jane said. "I don't think it would have made a difference."

"What are you talking about?"

"Seeing me with Ryan wouldn't make you hate me." Very methodically, she unclasped the front of her bra and threw it aside, revealing her big, mouthwatering tits. "I think it would have turned you on."

He shook his head. "I would've strangled him."

She shook her head right back, then removed her thong. She moved naked toward the bed. Offered him a tantalizing view of her firm ass as she bent down to open the top drawer of the nightstand. She pulled out a condom and the tube of lubrication they'd been using the past week.

"You would have loved it," she corrected, her blue eyes sizzling with heat. "Come on, Becker, tell me it doesn't turn you on—the thought of Ryan's cock plunging inside me. Tell me you don't get hard thinking about him inside my pussy while you fuck my ass."

His dick turned to marble, pushing against his zipper. Damn it. Damn *her*. She was right. Despite the jealousy pulsing through his veins, he *was* turned on.

Jane eyed him knowingly, then shot a pointed look at his bulging erection. "That's what I thought." She licked her lips, desire and anger battling on her beautiful face. "Come here, Becker. Take your goddamn clothes off and come here. Let's see how much it turns you on."

It was almost like a magnetic force drew him to her. His body was taut, muscles straining as he did what she asked and shucked his clothing. He walked over to her, naked, his cock eagerly jutting out at her.

Her touch wasn't gentle as she gripped his erection. "I want you in my ass," she said in a throaty voice.

Becker's pulse sped up like a racecar tearing toward the finish line. "Are you serious?"

"Dead serious." She teased his tip with her index finger, rubbing the drop of precome. "And I want you to pretend he's here with us."

He opened his mouth to protest, but she cut him off with a stern look. "You started this, Beck, and we're going to finish it."

She gave his cock one last caress, then lowered herself onto the bed and tossed him the condom. He rolled the latex onto his stiff shaft and joined Jane on the bed, reaching for the lube. He squirted a hefty amount into his palm, then flipped her onto her stomach and began to stroke her. Kneaded her firm cheeks with his hand. Circled her puckered hole with his finger, got it nice and slick. Jane gasped when he slipped the tip of his finger into her ass.

"Want me to stop?" he said hoarsely.

"No, keep going." She moaned as he pushed his finger deeper inside. "*Yes*, Beck, keep doing that."

His heart pounded, his groin so tight with anticipation he could barely move. Fuck, he wanted to be in that tight ass. He stretched her with his finger, rubbing lube over the delicate opening. A second finger entered the mix, then a third, until Jane was moaning wildly. She was on her hands and knees, but when he poised himself behind her, she rolled onto her side and said, "Like this. I want you to imagine him here with us, fucking me from the front while you're thrusting from behind."

A jolt of arousal shot through him. The picture she'd just painted wasn't supposed to turn him on, damn it. But it did. It fucking did.

Becker slid down and pressed himself into the graceful curve of her back. His balls were heavy, aching with the need for release. He shoved Jane's unruly red waves off her neck and kissed her nape, swirling his tongue over the little hairs there. She whimpered and wiggled her ass into him. She was slick from the lube, slicker from the sweet juices soaking her pussy. When he slid his hand between her legs and felt the moisture pooled there, he couldn't help but slide into her pussy for a few languid strokes. They both groaned, and Becker pushed in deeper, thrust harder, cupping a firm ass cheek with one hand and teasing her puckered hole with his other. He slid his finger inside, and she was so tight, he was paralyzed with lust. Fuck, he needed to be in there.

Sucking in a breath, he withdrew from her pussy, pressed his tip against that tight rosette and eased his cock inside.

Jane let out a cry of pleasure. "More," she begged.

He gave her more, sliding in another inch, but it still wasn't good enough for her. Whimpering, she pushed her ass out and forced him to fill her completely. Becker nearly fainted from the incredible sensation. She was so goddamn tight, it felt like a hot fist clenching his cock.

Jane shifted, her hand moving between her thighs, and then he felt pressure against his cock and realized she was fingering herself while he was buried in her ass. "Do you feel that?" she whispered.

He couldn't make his vocal cords work, but managed a groan.

"Imagine it's him." He felt her slip another finger into her pussy, at the same time his cock pumped in and out of her ass. "Can you see him, Beck? Can you see him pushing his cock into me?"

God help him, but he saw it. He saw Ryan's hips moving against Jane, saw Ryan's features tightening with pleasure. Each time she pushed her fingers deeper, he imagined it was Ryan's dick inside Jane. His pulse shrieked in his ears, his chest heaving from each ragged breath.

"You like it, don't you?" she said softly.

"Yes," he ground out.

"It turns you on."

"Yes."

"Good."

Becker closed his eyes and lost himself in Jane, thrusting into her with long, frantic pumps. Her husky moans drove him wild. So did the forbidden images swimming through his mind. Another man in bed with them. Another cock bringing Jane pleasure. When she began to shudder from orgasm, Becker let himself go too. He couldn't last long, not inside that unbelievably tight channel, not when Jane was writhing and moaning in the sexiest fucking way. He couldn't stop coming, couldn't stop driving in and out of her sweet ass.

When the pleasure finally ebbed, he felt shell-shocked. Jane's back was soaked with sweat, sticking to his own sweaty chest like glue. His heartbeat was out of control, his breathing unsteady. And when Jane finally rolled over so they were face to face and kissed him, he was nothing but a pile of mindless mush. Unable to think or breathe or move.

"Did it work?" she murmured, brushing her lips over his again.

He found his voice. "Did what work?"

"Did you get me out of your system?"

He met her gaze, and the vulnerability he saw there made his heart squeeze. Had he gotten her out of his system? He wanted to laugh. Yeah, right. If anything, he wanted her even more. He'd never come that fucking hard. While fantasizing about another man screwing the woman in his bed, no less.

A wave of unease swelled in his gut. Christ. What was he doing? Since the moment he'd met Jane, he'd been acting on impulse. Having sex with her in an elevator. Agreeing to a fling. Considering *threesomes*, for fuck's sake.

This wasn't him. He wasn't that guy. He was thirty-two years old and all he wanted was to settle down. Find himself a sweet, loving wife, have a couple of kids, build a nice, stable life for himself.

Instead, he'd once again wound up with a woman he couldn't have any of that with. Jane was incredible, yes, but she wasn't going to be the sweet, loving housewife he desired. She was ambitious, determined to win a Pulitzer. And she'd admitted more than once this week, when he'd broached the subject, that she had no desire to have kids any time soon. So what was he supposed to do? Wait around for another fourteen years the way he'd done with Alice?

"Becker?"

Her soft voice brought him back to reality. He realized he hadn't answered her question. "No," he confessed. "I didn't get you out of my system."

The corner of her mouth lifted. "Pity."

Ignoring the heavy weight pressing down on his heart, he released an unstable breath and said, "But I think I know how I can."

Confusion crossed her face. She let out a breath of her own, suddenly wary. "We're actually still on this topic? I'm leaving in three days, Beck. Let's just enjoy the time we have left."

"I...can't." He swallowed. "It's not fair to either one of us if we continue this...this fling, or whatever the hell we're calling it now. Three more days won't make a difference. In the end, I still don't want a relationship."

Her eyes narrowed. "You're lying."

He faltered. "What?"

Slowly, she disentangled herself from his arms and sat up. Her bare breasts rose with each breath she took. "You do want a relationship. This entire week, you've dropped hints about it, about the kind of life you want to have." Jane's cheeks turned pink with anger. "The life you described, well, it obviously requires a specific type of woman. In other words, not *me*."

He gulped again, fighting a pang of discomfort. "Jane, I think you're amazing, you know that."

Her eyes flashed. "Amazing, but not good enough, right?"

Before he could respond, she flounced off the bed and grabbed her dress off the floor. She threw it over her head without bothering with undergarments, and as she tied her halter back together, she shook her head at him. "You're an idiot, Becker."

His nostrils flared. "Why? Because I want a different sort of relationship this time around? I've already been with one career-minded woman who didn't want to settle down. I can't do it again." He locked his gaze to hers. "Tell me, Jane, what kind of relationship do you want?"

Hesitation flickered on her face. Finally she sighed and said, "I want to settle down. One day."

Becker couldn't stop the burst of disappointment that went off in his chest. Perpetually honest, that was Jane. Though, even if she'd tried to lie and convince him their life goals were aligned, he would've been able to see through her. Jane was very easy to read. Probably because she was incapable of lying.

"So why drag this out?" he asked softly, rising naked from the bed. He found his jeans and pulled them up to his hips. "I like you, Jane." His features twisted. "I more than like you. Fuck, a few more days and I can see myself half in love with you."

Her throat bobbed as she gulped. "I know what you mean."

"That's why we need to end it now." His chest constricted the second the words came out. "We want different things out of life. Giving ourselves three more days to get even more attached is a bad idea."

She didn't answer for a moment, and when she did, there was sadness in her tone. "You're right." She paused. "I'll just gather up my stuff and head back to my room."

Becker eliminated the distance between them and gently took hold of her arm before she could go to the door. "Hey, you can't just hurry off. Can we at least say a proper goodbye?"

Jane gave a faint smile. "You just fucked me in the ass. Can't that be our goodbye?"

His mouth twitched. Damn, he really would miss her sass. He swept his gaze over her, taking in the sight of her tousled red hair, messy and sweat-dampened from the sex. The way her dress slid over each curve of her petite body. Her full lips, red and bee-stung from their kisses. She'd never looked more beautiful.

"C'mere," he said gruffly, reaching for her.

Jane hesitated, then allowed him to draw her into his embrace. He held her tight, inhaling the sweet scent of her shampoo, smiling when her hair tickled the tip of his nose. Then he dipped his head, placing a tender kiss on her lips. She kissed him back, her tongue darting out for one brief moment to meet his, then retreating.

"It's been fun," she said lightly as she stepped out of his arms.

"More than fun," he corrected. He shifted awkwardly. "Will you send me a copy of the magazine when your article comes out?"

"Sure." She bent down and collected her underwear from the floor. Tucking it into her purse, she ruefully glanced at the other items of clothing strewn across the room. "Can you toss everything else into the duffel I brought over and have it sent to my room?"

"No problem." His throat suddenly felt thick, tight. "I'll see you around, Jane."

"See you around, Becker," she echoed.

She slung the strap of her purse over her shoulder and walked out of the room. As the front door clicked shut, Becker realized they'd just spoken the same parting words they'd exchanged that first day, when they went their separate ways after the elevator encounter.

Last time, the goodbye hadn't stuck.

This time, he had to make sure it did.

Chapter Seven

JANE WOKE UP THE NEXT MORNING TO THE SOUND OF HER CELL PHONE chirping out a tinny rendition of a Bon Jovi song. It was her sister's ringtone, which was the only reason she forced herself into a sitting position and grabbed the phone from the bedside table. She hadn't spoken to Liz since she'd driven down to San Diego from LA, and she wanted to make sure her older sister was doing okay. Being held hostage in South America wasn't an easy experience to forget, though Liz kept acting like it was no biggie.

"Hey, Lizzie," she said sleepily, rubbing her eyes.

"Hey, Janie," her sister teased. "Did I wake you?"

"Yeah, but don't worry, I had to get up anyway." She shifted the phone to her other ear and climbed out of bed.

"How's the writing going?"

"At the moment, it's not. But I'm planning on sitting down and finishing the first draft today."

"Did you end up getting an interview with Lieutenant Becker?"

Jane ignored the pain and regret that filled her belly. "No, he didn't agree to it."

"I thought that would happen." Liz chuckled. "He seemed like a very private man."

"He is."

"But that body — it's to die for, isn't it?"

Another spark of pain. Yep, Becker's body truly was amazing. But not as amazing as the rest of him. She'd spent nearly a week with the man, plenty of time to get acquainted with his other attributes. Like the gentle way he brushed her hair off her forehead. His rare smiles and even rarer bursts of laughter. His intelligence. The way he accepted her completely, appreciated her candid nature and total lack of inhibition.

Except…he hadn't completely accepted her, now had he? She hadn't been enough for him, when it mattered.

Irritation nipped at her throat. His ex-wife had screwed him up pretty badly, and now he was going out of his way to find a woman who probably didn't even exist. This wasn't the 1950s anymore. Chances were, he'd have a tough time finding that perfect, childbearing housewife of his.

Not that it was any of her business. She and Becker were over. The fling had ended. Now she needed to focus on other things, namely writing her article and going back to LA.

"Listen," her sister was saying, "Mom and Dad are planning a party for Ken's birthday. We're using one of his photos as the cover of the invitation, but Mom wanted you to write the text."

Jane bit back her surprise. Her family didn't usually make much of an effort to acknowledge her career. Sure, scribbling the text for an invitation wouldn't showcase her writing or anything, but it was the first time they'd bothered to include her in something. A rush of warmth filled her heart. Maybe almost losing Liz had made her parents realize their younger daughter was important too.

"Tell Mom I'll call her when I get home," Jane said. "I'd be happy to help out."

"Good." Liz's voice softened. "You sure you're okay? You sound…sad."

"I'm fine," she lied. "Just busy."

"Well, finish up that article and come home already. We'll go out for lunch when you get back, okay?"

"Okay."

The two sisters hung up, and Jane drifted into the bathroom. After she brushed her teeth and took a quick shower, she put on a pair of denim shorts and a yellow tank top, suddenly feeling a burst of inspiration. Talking to Liz had reminded her of the reason she'd come here in the first place. She picked up the laptop case sitting on the dresser and carried it over to the sitting area, which consisted of a tiny table and semi-comfortable chair. She pulled the computer out of its case, booted it up, and got to work.

She worked for four hours straight, only stopping to take a quick lunch break and order room service. It was nearly six o'clock when she finally leaned back in the chair and rolled her aching shoulders. Done. As she read over her work, she realized she'd completely forgotten about the interview she'd scheduled with Ryan Evans, but she decided she didn't need it. The story of her sister's ordeal was just as powerful without the interview.

And it was pretty damn good, if she said so herself. It probably would have been better if the magazine could print that gorgeous photo of Beck standing in front of the helicopter. But Becker had made his refusal clear.

He'd made a lot of things clear, hadn't he?

Stop thinking about him.

The voice in her head was firm, but it didn't deter Jane from thinking about him. From remembering all the time they'd spent together this week. Damn it. What was the matter with that man? The two of them were explosive together. Jane had never felt a connection like this with a man before, and she knew Becker had felt that same connection. Obviously it hadn't mattered to him as much as it mattered to her.

The ring of her phone jerked her out of her thoughts. Arching her stiff back to stretch it, she got up and grabbed the cell from the bed. An unfamiliar number flashed across the screen. Wary, she picked up. "Hello?"

"Finally," teased a male voice. "I was beginning to think you were avoiding me, and that was very upsetting. My ego is fragile."

She recognized the mischievous rasp of Ryan Evans' voice immediately. An unwitting smile reached her lips. "I'm not avoiding you. I've been working on my article and I tend to block out all outside noise when I'm writing. I take it you called before."

"Three times," he said with mock severity. "This is the most effort I've ever gone to for a woman."

"I'm flattered."

"You should be." Ryan finally grew serious. "So, did you still want to do that interview?"

Her gaze drifted to the laptop across the room. Technically, she didn't need Ryan anymore. She could just polish up the article, send it to Maureen tonight, and head back to LA tomorrow morning.

But that still meant she'd be alone tonight. Alone, most likely pigging out on room-service desserts, and thinking about Becker.

That did not sound like fun.

"Actually, I don't think I need the interview anymore," she answered. "But…I could use some company, if you're up for it."

"I'm up for anything when it comes to you."

His voice oozed sexuality, and Jane felt a blush creep into her cheeks. She thought about last night with Becker, how the two of them pretended Ryan was in the room with them. God, that had been hot.

Pushing the memory away, she cleared her throat. "Where do you want to meet?"

"I'm actually heading over to the Sand Bar tonight. I'm meeting Matt — Matt O'Connor, you met him yesterday — in a couple of hours, but I could meet you there now if you want."

"That sounds good."

"What's your poison? I'll order you something if I get there first."

"Margaritas," she said immediately. "I'm going to need a lot of margaritas."

JANE PASTED ON A SMILE AS SHE STRODE INTO THE SAND BAR, A SMALL but trendy bar located right on the boardwalk. The place was busy, filled with a mishmash of patrons, from surfers to a group of suit-clad men who looked like tax lawyers. On the phone, Ryan had told her the place had awesome chicken wings, but Jane was more interested in the alcohol it served. After yesterday's awful goodbye with Becker, she was looking forward to getting good and drunk.

Although the magazine had paid for her hotel room until Sunday, she'd already decided this would be her last night in San Diego. She was done with her article. She was done with Becker. Which meant there was really no reason for her to stick around. Might as well go home, focus on her job, and force herself to forget about the sexy Navy SEAL who'd rocked her world this week.

Ryan wasn't inside the bar when she walked in. She searched the crowded room and finally spotted him at one of the outdoor tables on a deck overlooking the ocean. She weaved her way toward him, ignoring the lewd whistle of a guy with spiky platinum hair, and the blatant ogling of a middle-aged man nursing a bottle of beer.

When she stepped outside, Ryan flashed an endearing grin and got to his feet. He was even sexier than she remembered, and completely opposite from Becker, who was strong and stoic, who exuded raw masculinity. Not that Ryan wasn't masculine. He had to be, with that lean, rippled body and the sexual energy it radiated, but he was laidback, cool in a very easygoing kind of way.

A little shiver danced up her spine as she remembered Becker's cock buried in her ass while she'd used her fingers to mimic Ryan inside her pussy. Arousal drummed through her blood, but quickly faded when she remembered Becker's subsequent goodbye. If she'd met Ryan first, maybe she would have hooked up with him. Now...well, she didn't want anyone but Thomas Becker.

Too bad he didn't want her.

"Did you have any problems getting here?" Ryan asked as he pulled out a chair for her.

The table he'd chosen seated two and was shaded by a huge red umbrella that fluttered in the evening breeze. On the horizon, the sun dipped into the water, filling the sky with brilliant shades of orange and pink. Jane set her purse on the wooden deck and sat down. "None," she said in response to his question. "I like it here. It's got a good atmosphere."

He sat down again. "That's why we come here. Oh, this is for you." He pushed the margarita glass across the table, the liquid coming perilously close to spilling over the rim.

"Thanks," she said gratefully. She picked up the glass, tipped it back, and drank nearly half of it.

Ryan's dark eyebrows shot to his forehead. He watched as she licked the salt from her lips, his blue eyes flickering with amusement. "So why the urgent need for company?"

She took another long sip, enjoying the lemony flavor of the alcohol as it slid down her throat. "I didn't want to be alone in my hotel room all night," she confessed.

Ryan looked intrigued. He dragged a hand through his dark hair and leaned back in his chair. "The Lieutenant is busy tonight?" he asked in a careful tone.

"The Lieutenant dumped me," she said glumly. Avoiding his eyes, she polished off the rest of her drink and signaled the waitress for another one.

When she glanced back at Ryan, he looked shocked. "Lieutenant Becker dumped you?"

She nodded.

His seductive blue eyes traveled down her face and rested briefly on her breasts, which practically poured out of her thin tank top. She hadn't bothered changing after Ryan's phone call. Just hopped in the car in her ratty cut-off shorts and practically see-through top. At least she was wearing a bra, though she could feel the heat of Ryan's gaze directly against her bare skin, teasing her nipples.

He finally lifted his gaze, shaking his head to himself. "Was he on drugs?"

"Nope." She shrugged. "He thinks I'm not his type."

Another flash of surprise from Ryan, followed by a lazy smile. "Janie, I think you're everyone's type."

She laughed. "Has anyone ever told you you're unbelievably charming?"

"I hear it all the time." He smiled devilishly, and a pair of adorable dimples creased his cheeks. Reaching for his beer, he took a long swig, then set down the bottle. He looked determined as he leaned forward on both elbows. "I have an idea. Want to know what it is?"

"Hell, yes."

He opened his mouth, only to get interrupted by the waitress, who deposited another margarita in front of Jane. With a quick thanks, Jane picked up the fresh glass and sipped, waiting for Ryan to continue.

"So here's what I'm thinking," he drawled. "For some reason, Lieutenant Becker was stupid enough to let you get away. I, on the other hand, would never commit such an atrocity."

She tightened her lips to stop from laughing. "Okay. And?"

"And I think it's a shame for you to spend your last few days in San Diego alone when you could be naked. With me," he finished, shooting her an innocent smile that revealed his straight white teeth.

Jane stared at him. "Oh my God. You're Man-Jane." She shook her head in bewilderment, wondering if this was how those chicks from *The Parent Trap* felt when they discovered they had a twin. "You're me."

Ryan wrinkled his forehead. "Is that a good thing, or a bad one?"

She pursed her lips as she mulled it over. "Well, it's bad for you, because I don't think I could sleep with a guy who reminds me this much of myself. It's weird. But it's also good for you, because I have no problem getting absolutely sloshed with a guy who reminds me this much of myself." She picked up her second drink and drained it.

Ryan offered a wolfish grin. "I still think revenge sex is a better way to get over Becker."

She flagged down the waitress and ordered another drink, this time a martini. "You never know," she said with a shrug. "I could get drunk enough that revenge sex might start looking pretty good."

His grin widened. "Fingers fucking crossed."

Chapter Eight

Becker spent the entire day going over the rental listings his realtor emailed, but if anyone asked him to describe any of the houses, he'd draw a blank. It was hard to focus when he couldn't quit thinking about Jane. Wondering what she was doing. Debating if he should call her up, tell her to forget everything he'd said yesterday, and take her to bed again.

He managed to fight the temptation, but by the time eight o'clock rolled around, he was anxious as hell. He'd gone to the hotel restaurant for dinner, convincing himself it was so he could get out of the cottage, but deep down he knew he was hoping to run into Jane. He hadn't, and now he was back in his room, absently flipping channels on the TV and wondering how the hell it was possible to miss someone so much, especially someone he'd only known a week.

Shutting off the TV, he finally gave up on trying to distract himself with mindless sitcoms. Maybe if he had someone to talk to about this. Someone who could offer some advice, tell him what to do. His head kept telling him to get over it, that Jane wasn't the right woman for him. She was too bold, too ambitious, breezing through life with her sassy smiles and act-before-you-think attitude. He didn't want another woman like that. He wanted to be with a woman who desired the same things as he did, not *one day* as Jane had said, but right now.

So yeah, his head knew all this. But his heart? His heart ached for Jane. Or maybe it was his cock doing the aching. Maybe she'd cast an erotic spell on him.

Regardless, he couldn't sit around here anymore, thinking about her. Before he could stop himself, Becker reached for his phone and scrolled through the contacts list until he came across one particular name. He hesitated. Fuck, did he really want to do this? Initiate some awkward male bonding time?

Do you really want to be alone? a voice countered.

With a sigh, he pressed send and waited.

Carson Scott answered the phone after two rings. "Hello?" the other man said easily.

"Uh, Carson, it's Becker." He cleared his throat, uncomfortable. He would've rather talked to Will Charleston, but Will lived too far away. Carson, on the other hand, was only five minutes away, having just moved into a building not far from the hotel. John Garrett lived around here too, but Becker definitely wasn't comfortable calling Garrett, who he knew the least out of all the men.

"Lieutenant?" The surprise in Carson's voice was unmistakable. "Hey. What's up?"

"Nothing really." He faltered. "I just called to see if you felt like having a beer. With me." For Christ's sake, could he make it sound any more like a date?

There was a pause. "A beer. Uh, sure," Carson finally agreed, still sounding confused. "I'm actually watching the Padres game right now. You want to come over here?"

"Yeah, I can do that. I can be there in ten."

"Cool." Carson rattled off his address and apartment number. "See you in a bit."

Becker hung up the phone and stared at it for a moment. He could call back. Cancel. Tell Carson he'd changed his mind. But what was the alternative? Channel surf some more and think about how much he wanted to see Jane again?

He was in the car five minutes later, driving toward Carson's building. This was the first time he'd made an effort to see one of his teammates outside of work, and as he pulled into the visitor's lot of Carson's low-rise, he found himself growing nervous. Shit, maybe he ought to turn around and go back to the hotel. He didn't know how to do the friend thing, sharing your feelings and all that crap. He'd always been a private person, and he felt a spark of annoyance toward Jane as he realized she was the one who'd driven him to make social contact.

If he hadn't met her, he wouldn't be so torn up in knots right now. He wouldn't need to seek out advice from a man he hardly knew.

Sighing, he got out of the car and stuffed his hands in his pockets, warily eyeing the quaint building that boasted redbrick walls covered by strands of ivy. The front entrance was small, featuring a series of mailboxes and intercoms. Becker searched for Carson's name, then pressed the button.

"Hello?" came a female voice.

Becker cleared his throat. "Uh, hey. It's Thomas Becker."

"Oh, hi! I'm so glad you're here. I need a second opinion about my Osso Buco. I'm buzzing you in."

An opinion about her *what?* Before he could decipher the weird remark, the door clicked open with a loud buzz. Becker walked through it and headed for the elevator.

Carson's apartment was on the third floor at the end of a narrow corridor with a clean tiled floor. Becker was just reaching his hand out to knock when the front door flung open and a stunning brunette with big green eyes appeared before him.

"Hi, I'm Holly," she said cheerfully. "Come in. Carson's in the living room."

He followed Holly into the small hallway, trying his best not to ogle her. She wore a pair of teeny black shorts and a bright green T-shirt, and though she couldn't have been much taller than five feet, she held a lot of energy in her petite body.

"I'm so glad to finally meet you," she said with a big smile. "Shelby and I wanted to throw you a welcome-to-the-team party when you first got here, but Carson said it wasn't your thing."

"Shelby?" he said blankly.

Holly shoved a wayward strand of brown hair off her forehead. "John Garrett's wife. She owns the bakery a few blocks from here. Oh, and she's pregnant!" Holly beamed at him. "Isn't that amazing? They just found out last week."

"Um..."

"For God's sake, sweetheart, leave the Lieutenant alone," came Carson's drawl. "I told you not to scare him off."

Holly linked her arm through Becker's as she led him into the living room, where Carson was sitting on the couch with a beer in his hands. "He's not scared of me," she said. "Right, Thomas?"

"Becker," Carson corrected.

Holly pursed her lips. "You don't like Thomas?" she said curiously.

He shifted awkwardly. "I like it." He shrugged. "People have just always called me Becker most of my life. I don't know who started it, but it stuck."

"Well, I like the name Thomas better," she answered. "It sounds very dignified." She let go of his arm and gestured to the couch. "Sit down. I'll bring out a sample for you."

"A sample?" Becker asked in a low voice as Holly bounded toward a doorway he assumed led into the kitchen. He sat on the long beige couch and accepted the bottle Carson offered him.

"She's trying out a new recipe," Carson explained. "Holly's a chef."

At Carson's explanation, Becker nodded, suddenly noticing the intoxicating aroma wafting in from the kitchen. Garlic, tomatoes, and a mixture of herbs. It smelled like heaven. Tasted like heaven too, he found out, after Holly returned with a small plate loaded with veal covered in a creamy tomato sauce and practically forced him to take a bite.

"This is amazing," Becker said in awe. "You're really good."

"Thanks." She took his empty plate. "I'm going to finish experimenting. You boys be good."

Holly left the room again. Becker's gaze drifted toward the television screen. The Padres game was at the bottom of the eighth, with the Padres leading by two runs, but he wasn't interested. He'd never been much of a baseball fan. Football was his sport of choice.

"So," Carson said, after the silence between them dragged on for far too long. "Not to be rude or anything, but what the hell are you doing here? We've known each other for seven months and you haven't once acted like you were into making friends."

Becker respected the other man's candor. It was probably what made him offer a frank answer of his own. "I've been an ass to you guys, haven't I?"

Carson's eyes flickered with amusement. "Yup."

"I'm sorry." He took a long sip of beer. "In case you haven't noticed, I'm not very good at socializing."

"I've noticed," Carson said dryly. He grinned. "But neither was Will at first, and I managed to draw him out of his prickly shell. I have faith in you too, Lieutenant."

"Quit calling me that. We're not on a mission."

"Sorry, it's a habit." Carson sipped his own beer, turning his gaze away from the screen to study Becker. "So why were you stir crazy? Did you get in a fight with that sexy-as-sin redhead you were with the other day?"

"Not really." He gave a noncommittal shrug.

"Then why the hell aren't you with her?"

Holly suddenly poked her head into the living room. "With who?" she asked, looking super interested. "Are you gossiping? If so, I want to know everything."

"I'm giving the Lieutenant love advice, babe. Mind your own business."

She groaned. "Oh God. Thomas, don't listen to him. He's terrible at giving advice."

Becker found himself grinning as Holly bounced back into the room. She flopped down on the armchair across from the couch, leaned forward and narrowed her eyes at Becker. "Okay, tell me everything. I'm much better at this kind of thing. Who is she?"

Discomfort tugged at his gut. He shot Carson a save-me look, but the younger man just shrugged as if to say, *There's no stopping it now.* So he turned back to Holly and said, "Jane."

Leaning back in the chair, Holly crossed her arms over her chest. "Jane. All right. What's the problem with Jane?"

"There's no problem. She's…great." He swallowed. "More than great, actually."

"Is she reluctant to get involved? Because that's what happened to Will." Holly offered a wide smile. "Luckily, I stepped in and saved the day, and now Will and Mac are happily married."

Carson set down his beer and pointed a finger at Holly. "Oh no. No, no, no, you are not doing it again." He shook his head at Becker. "She pretended to be Will's girlfriend to make Mackenzie jealous. Oh, and she let him *kiss* her."

"For show," Holly emphasized. "And it worked, didn't it?"

Carson growled. "What's next? You going to hire yourself out for weddings and bar mitzvahs?"

Despite the bickering and totally weird subject matter, Becker was extremely amused by Carson and his girlfriend. He could tell they were madly in love, even when they were grumbling at each other. And Holly reminded him a lot of Jane. Her sass, the stubborn tilt of her chin.

At the thought of Jane, his chest tightened. Damn it, why couldn't he stop thinking about her?

"So what's the problem?" Holly asked, fixing shrewd green eyes on Becker.

He opened his mouth, intending to lie and say there was no problem, but instead, he ended up telling them everything. His encounter with Jane in the elevator, the incredible week they'd spent together, his reluctance to get involved with her. He even spilled some details about his marriage, a topic he hadn't spoken about with anyone but Jane.

When he finished, Holly looked bewildered. "But it sounds like you really care about her. Why can't you be with her?"

A heavy breath rolled out of his chest. "She reminds me too much of my ex."

Next to him, Carson took another swig of beer and then set the bottle down with a laugh. "Actually, she sounds nothing like your ex."

He frowned. "Why do you say that?"

Carson shrugged. "Well, you described your ex-wife as — not to sound like an ass — a selfish bitch."

"Carson," Holly chided.

Becker smiled wryly. "No, he's right. Alice isn't the nicest person."

"But Jane is," Carson pointed out. "I played nine holes of mini-golf with her, and not once did I get the selfish bitch vibe from her."

"And you said she didn't even bug you about the interview," Holly chimed in.

"Yeah," he admitted.

"So she can't be as bad as your ex," Holly said confidently. "You said your ex-wife would do anything to get ahead in her career. Well, if Jane was like that, she wouldn't have given up until she got that scoop she originally came for. Instead, she accepted your answer and left it alone."

Holly had a point. Jane had completely dropped the issue of his interview, which was something Alice never would've done. "But..." He drained the rest of his beer, wishing the two of them hadn't put him on the spot like this. He could tell from their expressions that they thought he was an idiot for ending things with Jane, and the longer they stared at him, the more he started to wonder if maybe they were right. "She doesn't want the same things as me," he finally said.

"Marriage, family?" Holly prompted.

"Yeah."

"Can you honestly tell me those are things you plan to have right this second?" Holly rolled her eyes. "You can't just snap your fingers and find yourself a wife, unless you plan on ordering one from some weird Russian website. No matter what, you'll have to date someone, take the time to fall in love with her, see if there's a connection. At least with Jane, you know the connection is there."

Fuck, another good point. He was starting to regret ever coming here.

Carson threw in his two cents. "I think you should give her a chance. You're obviously falling for her, so why not see where things go? And if in a few months you find she's really not the right woman for you, then I promise I'll buy you that Russian bride myself."

Becker couldn't help but laugh. "Thanks. That means a lot to me."

Carson grinned. "Good, so go talk to her."

He leaned back against the sofa cushions, only to notice both Holly and Carson looking at him. "What?" he said defensively.

"Go talk to her," Holly burst out, looking frazzled.

Becker blinked. "Now?"

"No, next month," Carson said. "Don't get me wrong, we can crack open a few more beers and watch the rest of this boring-ass game, but wouldn't you rather be having make-up sex with your sexy redhead right now?"

Holly leaned forward again, looking intrigued. "Oooh, is she really that attractive?" she asked her boyfriend. When Carson nodded, she swung her head at Becker. "What are you waiting for? Get her back already."

BECKER'S CONFIDENCE WAS SKY-HIGH AS HE DROVE BACK TO THE HOTEL. Damn, Carson and his girlfriend ought to go into motivational speaking.

The two of them had pumped him up, made him feel like getting Jane back was the only course of action to take. And why shouldn't he? They were right. He *was* falling for her. He had fun with Jane, more fun than he'd ever had with a woman before. She made him laugh, which was pretty much a miracle considering that with Alice, he'd barely cracked a smile in over a decade.

He couldn't help wondering if he was being reckless. Maybe even foolish. Jane would be leaving in two days, heading back to LA, a good two-hour drive from Coronado. How would they ever even see each other? Which one of them would make the commute? Would Jane even consider doing it?

He forced himself not to dwell on the minor details. There was no point in thinking about any of that until he knew if Jane was even willing to continue their relationship once she left. Fuck, he hoped she would. Carson and Holly had made him realize how unfair he'd been to her. Her resemblance to Alice, now that he thought about it, was pretty fucking flimsy. Big deal, so they shared some common personality traits. When it came to the traits that mattered, Jane was not Alice, and never would be.

He parked the SUV in the guest lot and got out. His palms grew damp as he pulled his phone from his pocket. It was only a quarter to ten. Jane probably wasn't asleep yet. He dialed the front desk and asked to be connected to her room, but the anticipation fizzled after the tenth ring, when Jane still hadn't picked up. She'd either fallen asleep, or simply wasn't taking any calls.

It didn't even occur to him that she might not be in her room, not until the sound of a car engine caught his attention. An olive-green Jeep Cherokee pulled into the parking lot, and Becker's breath froze in his lungs when he spotted the two familiar figures in the vehicle. He discreetly ducked between his SUV and the minivan beside it, forcing his pulse to slow. Fuck. That couldn't have been Jane in that Jeep. Sitting next to Ryan Evans.

He peered out from his hiding spot, his hands curling into fists as he received confirmation. Across the lot, Evans hopped out of the Jeep, then bounded toward the passenger door to help Jane out. She tripped and stumbled into Ryan's arms, letting out a laugh that echoed through the deserted lot and hardened Becker's veins.

He stood there, frozen in place, as Ryan wrapped his arm around Jane's shoulders and bent to say something in her ear. She laughed again, and then the two of them headed for the path leading toward the hotel.

Becker watched them go, unable to move, unable to stop the simultaneous jolts of anger and betrayal.

One day. That's all it had taken for her to hook up with another man. And here he was, pining over her for the past twenty-four hours, second-guessing his decision to end things, coming here to win her back. What a fucking moron he was. What did he expect, that she'd be missing him too? She'd said so herself. She liked sex. And she'd been attracted to Evans. Not to mention her admission that she'd never had a relationship that lasted more than a few months.

Well, theirs had lasted a full week.

He slowly uncurled his fists, sucking in a long breath. Fuck. He needed to calm down. Needed to restrain himself, before he lost control, marched over to Jane's room and punched Ryan's lights out. Getting angry wouldn't achieve a goddamn thing. Either way, he'd completely deluded himself into thinking he and Jane could have something serious. How could they? Jane wasn't serious. She was fun and flirty and fucking another man right at this very moment. How could he get serious with a woman like that?

Tightening his jaw, he tore his gaze away from the direction Jane and Evans had gone. As much as it hurt to see them together, at least it'd snapped some sense into him. He and Jane had fucked for a week, and now she'd found a new bedmate. Big deal. He'd get over it.

He'd get over *her*.

He let out a ragged breath, straightened his shoulders and headed to his cottage, all the while trying to convince himself that getting over Jane would be absolutely no trouble at all.

Chapter Nine

"OKAY, ARE YOU GOING TO TELL ME WHAT'S BOTHERING YOU OR SHOULD I tell Mom and Dad so they can harass you about it?" Jane's sister demanded, her hands on her hips as she loomed over Jane.

Jane had been lying on her comfy couch, a carton of ice cream in her lap, when her sister had marched into her apartment as if she owned the place and started the interrogation. "I don't see what the big deal is," Jane said defensively, sliding up into a cross-legged position. "I took a week off work so I could chill out for a while. Why is that cause for concern?"

"Because you never take time off," Liz said, her blonde ponytail flipping as she plopped down on the couch. "You've practically lived in your office for the past two years."

"Well, I needed a break." She jammed her spoon into the carton and brought out a scoop of cookie dough ice cream, which she swirled around in her mouth before swallowing. God, ice cream was the best thing ever. She'd been back in LA for a week now, and so far the only thing that had managed to cheer her up was ice cream.

"Why?" Liz pressed. "What happened in San Diego, Janie? You've been depressed ever since you got back."

"I'm not depressed."

"Sad, then."

"I'm not sad."

Liz groaned with frustration. "I *will* call Mom. She'll get the truth out of you."

Jane sighed. She set down the carton on the glass coffee table and turned to her sister. "Fine, I'll tell you what's wrong, but please don't tell Mom, okay?"

Triumph lit her sister's eyes. "I *knew* something was wrong. Tell me everything."

Jane spilled her guts. She told Liz all about Becker, the wild sex, her growing feelings for him, how he'd ended it before it could even begin. She finished by confessing how she'd spent her final night in San Diego—drunker than drunk. She left out the part about Ryan being there, since it wasn't important. Nope, the only truly important thing was how desperately she missed Thomas Becker.

"Then call him," Liz said when Jane voiced the thought out loud.

"I can't. He made it clear he doesn't see a future with me. He wants some perfect, obedient little housewife who'll pop out half a dozen babies for him, and we both know I'm neither perfect nor obedient," she said wryly.

Her sister grinned. "No, obedient you most certainly are not. Not perfect either, but..." Liz's voice was laced with affection as she said, "You're an amazing woman, Janie. Any man would be lucky to have you."

"Too bad the one I want doesn't see it that way."

She went for the ice cream again, but Liz intercepted her, pushing the carton out of reach. "Thomas Becker is obviously an idiot. If he can't see what's right in front of him, then he doesn't deserve you."

Jane didn't answer. Liz was probably right, but that didn't mean she could simply erase her feelings for Becker. It was so messed up. She'd only spent a week with the man. One freaking week, yet she'd connected with him in a way she never had with any other man.

"Come on, get up," Liz ordered. She stood and held out her hand. "Let's go."

Jane allowed her sister to help her to her feet. "Where are we going?"

"Anywhere. You need to get out of the apartment and stop thinking about Becker."

She glanced down at her ratty sweatpants. "I'm not even dressed."

"Then get dressed. We'll go get a manicure or see a movie, or just walk down Sunset and window shop."

"I don't—"

"No argument," Liz interrupted. "Now get dressed so we can work on helping you put Thomas Becker right out of your mind, okay?"

The image of Becker's serious face and spectacular body floated into her mind, eliciting a spark of hurt. She quickly pushed it aside, taking a deep breath. "Let's go."

BECKER HAD NO CLUE WHY HE AGREED TO SHOOT POOL WITH CARSON tonight. Ever since the night he'd seen Jane and Ryan together at the hotel, draped all over each other, he'd avoided his fellow SEALs, especially Carson. There'd been a couple of messages on his cell phone from Carson, and one from Holly, the day after he'd stopped by their place, but Becker hadn't returned the calls. Those two were the reason he'd gone to see Jane in the first place, and look how *that* turned out.

Fuck. There he went, thinking about her again. It had almost become a twisted game, counting how many times a day Jane slid into his mind. The current tally was six, and pathetically, that was just in the last hour.

"I'm still waiting to hear why you've been avoiding me this entire week," Carson said casually as he racked the balls on the pool table.

"I'm not avoiding you," Becker lied.

"Yes, you are. But whatever, don't tell me why." Carson stepped back and gestured for Becker to break the neatly arranged balls. "At least tell me what happened with Jane."

"Nothing. It didn't work out." Averting his eyes, he bent forward, pulled his cue back and sent the white ball smashing into the others, making them scatter on the green felt like frantic rats.

He straightened his back and examined the table, annoyed to see that despite the excessive strength he'd put into the shot, not a single ball had landed in a pocket.

Behind him, he heard Carson let out a frazzled breath. "What do you mean, it didn't work out? She wasn't interested?"

Before he could answer, he caught a flash of movement in his peripheral vision. An irrational knot of anger coiled around his insides when Ryan Evans and Matt O'Connor strode up to the pool table. They knocked fists with Carson, but didn't offer the easygoing gesture to Becker, simply nodding in greeting.

Becker forced himself to nod back. Forced himself not to glare at Evans, or even worse, unleash an upper cut into the younger man's jaw.

Ryan hadn't done anything wrong. So what if he'd slept with Jane? No matter how much the notion infuriated him, Becker couldn't blame Ryan. Fuck, he couldn't blame Jane, either. After all, he was the one who'd broken things off with her.

Still, it took a considerable amount of willpower to maintain a civil attitude toward Ryan. Just looking at the guy, Becker couldn't help but imagine him in bed with Jane. Which brought a wave of discomfort to his gut, since he and Jane had done just that, hadn't they? Imagined Ryan in bed with them. The uncomfortable ache faded back into anger as he realized the fantasy had come true—for Jane, at least. She'd wasted no time climbing into bed with Ryan. Becker's chest hurt just thinking about it.

"One of you grab me a beer, will you?" Carson said to the two newcomers.

"Get your own beer," Ryan said, rolling his eyes.

"Come on, please? I'm about to kick Beck's ass here."

Matt took pity on Carson and headed toward the long counter on the other side of the room. As Carson leaned forward to take his shot, Ryan turned to Becker and said, "Have you heard from Jane?"

His entire body tensed. Seriously? Evans was actually bringing up Jane, to *him*, the man who'd been fucking her only the day before Ryan?

"No," he said stiffly. "I haven't."

Ryan must have sensed the hostility, because he backed off and wandered over to Matt, who was returning with the beers. Evans and O'Connor went to stand by Carson, leaving Becker free to focus on the game. He bent to take a shot, forcing himself to relax. Wasn't Ryan's fault things hadn't worked out with Jane.

He sank a couple of balls, zoning out the conversation of the other guys, then missed what could have been a sweet combo. He straightened up, waiting for Carson to shoot, and that was when he caught the tail end of Ryan's comment to Matt.

"—like, incredible head. That blowjob should go down in history, pun intended."

Becker pressed his hands to his sides, fighting back a rush of rage-tinged disbelief. Wow. Evans was a real asshole to talk about this shit in front of him. And to give O'Connor details about what Jane was like in bed? Sleazy as hell.

Matt laughed. "Did you spend the night?"

"Nah. Awesome BJ aside, the sex wasn't all that great."

Beck's fingers curled into fists. Okay, this was fucking disrespectful. If Evans said even one more word...

"I like my women moaning and squirming and you know, getting into it. She just lay there, looking bored, making me do all the work." Ryan shrugged. "She was tight as hell, though—"

Becker snapped. One second he was standing by the pool table, the next he was shoving Evans hard against the wall. He seized the other man by the collar and shook him, his vision nothing but a red haze

"Don't fucking talk about her like that," Becker growled.

Shock flooded Ryan's face. "What the fuck are you doing, Lieutenant?"

He shook the younger guy again, his jaw so tight that his teeth started to hurt. "This isn't a locker room," he spat out. "Show her some goddamn respect."

A hand suddenly clamped down on Becker's shoulder. "Beck, let him go," came Carson's even voice.

Becker didn't ease his grip. Glaring at Ryan, he said, "If I hear you talking about Jane in that way again—"

"Jane?" Ryan interrupted, his eyes widening.

"What, you forgot her fucking name already?"

There was a short pause, and then Ryan sighed. "We weren't talking about Jane, man. We were talking about Cynthia."

Becker blinked. "Who?"

"Cynthia, the chick I hooked up with last night."

The air went rushing out of Becker's lungs. Cynthia? He looked into Ryan's eyes, saw the genuine confusion there, and cursed under his breath. Shit.

Slowly, he released Evans from his kung-fu hold and took a step back. As he noticed the curious eyes focused on him, not just from his team members, but the stares of the other bar patrons, he grew uncomfortable. *Shit.*

"I'm sorry," he muttered, his voice hoarse. "I thought you were... talking about her."

Ryan straightened the collar of his shirt, a flicker of annoyance entering his eyes. "That wasn't cool, Lieutenant."

"I know." He drew in a breath. "I'm sorry. I thought…"

"You thought I fucked her," Ryan finished knowingly. "Yeah, well, I would've, if she'd wanted me. But she didn't. I took her back to her hotel room where she spent half the night crying."

Becker swallowed his surprise. "Why was she crying?" he asked gruffly.

"Because you dumped her, you idiot."

"You can't call your superior officer an idiot," Carson said. He smirked. "But I can." He cast an irritated look in Becker's direction. "You're an idiot. You didn't even talk to her, did you?"

"No," Becker admitted.

"Why the fuck not?"

"Because…" He let out a sigh. "Because I thought she slept with *him*," he said, jerking his thumb at Ryan. He stared at the other guy in remorse. "I saw you two in the hotel parking lot. You had your arm around her, and you walked inside together. I assumed you…you know."

Ryan flashed a grin. "Like I said, I totally would have. But she's in love with you. She spent the entire night downing margaritas and talking about what a jerk you were for ending things, then she cried, then… well, then there was the vomit thing, and finally she went to bed." He gave a pointed look. "I slept on the floor, by the way. I only stayed the night because I didn't want her to be alone."

Becker had no idea what to say. He felt like a total asshole for making assumptions. And he felt like an even bigger asshole when he pictured Jane's silky-smooth cheeks soaked with tears. *He'd* caused those tears. He'd built up this foolish image of his perfect woman, a woman who was the complete opposite of his ex-wife. But who the fuck needed perfection? And why on earth would he ever want a sweet, docile wife when he could have his feisty, stubborn Jane?

"I'm an idiot," he mumbled under his breath.

Carson overheard the remark and said, "Trust us, we know."

JANE'S HANDS WERE FULL OF SHOPPING BAGS AS SHE CLIMBED THE STAIRS leading up to her third-floor apartment. Her building didn't have an elevator, but considering her claustrophobia, that was a blessing. Besides, hiking up all those stairs was good exercise. But also super irritating when trying to make the climb with a million shopping bags. Liz had been right, though. All she'd needed to do was get out of the house and already she felt much better. Of course, a shiny pair of Manolos and three new dresses could make anyone feel better.

Shifting the bags from her right hand to her left, she dug around in her purse in search of her keys, head bent as she headed down the corridor toward her apartment. She'd just grabbed hold of the key ring when she lost her grip on the purse. It went flying to the floor, its contents spilling onto the carpeted hallway floor.

"Argggggh," she said irritably.

"Need some help?"

The familiar voice caused her to drop the bags she was holding. Those fell too, joining her purse on the ground, but Jane was too stunned to pay attention to the discarded items. Becker was standing by her door, clad in a pair of khakis and a blue button-down shirt over a white T-shirt. Apprehension clouded his eyes, along with a spark of heat that burned brighter when their gazes locked.

"What are you doing here?" she squeaked.

"I wanted to see you," he said simply.

She swallowed. "Why?"

"Because I missed you."

Her heart did a little flip. She wanted to throw her arms around his strong, corded neck and kiss him, but she forced herself to stay put. She didn't fully trust this. Didn't fully trust *him*. What had changed? A week ago, he'd been telling her he didn't want to get attached to her, that her goals were too different from his, and now here he was, standing in front of her.

"You drove two hours to tell me you missed me? You could have just picked up the phone," she said quietly.

"No," he disagreed. "I couldn't."

"Why?" she repeated.

Becker stepped closer. She could see his pulse throbbing in his throat. "Because I need to say this in person."

She bit her lower lip. "Say what?"

He moved even closer. "That I'm in love with you."

Jane's mouth ran dry. "What?"

"You heard me," he said roughly. "I've fallen for you, Jane. And I was a total jerk for ending things the way I did."

"Yeah, you were," she agreed.

"I was going to tell you I made a mistake. I realized it the day after." His features creased with something that resembled guilt. "I came to find you that night at the hotel. Only when I got there, I saw you and Ryan in the parking lot, and I..."

"You thought I slept with him," she said flatly.

Shame swam in his eyes. "Yes. I jumped to conclusions. I..." His voice wobbled. "I figured it confirmed what I was thinking all along, that you weren't my type...you weren't serious about me."

Jane let out a shaky breath. "I was serious about you."

"Past tense?" he said, watching her carefully.

She met his gaze, and the hope and trepidation she saw there sent a rush of warmth flooding through her. "Present tense," she said softly. "I *am* serious about you."

He didn't speak for a moment. For so long, in fact, that she started to worry. But when he finally opened his mouth, it was worth the wait.

"I'm sorry, baby. I'm sorry for comparing you to Alice, for telling you you're not my type, and most of all, for believing you'd jump into bed with the first warm body you came across." He stepped forward, one callused hand reaching out to stroke her cheek. "Can we start over?"

A part of her wanted to scream *yes!* But she tamped down the eager response and studied Becker's handsome face. "How will we make a relationship work, Beck? We live in different cities."

"Two hours away, that's all. And I promise you, I'll come up here whenever I can. I'll spend every available second making you happy, Jane."

Pleasure skittered up her spine. "Wow. You actually sound like you mean that."

"I do mean it." He smiled. "We can figure this out as we go along. I'll do the long-distance thing for as long as we have to. All I know is that I want to be with you. I'll take whatever I can get."

"What about the passive housewife you wanted?" she teased.

"Screw passive," he said fervently. He bent his head close to her ear. "I want aggressive, Jane. I want fiery and bold and honest. I want *you*."

And there it was. The three little words that made her melt. The three little words she'd wanted to hear since the moment Becker told her she didn't fit his blueprint for an ideal woman. Well, screw the blueprint. She'd known all along that she was exactly what he needed. Someone who made him laugh, someone who challenged him and excited him and turned him on. And now he knew it too.

She offered an innocent grin. "Took you long enough to figure it out, huh?"

"So I'm a little slow on the uptake. Don't rub it in." He planted his hands on her waist and yanked her toward him.

The second their bodies met, a ribbon of heat uncurled inside her body, making her skin burn.

"I missed you," Becker said gruffly.

Jane's eyelids fluttered closed as he leaned in to kiss her. When their lips touched, a thrill shot up her spine. "I missed you too," she whispered against his mouth.

They kissed again, and Jane was breathless by the time they finally broke apart. Her heart thudded wildly against her ribs, her nipples tingling, her panties soaked. "For the love of God," she blurted out. "Help me pick up all these bags so we can go inside."

Becker's eyes twinkled. "If I help, do you promise we can do naked things?"

She bit back laughter. "Oh, we'll definitely be doing naked things."

"Good," he said, giving a satisfied nod.

And then he helped her gather up the fallen bags, followed her into the apartment, and shut the door behind them.

The End

Up next: Ryan's story! Keep reading for Heat of the Night...

Heat of the Night

An Out of Uniform Novella

Elle Kennedy

Chapter One

"So this is the new place," Jane Harrison remarked, glancing around the courtyard of the low-rise apartment building. She admired the perfectly kept lawn and colorful flowerbeds around the edge. "I like it."

"Me too," Ryan Evans admitted.

His gaze strayed to the rectangular pool, where his teammate, best friend and new roommate, Matt O'Connor, was swimming laps. He and Matt had moved in three weeks ago, and so far the arrangement was working out nicely. They'd always gotten along, being the two youngest members of SEAL Team Fifteen, and now its two remaining bachelors. All the other men had settled down over the past few years, handing the manwhore torch to Ryan and Matt, who used it to burn the sheets with the endless supply of willing women in San Diego.

Hell, he and Matt had only been in the building three weeks and already they'd wound up in bed with their upstairs neighbor, Christina, a sexy blonde looking for some fun after a break-up with her beau. Ryan's teammates constantly told him he should think about finding one woman to settle down with, how "rewarding" it was, but Ryan wasn't interested. Not now, anyway. The only woman he spent more than a week with was standing right beside him, and she happened to be engaged to his commanding officer.

"Beck and I are thinking of finding a house in this area," Jane said, her long red ponytail bouncing as she continued looking around.

"Didn't he just buy a house near the base?" Ryan asked.

"No, he's renting. He didn't want to buy until he knew whether I'd be leaving L.A. Now that I left the magazine, we're ready to find a place."

Ryan frowned. "You left the magazine? Since when?"

He couldn't believe Jane would even consider leaving her job at *Today's World*. Since the moment he'd met her, he could tell she loved her work.

In fact, that was the main obstacle for her and Lieutenant Becker, the fact that Jane's ambitions meant she wouldn't be a housewife any time soon. Ryan still didn't get why Beck had been so turned off by that. Jane was the greatest woman Ryan had ever met. Fuck, if he'd met her first, maybe he wouldn't be having threesomes with Matt and their new neighbor. But Jane was head over heels in love with Beck, and Ryan respected that. He just hoped Becker hadn't pressured her to quit her job.

"It was my choice," Jane added, reading his mind. "I'll do some freelance work until the baby comes."

Ryan's gaze flew to hers. "The *baby*? Holy shit, you're pregnant?"

"Seriously, you're telling me you didn't notice that my boobs got enormous?"

"They were enormous to begin with."

"Yeah, but now they're extra enormous." Her eyes sparkled. "It's worth it, though."

"You sure about that? Six months ago you had no intention of being a wife and mom. Don't tell me you planned this."

"No, it wasn't planned," she admitted. "But the second I looked down at that pee stick and saw the pink plus sign, something changed. Honestly, Ry, I'm so freaking excited about this baby. I never thought I'd be this happy, but I am. And before you ask, yes, Beck and I plan to get married. Maybe in a few months."

Ryan studied her face, looking for any hint that she might not be completely honest, but Jane's expression conveyed pure bliss. Shit. She was actually cool with all this. Which meant he had to be cool, too, no matter how apprehensive the news made him. Hit a little too close to home, that's all. His mother never wanted a kid — Ryan's father rushed her into it — and she'd been miserable and angry during Ryan's entire childhood. So…yeah. He really hoped Jane was sure this was what she wanted.

"So…" Jane eyed him expectantly. "Do I get a hug, or what?"

He found himself experiencing a pang of longing as he pulled the petite redhead into his arms and held her close. Damn. Why hadn't he met her first?

Fuck. He seriously needed to put an end to all this inappropriate yearning. It was all sorts of wrong.

"I'm happy for you," he murmured, planting a quick kiss on her forehead.

Jane was beaming as she pulled back. "Thanks. That means a lot."

"Hey! Where's my hug?" Matt teased. A moment later, he ascended the ladder at the edge of the water and hopped up on the pool deck. Water dripped down his bare chest and off his navy-blue swim trunks, and his shaved head glistened under the hot afternoon sun.

"Janie's preggers," Ryan called as Matt grabbed a towel off the nearby chaise lounge.

"No shit!" Drying off, Matt made his way over to them, shooting Jane a big, genuine smile. "Congrats, darlin'."

Jane grinned back, pretending to fan herself. "I love it when you call me darlin'. Where you from again, Matty? Georgia?"

"Tennessee," Matt drawled, thickening his accent, which barely made an appearance after all his years of living out west. "I'm flying out there in a couple hours, actually. It's my mama's birthday tomorrow so I'm heading home for a quick visit."

"Nice, have fun. I should get going too," Jane said, shifting her purse to her other shoulder. "Beck and I are going to look at a few places."

She gave each of them a hug and kiss on the cheek, even Matt, who was still all wet. Then she offered her usual cheerful wave and flounced off, while Ryan watched after her, feeling slightly dismayed.

"Get that look off your face." Matt sighed, slinging his towel around his neck. "She's off-limits."

"I know she's off-limits." Ryan's lips tightened. "You don't have to remind me of that every time she's around."

"Yeah, I do. Because I see the way you look at her, and it's not healthy, man. She's having a baby with Beck, for chrissake."

Ryan didn't answer. He should've never told Matt about his attraction to Jane, but Matt had the uncanny ability of knowing things without Ryan saying a word. They'd gotten drunk a few months ago and when Ryan mentioned Jane's name in some random, unimportant sentence, Matt set down his beer and said, "You have a thing for her, don't you?" Just like that. Ryan ended up confessing his completely improper feelings, which he now regretted, seeing as how Matt rode him about the issue whenever he could.

"You need to distract yourself," Matt said as they drifted toward the back entrance of the building. "Go out tonight or something."

Ryan shrugged. "Don't feel like going out."

"Then visit Christina." Matt grinned. "I mean, I know she likes me better, but since I won't be around I'm sure she'd be willing to settle for second best."

"Funny."

They entered the stairwell and climbed the two floors to their apartment. Matt immediately made a beeline for his bedroom, calling out, "Gotta finish packing."

Ryan headed to the kitchen and grabbed a beer from the fridge before flopping down on the living room couch. He took a long swig of beer, hoping it would soothe the lump of sadness and faint bitterness stuck in the back of his throat. Damn, he was pathetic. He had absolutely no business wanting Jane. She was his friend. She was Becker's pregnant fiancée. And besides, what could he really offer her, even if she was available? He'd never been in a long-term relationship before, wasn't sure he even wanted one.

Matt was right. He needed a distraction.

The red numerals on the Blu-Ray player's clock read 4:30. Christina volunteered at the hospital every afternoon until five, then worked as a bartender at a local bar until midnight. She wouldn't get home until close to one, which meant he had about, oh, eight hours to kill before he could pay her a visit.

Ryan leaned his head back on the sofa cushion and forced all thoughts of Jane, Becker and their new baby from his head. Fuck, it was going to be a long night.

ANNABELLE HOLMES TOOK ANOTHER SIP OF HER VANILLA AND LAVENDER tea and glanced down at the lined sheet of paper in front of her. She stared at her own loopy handwriting, wishing she hadn't written anything down. It made the words feel a little too…real. And they weren't real. They were fiction, fantasy, just a silly exercise meant to prove to Bryce that the speech he'd unleashed on her two days ago was pure and total bullshit.

I need to walk on the wild side, Annabelle.

Translation: the vanilla sex we've been indulging in is boring the shit out of me.

It wouldn't hurt either one of us to experiment.

Translation: you're a prude in bed and I'd like to screw around with someone a tad more adventurous.

The funny thing was, there was only one prude in the bed she and Bryce had shared for five years, and it sure as hell wasn't her. She couldn't remember how many times she'd suggested they spice things up, how many hints she'd dropped about straying from the missionary and exploring the raw, wild and indecent.

How quickly Bryce forgot. He'd implied that she was the one holding back, promptly following that zinger with the admission that he wanted to take a break, play the field and let loose before they made any serious decisions about their relationship. She'd been tempted to laugh, because, really, they'd pretty much been engaged since they were six years old — their relationship had never been anything *but* serious.

How could he be so freaking insulting? At first she'd been hurt and depressed, but after Bryce left the San Francisco condo they'd shared for five years, leaving her alone and upset, she'd gotten pissed off. And now here she was, two days later, staying in a strange apartment in San Diego and jotting down a list of every naughty act she'd ever fantasized about. She still wasn't sure what she was going to do with the list. Rip it up? Deliver it to her insensitive ex?

Annabelle looked at the list again, feeling her cheeks grow warm as she read the last item she'd written. *Have sex with someone else — while you watch.*

She took another sip of tea and added another item. *Sex in public (preferably a place without security cameras).*

Now that would be fun, seeing the suddenly-uninhibited Bryce pull down his Armani trousers and risk a random passerby seeing his cock.

She snorted. Yeah, right.

The cell phone next to her glass began to ring. She didn't need to look at the caller ID to know who was on the other end of the line. Her parents nearly had joint coronaries when she'd announced she was going to San Diego for a few weeks. They hated that she was "slumming it", though Christina's apartment was hardly a hovel. The building was small, but pretty and clean, and Annabelle was looking forward to taking a dip in the pool tomorrow morning. She couldn't remember the last time she'd gone swimming anywhere other than her father's country club.

"Hello?" she answered.

"When are you coming home?" came her mother's shrill voice.

"I already told you, Mom. I'll be here for a few weeks."

"But what about the anniversary dinner?" Sandra Holmes sounded crushed.

"I said I'd be home for that," she reminded her mother. "I'll be back for the weekend, and then fly back to San Diego, okay?"

Her mom let out a loud, put-upon sigh. "I don't like knowing you're all alone out there, living in a hippie's apartment, carousing around in an uncivilized city."

Annabelle snorted. "First of all, Christina is not a hippie. She's studying to be a doctor. Secondly, San Diego is a perfectly civilized place. Chill out, Mom. I won't be here forever. Christina comes back in a month, so I'll have to leave then anyway."

Never satisfied, her mother went on for a few more minutes about all the hazards Annabelle would face in such a dangerous city, but she tuned it all out. Thank God for Christina. If she hadn't run into Christina's parents at the market two days ago, she wouldn't have known their daughter would be out of town for the month, and then she would've had to move in with her parents. Eek.

"And why would she just leave you there in that apartment alone?" her mother was reprimanding.

She suppressed a sigh. "I told you, Christina eloped with her boyfriend. When I spoke to her, she said I could use the place until she gets back."

"I never liked that girl," Sandra said in a frosty tone.

No kidding. Sandra disliked all of Annabelle's college friends, including Christina. She also disliked Annabelle's co-workers, her boss, and pretty much anyone her daughter got close to. Except for Bryce, of course. Sandra *loved* Bryce. The Holmes and Worthington families had been close for years. Throughout Annabelle's entire childhood and adolescence, all she'd heard from her mom was what a wonderful husband Bryce would make.

"Christina is awesome," Annabelle said in her friend's defense.

Her mom ignored the remark. "Your father and I want you to come home. Oh, and Paulette Worthington and I wanted to sit down with you to talk about the details for the wedding."

Annabelle held her tongue. She hadn't told her mother about her and Bryce, so Sandra was still under the impression a wedding was in the foreseeable future. No point bursting that dream yet, not until she figured out for sure what she wanted to do about Bryce.

"I'll call you when I know when I'll be home," she said instead. "Talk to you later, Mom."

"Annab—"

She hung up, then quickly powered off the phone so her mother wouldn't be able to call back. Jeez. Talk about overbearing. She knew her parents loved her, but sometimes she wanted to strangle them. They were snobby, overprotective, presumptuous, and had total tunnel vision when it came to Annabelle's future. Marry Bryce, move into a mansion on Nob Hill, spend the afternoons at the country club, the evenings entertaining San Francisco's elite. If it weren't for her job, Annabelle might have left San Francisco years ago, but she'd been lucky to land a position at one of the top event planning companies in the Bay Area, and as much as she hated her parents' interference in her life, she loved her work.

Fortunately, her boss had given her the month off, which meant she could take a breather and really think about what she wanted out of a relationship. Yeah, Bryce had dumped her, but their lives had been intertwined since they were children, and she knew eventually he'd try to win his way back into her life.

Question was—did she want to let him back in?

Sighing, she crumpled the silly list she'd been constructing and tossed it on the hardwood floor beside the bed. This was stupid. She wasn't going to give the list to Bryce. A list of fantasies wouldn't erase the hurtful words he'd spoken two days ago, and it sure as heck wouldn't help her figure out what she truly wanted from a relationship.

Rising from the bed, she headed into Christina's small bathroom and got ready for bed. Brushed her teeth, exfoliated, combed her unruly brown waves, and then slid into bed and settled beneath the covers.

She planned on using this time off to really think about her life and the choices she'd made. Particularly her choice in men.

Did she really love Bryce? His break-up words had upset her, but was that because she was genuinely in love with him, or because the fairytale life her parents had outlined for her since she was a kid had now gone up in flames?

She rolled over, gritting her teeth. *Don't think about it now. Figure it out in the morning. For now…just sleep.*

THE UPSTAIRS APARTMENT WAS DARK WHEN RYAN LET HIMSELF IN WITH the spare key Christina had given them. Christina might very well be the coolest chick he'd ever hooked up with. She'd just broken up with her boyfriend when Ryan first met her, and she was so completely comfortable with her sexuality it almost scared him. She hadn't had any qualms about having a hot threesome with him and Matt the night after they'd met, and she'd teased that if one or both of them didn't make use of the open invitation she'd extended, she'd be very pissed off.

He crept down the narrow hallway toward the bedroom. He'd texted her with the heads up that he was coming by, and although she hadn't responded, that didn't mean anything. Christina didn't respond to half the messages he sent her.

His dick was already semi-hard as he approached the door. Fuck, this was exactly what he needed. A night of no-strings sex was guaranteed to make him forget about Jane's announcement. A baby. God. Not that he'd ever really thought there'd be a chance for him and Jane, but this pregnancy pretty much snuffed out even the faintest spark of hope.

Ryan pulled his T-shirt over his head as he entered Christina's bedroom. His jeans were next, dropping to the weathered hardwood next to his discarded shirt. He could make out Christina's form in the shadows, curled up on her side under a puffy blue comforter.

He grinned in the darkness. These were his favorite kind of wake-up calls. Hers too.

He moved to the bed and lifted up the edge of the comforter, easing his way under the heavy cover and spooning Christina from behind.

Lowering his head to her neck, he breathed in the appealing scent of...
orange blossoms? She usually smelled like plain old Ivory soap, but Ryan
wasn't complaining. He liked this new scent. A lot.

"You smell delicious," he rasped into her ear, one arm reaching around
her waist to pull her closer.

She whimpered in her sleep, wiggling her ass against his now-throbbing
erection. Wow. He was crazy turned on. Not that Christina didn't usually
turn him on, but this was...different. She felt soft and warm against
him, and that scent drove him crazy. He suddenly couldn't wait to be
inside her.

"Open your eyes, baby," he murmured.

She mumbled something in protest.

He grinned again. "Fine, keep 'em closed. But can you roll over for
me?"

She shifted, and he helped her along by cupping her ass cheeks and
moving her onto her back. He frowned as he ran his hands over that
ass, which was much rounder and sweeter than he remembered. And
come to think of it, her hair was longer too. Five days ago, when he'd
last seen her, she'd had a short blonde bob. Now her hair cascaded
down her shoulders in soft waves. And the tits beneath her thin tank
top seemed bigger—

Clarity sliced through his mind at the same time the woman beneath
him blinked her eyes open. A pair of brown—not blue—eyes stared
up at him in shock.

Ryan shot up, surprise slamming into his chest. Fuck. Oh, fuck. This
was *not* Christina.

"Oh my God," came a high, terrified voice.

Nope, definitely not Christina.

He opened his mouth to apologize just as the curvy, curly-haired
female bounded to the edge of the bed, shoved the comforter up to her
neck, and said, "Please don't hurt me!"

Chapter Two

RYAN WAS OFF THE BED SO FAST HE NEARLY TRIPPED OVER HIS OWN FEET. He didn't get embarrassed easily, but the sight of the terrified woman on the bed brought a wave of mortification to his gut. Shit. He'd fondled a complete stranger. Where the *hell* was Christina?

He opened his mouth to explain, but the stranger he'd just felt up was suddenly on her feet too. The next thing he knew, she hurled the little lamp on the bed table at his head.

Ryan caught it effortlessly. "Hey, listen!" he shouted. "I'm not here to —"

But the woman wasn't listening. Instead, she'd started babbling. "Seriously, you don't want to do this. I have, like, eight different types of STDs, so your health is at risk and really, who wants to be at risk?" Words kept popping out like coins from a slot machine. "I'm actually doing you a favor here, dude. You should go find someone else to rape — wait, that's not what I meant! Don't find anyone else! You shouldn't be doing this to any woman, ever, I'm not encouraging it at all, I'm just saying…" She trailed off, and that spark of fear returned to her face. She looked around wildly, as if scanning the room for another weapon.

Ryan stared at her for a moment, bewildered.

Then he burst out laughing.

A pair of chocolate-brown eyes glared at him. "Seriously? You're *laughing* at me?" Her tone hardened, and one slender arm stuck out and fumbled for something on the nightstand. "I'm giving you five seconds to get the hell out of here, you…you predator!" She made a victorious sound as she found what she was looking for — a cell phone. "I'm calling the police, asshole!"

Ryan's laughter died in his throat. No matter how entertaining he found this woman, he wasn't in the mood to be dragged off to jail. "Hey now, wait," he said immediately, setting the lamp she'd thrown at him down on the floor. Then he held up his hands in surrender. "This is just a misunderstanding, babe."

"Babe? I am *not* your babe." Her finger jammed on the phone screen. "Nor will I be your rape victim so—"

"I'm not here to rape you," he cut in, running a frazzled hand through his hair. "Would you just shut up for a second so I can explain?"

Her eyes flashed, but her mouth promptly closed.

Ryan drew in a calming breath, collecting himself, all the while noticing just how freaking hot this woman was. Along with her vibrant brown eyes and amazing hair, she had delicate features that included a cute upturned nose, high cheekbones and sexy pink lips, the bottom one fuller and poutier than the top. Was she a friend of Christina's? And if so, why had Christina never introduced them?

"You're not explaining," she said, shooting him a dirty look.

Ryan sighed. "Look, I came here to see Christina, okay? I thought you were her when I got into bed with you."

"Christina?" she echoed.

"Yes. Christina. You know, the woman who lives here." He frowned. "So who the hell are you and why are you in her bed?"

"Nuh-uh. Who the hell are *you* and what are *you* doing in her bed?" she shot back.

Frustration crept up his spine. "Are you always this fucking difficult?"

"Are you?"

Ryan released another breath. He suddenly felt extremely awkward standing there in his blue-and-white-checkered boxers, but he made no move to pick up his clothes. He was scared to turn away from this woman. Who knew what she'd do if he took his eyes off of her.

"Okay. Let's calm down," he said quietly. "I'm Ryan, all right? I live downstairs. What about you?"

"I'm Annabelle," she answered reluctantly. "Christina's letting me stay here for a few weeks."

He rolled his eyes. "See how easy that was? So where exactly did Christina go?"

"Vegas. She eloped with her boyfriend Joe."

Surprise jolted through him. "She told me they broke up."

"They did." Annabelle shrugged. "But then he sent her a bunch of flowers and a super sweet card begging her to take him back, so she did, and then he proposed, so she said yes, and now they're in Vegas. Anything else you want to know?"

The disappointment he experienced at the news that Christina was back with her boyfriend was almost nonexistent. That was the nice thing about flings. You didn't get attached, didn't feel crushed when the other person left. If anything, he was happy for Christina. She'd admitted that she still loved her ex, but the guy had been too much of a selfish jerk to appreciate the good thing they had. Evidently the jerk smartened up.

Still holding the phone in her hand, Annabelle took a couple of steps toward him, her bare feet slapping the hardwood floor. Her pink tank top did nothing to contain the soft jiggling of her tits. And those little boxer shorts she wore hugged her firm thighs, revealing smooth, shapely legs and tiny feet with red painted toenails.

Despite himself, Ryan's cock twitched inside his boxers. He was ridiculously turned on, and in his state of undress, he couldn't really hide it either. His dick poked against the front of his boxers, providing a tent that could accommodate an entire campsite.

Annabelle's brown eyes widened slightly as her gaze dropped south. "Seriously?" she blurted out. "Can't you keep that thing under control?"

Another laugh bubbled out of his throat. "You should take it as a compliment."

Her cheeks turned bright red. "Look, as fun as this is," she said, sarcasm ringing in her voice, "could you please leave? I was trying to sleep before you burst in here like you own the place." Her eyes narrowed. "Were you involved with Christina?"

"Kind of. Nothing serious, though." He offered a dry smile. "Actually, not serious at all, considering she eloped to Vegas with another man."

"You don't look too beat up about it."

Ryan shrugged. "I'm not. Like I said, it wasn't serious."

"Good. Great. Now that we've cleared that up, could you please go?"

She was making a very good point. He *should* go. Now that his plans for a night of wild sex had shot up in smoke, he had no reason to stick around and chat with Christina's weird houseguest. On the other hand, Annabelle was super hot, and he was super horny, so...

As if reading his mind, Annabelle held up the phone and said, "Don't even think about it, pal. Touch me and I'll call nine-one-one."

He grinned. "Come on, you know you're tempted."

Her cheeks grew redder. "Tempted to do what?"

"To get back in bed. With me." He cocked one brow. "And I can assure you, we'd have a really good time…"

She stared at him for a moment. Then she let out a laugh. "Oh God. Do women actually fall for that stuff?"

He frowned. "Yes."

"Yeah, well, I don't." She rested one hand on a curvy hip and nodded at the pile of clothes next to the bed. "Okay, time for you to go, Robert."

"Ryan."

"Whatever."

He found himself grinning again. Damn, he liked her. It was rare to come across a woman who was immune to his charm, and even rarer to find one who managed to keep his interest for more than five minutes. He had no idea where Annabelle had come from or how long she planned on staying in the building, but he hoped she stuck around for a while. Or at least long enough for him to get his hands on those delectable curves again.

"Why are you still here?" she grumbled. "I'd like to get some sleep sometime this century."

His lips twitched. He wondered if she brought that sexy sarcasm to bed with her. "I'll get right out of your way," he said graciously.

He strode to the side of the bed, making sure his bare arm rubbed against *her* bare arm as he walked by. He heard a soft intake of breath, but when he glanced over, she just looked annoyed.

Bending down, he collected his jeans and T-shirt from the floor and tucked the pile of clothes under his arm. Somehow he doubted she would grant him the time to get dressed.

"Do you have a key or did you break in?" she asked sternly.

"Spare key. I left it in the living room." Impulsively, he cast a devilish grin. "What do you say I keep the key and come by tomorrow night?"

Annabelle laughed.

He pursed his lips. "Was that a yes?"

Another laugh, this time with the words, "Hell, no" mingled in there.

"Your loss," he said with a sigh.

Those liquid brown eyes glimmered with amusement. "Yeah, I'm sure it is."

He found it difficult to walk to the door, particularly since his cock was still rock-hard and refusing to go down. But monster erection aside, he found it difficult to walk away from *her*. He couldn't remember the last time he'd had so much fun with a woman who wasn't Jane. Unfortunately, the fun was one-sided. Annabelle was now tapping her foot all sexy-like, eager to see him go.

She trailed after him down the dark hallway toward the front door. "G'night now, it was awesome meeting you."

"Sweet. It was nice meeting you too."

"Uh, no. I was being fake nice." She huffed. "Honestly, Roger—"

"Ryan—"

"—I'm not trying to be rude, but I'm exhausted. I want to go to bed—" She raised a hand before he could open his mouth. "Alone. I want to go to bed alone, and fall asleep alone, and wake up in the morning, alone. Okay?"

"Like I said, your loss."

The corners of her pouty mouth lifted, just a little. Oh yeah. She liked him. He could always tell when a girl liked him, and this one, no matter how grumpy and off-putting she was trying to be, *totally* liked him.

"How long are you staying here?" he asked, pausing in the doorway before she could boot him out.

She eyed him suspiciously. "Why do you want to know? Are you planning on sliding into bed with me tomorrow night?"

"Will you be here tomorrow night?" he countered.

Annabelle hesitated. "Yes. I'm here for three weeks."

Ryan gave himself a mental high-five. Oh yeah. Three weeks. He could definitely work his magic on her in three weeks. Hell, he'd probably only need three days, maybe less, to win over this chick. *Why* he wanted to win her over so badly eluded him, but who cared why? As long as it distracted him from the fact that Jane was having a baby with Becker, he was cool.

"Well, I look forward to seeing you again, then," Ryan said, letting his gaze sweep from her face down to her cleavage and then back up.

She rolled her eyes. "We're not going to see each other again. I plan to diligently avoid you."

"Good luck with that."

"Good night, Rick."

"*Ryan.*"

With a sweet smile, she gave his butt a little shove and pushed him out the door. "Good night," she said again, and then the door closed in his face.

Ryan's mouth stretched out in a grin as he listened to the sound of the lock clicking into place. "'Night, Annabelle," he called.

Still holding onto his clothes, he climbed down the stairs to his own apartment. Matt had left hours ago, and the apartment was dark and quiet as he locked up and headed for his bedroom. He was too keyed up to sleep—meeting Annabelle had been way too much fun, and his erection refused to subside.

Sighing, he dropped his clothes on the chair near the bed. As he was debating whether to jerk off or watch TV, a flash of yellow caught his eye. Furrowing his eyebrows, he stepped toward the chair and picked up his jeans, then watched as a piece of yellow legal paper fluttered to the hardwood floor.

He bent to pick it up. Feminine handwriting was scrawled across the page. Unable to fight his curiosity, he smoothed out the sheet and read the first line.

His jaw promptly fell open. It wasn't only the intriguing heading that caught his attention—*I'm Up For This. Are You?*—but the dirty little items that followed. He read each one. Twice.

Ryan broke out in a slow smile. Well…damn.

Hot fucking damn.

No matter how hard she tried, Annabelle couldn't get her late-night visitor out of her mind.

She spent the morning answering emails and trying to not think about Ryan, but every five seconds, the memory of his gorgeous face and drool-worthy body floated into her mind like a piece of driftwood. Hands down, he was the hottest guy she'd ever met. When she'd woken up to find those playful blue eyes on her and that lean, muscular body pressed against her, she'd thought she was dreaming.

During their entire exchange, she'd been fighting little sparks of desire. Her breasts had felt so heavy and tingly she'd had to cross her arms over her chest. If he'd stayed for even five more minutes, she probably would've jumped him.

So why did you throw him out?

Uh, Bryce? she reminded the voice in her head.

You mean the guy who dumped you?

She ignored the taunting reply and headed for the bathroom to get a towel. Fine, so maybe she didn't owe anything to her as-of-two-days-ago ex, but she wasn't the type of girl to hop into bed with a stranger. She was Annabelle Holmes. Her parents had raised her to be a perfect lady, and ladies didn't have sex with random men, no matter how appealing they might be.

She found a towel and slung it over her shoulder, then left the apartment and walked downstairs. The courtyard was empty when she stepped outside, and the pool looked so inviting she had her shorts and tank off before she even reached the deck. Tilting her head, she let the sun's rays heat her face. Beads of sweat formed between her breasts, but she welcomed the heat. She was happy to finally get a chance to wear this teeny yellow string bikini. It never got this hot in San Francisco, and the change of scenery was refreshing.

Kicking off her flip-flops, she moved to the edge of the pool, took a breath, and dived cleanly into the deep end.

The cold water engulfed her, feeling like heaven as she swam underwater for a few moments. God, what a gorgeous day. Despite the fact that she missed her job, she was looking forward to a few weeks of downtime. Doing nothing but swimming and tanning and exploring San Diego. She closed her eyes and floated on her back for a while, relishing the solitude, but her me-time was cut short at the sound of footsteps.

Her eyes popped open in time to see Ryan approaching the deck, his blue eyes seeking her out and dancing playfully.

She was so surprised she sank in the water like a stone. Sputtering, she broke the surface, droplets dripping from her hair and into her eyes. "You," she squeaked.

"Me," he confirmed.

She was suddenly grateful to be submerged in cold water, because the sight of him made her extremely hot. He wore blue surf shorts and a sleeveless basketball jersey, and his chin was dotted with dark stubble. God, why did men look so good when they were all scruffy? Bryce never sported any scruff—the guy shaved like three times a day just to make sure his aristocratic face remained pretty-boy smooth. But Ryan…oh boy.

Putting on an indifferent voice, Annabelle raised a brow at him. "Didn't we say everything we needed to say last night? You know, when I asked you to leave?"

He shot her a lazy smile. "You may have said what you needed to, but I have one more thing to say."

"Oh, really? And what's that?"

"Yes."

Treading water, she shoved wet strands of hair off her forehead. "Yes what?"

Slowly, he reached into his back pocket and removed a wrinkled piece of paper.

Annabelle's eyes widened at the familiar scrap of yellow. No. That couldn't be the same sheet she'd been using when…shit. Shit, where had she put the list? She searched her brain, finally remembering she'd tossed the fantasy list on the floor before she went to bed. The floor…where Ryan had dropped his clothes before he'd crawled into bed with her.

"Yes to this question," he said, holding up the page. "*I'm Up For This. Are You?* Well, babe, *yes*. I am definitely up for it."

Heat scorched her cheeks. Scrambling up the metal ladder, she hauled herself out of the pool and shot a wet arm in his direction, trying to grab the list.

Grinning, he held it out of her reach. "Finders keepers," he mocked.

"What are you, five? Give it back. That's personal property," she snapped.

Rolling his eyes, he obligingly handed her the list, which got soaked the second her wet hand clutched it. The ink began to smear, and for some asinine reason, she fanned the sheet to stop the smearing. What was the matter with her? A total stranger had just become privy to all her secret fantasies and she was trying to *preserve* the words? She ought to be burning the damn thing.

"Don't worry," Ryan said graciously. "I memorized it."

She set her jaw. "You had no business reading that."

"Maybe not, but I did, and now it's branded into my memory. It kept me up all night, you know. There I was, tossing and turning, wondering where we should go to take care of number four. A park? Out here in the pool? The back alley of a bar? Damn, the possibilities are endless, Annabelle."

Number four? What was he—her cheeks burned. *Sex in public (preferably a place without security cameras).* Oh God. She couldn't believe he'd actually memorized it. The last time she'd been this embarrassed was back in the third grade when her frenemy Joan poured water on her crotch and proceeded to tell the entire class she'd peed her pants.

"*We* are not going anywhere," she said stiffly. "I, on the other hand, am leaving now." Her back was ramrod straight as she stomped toward the chair where she'd dropped her towel.

She felt Ryan's eyes on her as she dried off, and knew he was ogling her tiny bikini. A sick part of her was even a bit flattered, but the embarrassed part overruled it, pushing her to dry off faster and wrap the towel around herself.

"So is that a no?" Ryan asked casually.

"Huh?"

"You won't let me help you?" he clarified.

She frowned. "Help me do what?"

"Cross out all the dirty items on your dirty list." He offered a charming smile. "Look, it's obvious you can't carry out some of those, uh, activities, alone. I'm just offering my services, babe."

"Again with the babe?" She huffed out a breath. "I don't want or need your help. That list was intended for someone else."

He paused. "You got a boyfriend?"

"Yes." She hesitated. "No. Well, maybe."

"Which is it—yes, no or maybe?"

She fought a wave of exasperation. "All of them, okay! I have a boyfriend, a sort of fiancé, but we're on a break right now. Not that it's any of your business."

"A sort of fiancé?"

"It's a long story." She grabbed her clothes, then slipped her feet into her flip-flops. "You are the pushiest guy I've ever met, you know that?"

A thoughtful expression flitted over his face. "I've never been called pushy before. Endearing, sure. Charismatic. Drop-dead gorgeous. A real-life Michelangelo's *David*. But never pushy."

A laugh slipped out of her throat before she could stop herself. "A real-life Michelangelo's *David*? Wow. You are so full of yourself, I don't even know what to do with that."

"You could do me," he said glibly.

Her thighs quivered. Just a little. Oh, for Pete's sake. She needed to get away from this guy. He was too freaking tempting, and right now she needed to avoid temptation. She'd left San Francisco to think about her relationship with Bryce, not jump into a fling with a guy who had major over-confidence issues.

"I won't even dignify that with an answer. I'm leaving now."

He shrugged. "Suit yourself."

She was halfway across the lawn when he called, "Annabelle!"

Reluctantly, she turned. "Yeah?"

"If you change your mind, I'm in Two-B." His handsome features were the epitome of cocky.

She kept walking, not allowing herself to breathe until she was inside the building. Her breath came out in a shaky puff. Jeez, why did he have to be so damn attractive? If she were here under different circumstances, then maybe…maybe she'd act out all of her wildest fantasies with this guy. But her heart still belonged to Bryce. Kind of. God, she wasn't the least bit sure how she felt about Bryce. They'd been in a serious relationship since she was eighteen years old, living together when she turned twenty, officially engaged when she was twenty-three. And yet he'd broken things off as if their relationship didn't mean a thing to him.

Not a break-up, time off, a condescending voice reminded her.

Right, "time off" was how he'd phrased it. Well, she hadn't wanted time off. He'd gone and made that decision for the both of them.

With an unhappy sigh, she went back to Christina's apartment, cursing Ryan for ruining her day. All she'd wanted to do was lounge around in the pool, and now she was back in the apartment, sulking again.

A beep caught her attention before she could head into the bedroom to change. Her cell phone sat on the kitchen counter, indicating she had a new voicemail. She figured it was her parents, as usual, but when she glanced at the screen, she saw the missed call was from Melinda, one of the assistants at Annabelle's company.

"Shit," she muttered. She hoped there wasn't some big emergency at work. Her boss had assured her she wouldn't be missed, since October was a slow month for them.

She dialed into her inbox and waited for the message to play.

"Hey, Annabelle," came Melinda's somewhat hesitant voice. "I know you're on vacation, and I hate to bother you, especially with something like this." A pause. "I was hoping you'd pick up, I hate to mention this in a voicemail, but…um, did you and Bryce break up? I only ask because I saw him last night at the Sheppard event and he was, um, with someone. They looked pretty close, too. I wasn't sure if you knew about it and I don't want to be the bearer of bad news, but I just thought you should know. Anyway…uh, I'll see you when you get back."

Click.

"To delete this message," a mechanical voice chirped, "press one. To save, press two. To — "

Annabelle hit the *end* button, then stared at the phone for several long moments. Anger clawed up her spine, settling in the back of her throat in a thick, bitter lump. He'd already started seeing other people? What the *hell?* They were engaged! Sure, he hadn't bought her the ring yet, but he'd proposed, and their respective parents were already planning the wedding.

Annabelle drew a deep calming breath, willing herself to relax. She couldn't believe it. Obviously he'd been dead serious when he said he wanted to see other people. He was already gallivanting all over San Francisco, getting *close* to some woman at a nightclub event that *her* company had planned. What. An. Asshole.

Meanwhile, here she was, fighting off the advances of a ridiculously appealing guy, out of respect for Bryce.

Well, screw him. He didn't deserve her respect.

If anything, he deserved a healthy dose of payback.

Annabelle straightened her shoulders and headed back to the front door. She didn't bother getting dressed. Instead, she walked out the door wearing her teeny-weeny bikini and hurried down the stairs. When she reached the second floor, she glanced up and down the hall until she saw it.

2B.

She stood in front of the door for a second, steadying her breathing and collecting some courage.

She could totally do this. In fact, she *wanted* to do it. She wanted it very, very badly.

Lifting her hand in determination, she knocked on the door.

Chapter Three

Ryan was not at all surprised to find Annabelle on his doorstep. If anything, he wondered what took her so long. He had enough experience with women to know when one was into him, and no matter how many times Annabelle tried to brush him off, he had no doubt that she wanted him. Still, he wasn't going to let her off the hook so easily.

"Finished playing hard to get?" he asked pleasantly.

Her mouth tightened. "You're going to make this hard for me, aren't you?"

"Yep."

He opened the door wider and gestured for her to come in. She did, but looked very reluctant doing so. Wary, she glanced around the apartment, taking in the leather couch, the state-of-the-art entertainment system and the two beer bottles on the glass coffee table. It was the typical bachelor pad, but Ryan didn't care. He was, after all, a bachelor.

"Do you have a stripper pole in the bedroom?" Annabelle asked dryly.

"If I did, would you do a sexy dance for me?"

"Nope."

"Figured I'd ask."

Looking awkward, she leaned against the arm of the sofa, her abundant curves practically pouring out of her indecent yellow bikini. She looked good enough to eat, but Ryan kept his distance. Women always needed to set some ground rules, and this particular woman probably had a whole slew of them. He already knew she liked to make lists.

"Three weeks," she began. "I'm here for three weeks, so that's all you're going to get from me."

He couldn't help but laugh. "You make it sound like you're doing *me* a favor. I think it's the other way around, Annie."

She bristled. "Don't call me Annie."

"Whatever you want, babe."

"Don't call me babe either." She rested her hand on the couch and tapped her fingers nervously. "So, um, about the list…"

He patiently waited for her to continue.

"It wasn't serious or anything." Her brown eyes avoided his. "I was just joking around."

"Liar. You're dying to do each and every thing on that list."

He could see her biting the inside of her cheek. "Maybe some things."

Ryan took a step closer. Her breath hitched. He could see her pulse throbbing in her throat, and a faint flush had spread just above her tits. Oh yeah. She was totally turned on. Good. "How about we start with good old number one, then?"

He stopped when they were only inches away. Her breasts were practically touching his T-shirt. He couldn't wait to feel her nipples poking against his bare chest. "What's number one again?" she asked, sounding breathless.

"Sex somewhere other than a bed," he recited.

She sighed. "Jeez, you really did memorize it."

"Couldn't help it. I have a photographic memory."

"Or you're just a pervert."

"That too." He flashed her a grin. "You like me, though."

"Maybe."

He eliminated the last inch between them, pressing his body against hers. A shaky breath flew out of her mouth. "Maybe?" he teased.

"Fine, I like you," she conceded. She paused, then tilted her head. "So, um, how do we do this?"

He froze. "Don't tell me you're a virgin."

"I'm not a virgin," she huffed. "I just haven't had sex with many strangers, okay?" She hesitated again. "Do you want me to take my bikini off?"

Ryan let out a low chuckle. "That's a good start."

His pulse sped up as she raised her arms and reached for the tie behind her neck. Anticipation coiled in his gut.

Then she stopped. Rather than untying her bikini top, she narrowed her eyes and said, "I think you should do it first."

"Do what?"

"Get naked. Because really, why should the girl always undress first? You're so sexist, Roger."

He sighed. "Do you always have to overanalyze every last detail?"

"Yes."

"Fine. Then overanalyze this."

Before she could respond, he captured her mouth with his. The kiss shut her up completely, and soon she was rubbing her tits against his chest like a contented cat. Fuck, she tasted sweet. Ryan slipped his tongue in her mouth, licking and exploring, while his hands drifted south to rest on her firm ass. She gave a soft whimper, then deepened the kiss. When her tongue entered his mouth, he groaned, as blood pooled in his groin and his cock thickened against her belly.

She reached down between them and rubbed him over his shorts, eliciting another groan from deep in his throat. The who-undresses-first debate went up in flames and soon they were both tugging at their own clothes. Her bathing suit was flung across the room, his shorts ended up under the couch, and who knew what happened to his T-shirt. Ryan didn't care. His entire body was on fire. So was Annabelle's, judging by the rosy flush rising on her smooth, golden skin.

"Fuck, you're sexy," he rasped.

She had an hourglass figure, with a curvy ass he couldn't help but dig his fingers into. And her pussy was completely bare, which made his mouth go dry and his tongue tingle. Damn, he couldn't wait to taste her. His cock bobbed against her stomach as he drew her close again, kissing her hard and deep. Then he slid down to his knees and pressed a soft kiss right between her legs.

Annabelle gasped, teetering on her feet. "Oh, God. That's...so good."

Steadying her with his hands, he dragged his tongue up and down her slit in featherlight strokes. Her soft moans egged him on. He loved hearing a woman moan for him.

He hated taking his mouth away, but Annabelle kept swaying like she might keel over, so, with a laugh, he gripped her hips with his hands and said, "Get down here."

The living room floor probably wasn't the most comfortable site in the world, but Annabelle didn't even blink as she stretched out on her back, her body spread out beneath him like a juicy holiday feast.

"I feel like such a slut," she breathed, looking half-amused and half-worried. "We don't even know each other."

"Yeah, but I'm dying to get to know you," he replied, settling himself between her thighs.

His cock ached to slide inside, but he wasn't finished with her yet. Straddling her, he bent down to kiss one of her distended nipples, sucking it deep in his mouth. She made a sexy little sound and then tangled her fingers in his hair and pulled him even closer. He suckled and licked, cupping her tits with both hands and kissing all that smooth, silky flesh.

"You are such a tease," Annabelle said, breathless and excited. "Will you just get inside me already?"

"Sure." He slipped one hand between her legs and pushed two fingers in her pussy.

They both groaned.

She was soaking wet. He quickly slid down her body again, his mouth desperate to lap her up. He swirled his tongue over her clit, then dragged it down her wet folds and thrust it deep inside her.

Annabelle moaned, her hips moving restlessly as he went down on her. "You're good at that," she mumbled. She made a wheezing sound. "And if you say it's because you've had a lot of practice, I'll slap you."

He laughed against her pussy. Yep, sarcastic even during sex. He'd known she would be, and damn, he loved it. He also loved driving her wild, flicking his tongue over her clit, licking every inch of her until she was moaning uncontrollably. Her sweet taste made him dizzy with lust, and his cock throbbed, hard and full and dying for release.

Annabelle moved her hips faster, her breathing heavy, but just as he felt her clit pulse against his lips, he drew back. He had a crazy urge to see her eyes when she came. Abruptly, he shot to his feet, his cock poking out like an angry sword.

"Where do you think you're going?" she grumbled.

"Condom," he said hoarsely.

He went from the living room to the bathroom and back to the living room in less than ten seconds. Ten seconds after that, he had a rubber on and was entering Annabelle with one swift thrust.

"Oh Jesus," he hissed out. She was so tight he nearly exploded from the feel of her inner muscles clamped around his dick. "Are you always this tight?"

"Probably. You want me to poll my other lovers?"

A laugh lodged in his throat. "No, please don't."

"Okay." She pressed her palm on his chest and stroked his pecs. "Can we stop talking now?"

Her touch seared his skin, causing beads of sweat to pop out on his forehead. He liked her touch. He liked everything about her — her brown hair fanned out on the floor, her rigid dark-pink nipples, the leg she'd hooked around his waist, the kung-fu grip of her pussy. She looked so fucking hot lying there beneath him, and he had no problem shutting up. In fact, he lost all capacity for speech as he started to move.

Annabelle moved with him, lifting her ass and meeting him thrust for thrust, while her fingernails dug into his back, eliciting little sparks of pain mingled with pleasure.

"I need...fuck," he swore. "I need to be deeper."

With a husky growl, he grabbed hold of one of her legs and lifted it up to his shoulder, pushing his cock into her as deep as it would go. Annabelle cried out, a wild throaty sound ringing with pleasure. He nearly came right then and there as he watched her hand slide down her body so she could rub her clit.

Biting her bottom lip, she met his gaze, and then she came.

It was the sexiest thing he'd ever seen, and he wasn't far behind her, especially when she lifted her head to his shoulder and bit his flesh, still whimpering and rocking beneath him. Ryan let go, shuddering as a burst of pleasure rocketed through his body, nearly stopping his heart. His climax made the world spin, and by the time his shoulders sagged and his chest collapsed onto Annabelle, he felt ravaged and exhausted and so fucking sated.

Under him, Annabelle was breathing as heavily as he was, and he suddenly realized he was probably crushing her. He gingerly rolled onto his side and, wincing, peeled the condom off his still-hard dick, He raised himself up on one elbow so he could peer down at her, grinning at the dazed look in her eyes.

"I guess we can cross number one off the list," he drawled.

"Oh yeah," she agreed, still sounding breathless. "That was surprisingly good."

"Surprisingly?" he echoed in mock anger.

"There was always the chance you were all talk and no action," she replied sweetly. "Overconfident men usually suck in bed."

"I do not suck in bed."

"I know. Like I said, you're surprisingly good."

"More like incredibly awesome."

She gave him a sugary smile. "It's nice to have a healthy ego."

He planted a quick kiss on her lips, then pulled back and admired her perfect features. "You really are beautiful, you know that, Annabelle?"

Her cheeks turned pink. "You already got me in bed — well, on floor — so you don't need to sweet-talk me."

"I'm not sweet-talking. It's true. You're beautiful."

He figured she'd object again — all she ever seemed to do was object — but instead she smiled shyly and said, "Thank you."

Those two words were laced with so much wonder that he had to ask, "Hasn't anyone ever told you that before?"

A tiny frown marred her forehead. "No. My parents, sure, but you're the first man who's ever said that."

"Then the men you've dated before are complete morons." He dragged his fingertips down her bare arm, then rested his palm on her stomach and rubbed the soft skin there. "You're gorgeous, Annie."

"So are you, Rick."

He chuckled. Man, he really liked this chick. Her well of sass never seemed to run dry, and he found himself laughing constantly when she was around. Plus, the mind-blowing sex didn't hurt.

Next to him, Annabelle shifted, arching her back to form a little bridge with her naked body. "God, my back kills."

"Isn't it worth it, though?"

She mulled it over. "Yeah, I guess it is." She raised herself up on her elbows. "I should probably take off."

"What's the rush?"

Discomfort flitted through her gaze. "I figured you had, I don't know, things to do or something." She paused. "And it just occurred to me I don't know a thing about you, except that you live in the building and were sort of involved with Christina."

"I'll tell you what — if you stay I'll tell you every last thing about myself."

He sensed her reluctance, and an odd spark of panic lit in his gut. He didn't want her to go. Weird, since they'd only met yesterday. But for some reason, he wanted her to stick around.

"Come on," he urged. "It'll be fun. We'll order some pizza or Chinese, spend the afternoon and night naked, and get to know each other."

The corners of her lush mouth lifted. "That does sound kinda appealing."

"It'll be fun," he reiterated.

Her smile widened. "How much fun?"

Ryan placed his palm on her thigh and stroked gently. "*A lot* of fun."

Chapter Four

A SHRILL RINGING WOKE ANNABELLE UP AT FIVE IN THE MORNING. AND it wouldn't stop. It kept ringing and ringing and ringing, and next to her, Ryan made no move to pick up the phone. Groaning, she buried her head under the pillow. Ryan shifted beside her, letting out a groan of his own.

"Who the fuck is that?" he mumbled.

"This isn't fun," she mumbled back. "You promised me a fun sleepover and then stuck me with a five o'clock wake-up call. I'm very unhappy at the moment."

The phone mercilessly stopped ringing. For half a second.

Then it started right back up again.

Annabelle shot up into a sitting position. "If you don't answer it, I will kill you."

Groaning again, Ryan stuck out his arm and began rummaging around for the phone. He finally got it, hit the talk button and lifted it to his ear. "What?" he barked.

Annabelle heard a male voice, but couldn't make out any of the words. Ryan, however, sat up abruptly, a sleepy grin filling his face.

"Seriously? *Now?*" He paused. "Okay. Yeah, definitely. We're on our way."

"We?" Annabelle demanded, rubbing her tired eyes.

He ignored her. "Huh? No, that's Annabelle...yeah, long story...she's kind of strange but—"

"Kind of strange?" she yelled.

"—pretty cool," he finished. "Yeah...okay, see you in twenty. Tell her to hold it in until I get there because I totally want to see the head when it—hello?" He glanced at Annabelle. "Bastard hung up."

Ryan got up, suddenly as alert as a guard dog. He moved around the bedroom, grabbing pieces of clothing, as Annabelle sat on the bed, shaking her head in confusion. "What on earth is happening?"

"Shelby's having her baby," he said without breaking his stride.

"Who?" She went pale. "Don't you dare tell me you got some girl pregnant."

"She's Garrett's wife." He sat on the edge of the bed so he could roll on a pair of socks. "Garrett's one of my teammates. I mentioned him yesterday, remember?"

She only sort of remembered. She was still having a tough time reconciling the fact that Ryan was a Navy SEAL. In between rounds of super awesome sex, they'd spent all of yesterday talking about their lives. When she asked him what he did for a living, she figured he'd say something like "pro surfer" or "personal trainer" or maybe "gigolo". A SEAL, she did not expect. Sure, he had the most extraordinary body, all toned and muscled and hard just about everywhere, but she couldn't imagine him holding a gun, or creeping through the jungle, blowing things up, taking down terrorists…hmmm, okay, it was actually kind of hot when she thought about it.

"His wife is having their baby and Carson says it'll be any minute now," Ryan said, jarring her from her thoughts. "I'm gonna be an uncle, babe!"

Although she didn't know Shelby or Garrett or Carson, Ryan's enthusiasm was contagious. "God help that baby," she said with a laugh.

He stood at the foot of the bed with an expectant look. "C'mon, get up. We have to go to the hospital."

Her enthusiasm faded. "Why? I don't even know these people, Ryan. I don't want to intrude."

"You won't be intruding." He waved a dismissive hand. "They'll all be happy to see you, especially Holly."

"Who's Holly?"

"I'll tell you in the car. Now get up already."

Annabelle slid out of bed, then paused, realizing she was totally naked. Almost immediately, Ryan's eyes darkened to a midnight blue, and she could see the arousal in his gaze.

Funny enough, she didn't feel self-conscious. She'd never walked around naked in the condo she shared with Bryce. Neither did Bryce, for that matter. As their moving-in present, he'd bought them matching robes. To preserve her modesty, she'd thought, but that was before she'd discovered he was a prude.

"I need to go upstairs to get some clothes. I only have my bikini here," she reminded him.

Ryan offered a wolfish grin. "Wear it to the hospital."

She snorted. "You wish."

"I do wish. All my friends would be jealous."

Laughing, she went over to the chair and picked up one of the T-shirts lying there. "Can I wear this?" Without waiting for him to agree, she slipped the shirt over her head. It hung down to her knees.

"You look seriously cute in my shirt," he said, then elicited a startled squeak from her by planting his hands on her waist, pulling her close and kissing her.

His lips were so soft, so warm. Annabelle's toes curled as his mouth moved over hers in a teasing caress. The man knew how to kiss. He knew how to do everything, in fact. They'd had sex three times already, and each time he pushed that thick cock into her, it took her breath away. Not that she was surprised. Just looking at him, you knew he'd be good in bed.

What would Bryce think if he could see her now?

The notion brought a pang of guilt to her belly, followed by a bolt of anger. Screw Bryce. Who cared what he thought. He hadn't thought twice before hooking up with someone else, so why should she?

"Okay," Ryan groaned, breaking the kiss. "If we keep doing that, we'll never get to the hospital." He gave her butt a gentle slap. "Let's get a move on."

"Do we have to?"

"Yep. Don't worry, Annie, it'll be fun."

She didn't bother to correct him this time, because she knew he'd simply pick another annoying nickname, and truth be told, she was beginning to like it. Nobody had ever called her Annie before. Her mother maintained that the nickname sounded too "common". Annabelle was a name that screamed wealth and prestige, according to Sandra Holmes.

Ryan waited somewhat impatiently as Annabelle got dressed upstairs, but she refused to rush. She still wasn't sure why he insisted she come with him. She didn't know any of his friends, and the birth of a child seemed like a stupidly inappropriate place to bring a girl you'd only known for two days. Yet for some reason, she wanted to go. She liked Ryan. She was drawn to him. And she couldn't help but be curious about his life.

They left the building fifteen minutes later. Ryan led her to an olive-green Jeep parked at the back of the lot. He didn't open the passenger door for her, and she resisted making a sarcastic remark about chivalry. Bryce always opened her door, which drove her crazy. She was perfectly capable of opening her own door, and when Bryce did it, there was nothing chivalrous about it. It felt more patronizing if anything.

"So what's the deal with this Bryce guy?" Ryan asked as he started the engine. "Am I helping you cheat on him? 'Cuz I'm not sure how I feel about that. I do have a moral code, you know."

She grinned. "Yeah, I'm sure you do." The smile faded as she pondered his question. She'd told him about Bryce earlier, but mostly skimmed over the details. "I guess Bryce and I are broken up."

He shot her a sideways look before turning his attention back to the road. "Were you really engaged?"

"Pretty much since we were six years old," she said wryly. "He officially asked me two years ago. Our parents were thrilled."

"Your parents aren't the ones getting married. How did *you* feel about it?" Ryan asked roughly.

She bit her bottom lip. "I...was happy, I guess. I've wanted to marry Bryce since we were kids. I thought he was a wonderful guy."

"Thought?" Ryan echoed, picking up on the past tense.

To her dismay, they reached a red light, which allowed him to turn his head and study her. His blue eyes flickered with curiosity, and discomfort rose up her spine. The last thing she wanted to do was tell Ryan about Bryce's parting words, about what a priss she supposedly was.

"He said some mean things before he left," she finally admitted.

Ryan's jaw hardened. "What kind of mean things?"

She shrugged and casually glanced out the window. "You know, about me, and our sex life, and..." She gritted her teeth. To hell with it. "He pretty much called me a prude, okay?"

Ryan was silent for a few seconds. Then he burst out laughing.

"It's not funny," she said, her cheeks burning up.

"Sure it is." He chuckled again. "It's also not true. Don't tell me you believed him, babe."

Annabelle didn't answer.

"Aw, fuck. You did, didn't you?" He sounded amazed. "Is that why you wrote that list? Come on, Annabelle, you should know better than to listen to some asshole. I just spent the entire day and night with you, and I can assure you, you're no prude."

"Um, thanks?"

They reached the hospital and Ryan parked the Jeep. Shutting off the engine, he looked at her and shook his head. "Don't even think about that ass anymore, okay? Because I know for a fact that you're the sexiest, hottest, wildest fuck a guy could ever have."

Despite the lewd words, she found herself laughing. Her heart may have skipped a couple of beats too.

Ryan hopped out to grab a parking ticket from the machine. When he came back, he shoved the ticket on the dashboard, while Annabelle got out of the Jeep and slung her purse over her shoulder. "Are you sure they won't mind that I'm here?" she asked once more.

"Trust me, they'll be ecstatic."

Chapter Five

HE WAS RIGHT. WHEN THE TWO OF THEM ENTERED THE LARGE WAITING room in the fifth-floor maternity ward, a brunette with bright green eyes and a blue-eyed redhead jumped up and swarmed Ryan and Annabelle like two excited bees. Ryan made the introductions, but the two women kept babbling about how exciting this was and how happy they were for Shelby that Annabelle had a tough time keeping up. The brunette was Holly, and the blond man with the killer smile was Carson, her fiancé. Jane was the redhead, and she introduced Annabelle to *her* fiancé, Thomas Becker, a man with short brown hair and a body that belonged in an action movie.

"Don't worry, you'll get used to them," Becker said dryly as Holly and Jane continued to talk Ryan's ear off.

"She's only three centimeters dilated," Holly was explaining. "Garrett came out an hour ago and said the doctor thinks it might be a while."

"Are Will and Mac coming?" Ryan asked.

"They'll be here in a few hours," Carson supplied. "Mac wasn't feeling well last night, so Will wants to let her sleep a while longer."

"She's pregnant," Holly told Annabelle. "And Will is totally overprotective. He thinks she'll lose the baby if she sneezes, but we keep telling him to quit worrying. Unless she has a vision of it or something, *then* he should worry."

Annabelle was lost again. She figured Will was another SEAL, but all this talk of pregnancy and visions made her head spin. It spun even more when Ryan shook hands with Becker and congratulated him for apparently getting Jane pregnant, though something in the exchange felt…forced. Ryan was smiling, his voice ringing with sincerity, but Annabelle could swear she'd heard a twinge of sadness.

She discreetly glanced from Ryan to Jane, but the redhead was staring up at her soon-to-be husband adoringly and Ryan looked perfectly unruffled.

Huh. Maybe she'd just imagined it.

"Shit, I'm starving," Carson mumbled. "Anyone want to make a trip down to the cafeteria?"

Ryan and Becker chimed in. Annabelle didn't have a chance. Her stomach had grumbled the second Carson said *cafeteria*, but Holly was suddenly gripping her hand. "Bring us some sandwiches or something," Holly chirped to the men, then tugged on Annabelle's hand and practically forced her butt into a chair. "Sit with us, Annabelle."

She found herself sandwiched between Holly and Jane, who stared at her in curiosity. "How did you and Ryan meet?" Jane asked.

"Is it serious?" Holly demanded.

"Um…it's only been two days," she said awkwardly.

"But you like him?" Holly pressed.

"Yeah, definitely." Before they could grill her again, she changed the subject. "How did you and Carson meet?" she asked Holly.

With a grin, Holly revealed that she and Carson had indulged in a one-night stand at a nightclub only to run into each other weeks later at Shelby and Garrett's wedding. Then Jane chimed in, confessing she'd met Becker in an elevator, where they'd gotten stuck and passed the time by having hot sex.

Annabelle laughed, thinking of her first meeting with Ryan. Unable to stop herself, she told them the story of how she'd woken up to find a total stranger in bed with her. Both women hooted with delight when she finished.

"Oh, that's priceless," Jane said. "I can't believe you threw a lamp at him."

"He deserves it," Holly said, rolling her eyes. "I've wanted to throw a lamp at Evans since the day I met him." Annabelle knew Holly was just teasing; the affection in her voice when she spoke of Ryan was easy to pick up on.

"Yeah," Jane agreed with a grin. "He's incorrigible. I've been tempted to do some lamp-throwing myself."

"So, have you and Carson set a date?" Annabelle asked Holly.

"Not yet." Holly made a face. "We're too busy arguing about who'll cater the wedding."

"Having trouble picking a catering company?"

"No, he won't let *me* do it," Holly complained.

"The bride can't cater her own damn wedding," came Carson's annoyed voice. He stepped into the waiting room, with Ryan and Becker in tow, and glared at his soon-to-be wife. "You're just going to have to pay someone else to do it."

"I'll prepare everything the night before," Holly insisted.

Annabelle smothered a laugh as she listened to them argue. She could tell they were madly in love, which brought a tiny pang of envy to her chest. Had she and Bryce ever acted that way, loving and teasing and so obviously infatuated with each other?

"I got turkey and ham," Ryan said, holding up two sandwiches covered in plastic wrap. "Pick one."

She reached for the ham and unwrapped the sandwich. Jane got up to sit with Becker, digging into the potato chips he'd brought her, and Holly and Carson split a tuna sandwich.

John Garrett walked into the waiting room while the women were eating, looking completely frazzled. Annabelle noted he was extremely good-looking, with dark hair, intense eyes and a long sexy bod. Even the lines of exhaustion creasing his face didn't take away from his handsomeness. Jeez, did the Navy only allow sex gods to enlist or something?

"Six centimeters," Garrett announced, raking both hands through his hair. "Shit, I'm dying in there."

"Is she okay?" Holly asked, her green eyes wide with concern.

"She's fine, considering." Garrett looked like he was going to keel over any second. "But she keeps yelling at me, and I'm pretty sure she broke one of my fingers during the last contraction." He held up his hand and sure enough, his pinkie was red, swollen and bent at a slight angle. And yet he didn't seem the least bit concerned about it. A few minutes later, he said he'd keep them posted and went to be with his wife again, broken finger and all.

Annabelle was impressed. Maybe it was a military thing, but she'd never seen a man look so calm. She shot a sidelong glance at Ryan, wondering how he'd react in this type of situation. His wife yelling and in pain, clinging to his hand so tightly she broke one of his fingers. She got the feeling he'd be calm too.

"So," Ryan said after Garrett was gone. "How long do you think this'll take?"

"Not long," Carson said at the same time Holly replied, "Probably hours."

Ryan groaned, evidently smart enough to know that the woman was always right.

Two hours passed before they knew it. Then three and four. By the time hour number five ticked by, the waiting room had become quiet. Annabelle yawned and stretched her legs out, leaning closer to Ryan. In the corner of the room, Jane had fallen asleep on Becker's shoulder and he was absently running his fingers through her hair. Carson was asleep too, head lolled to the side, while his fiancée buried her nose in a paperback novel.

Annabelle jumped when she felt Ryan's lips brush across her earlobe. "This is so boring," he whispered.

She smiled. "It's hard work pushing out a baby. I doubt Shelby is finding it boring."

"Yeah, well, Will and his wife have the right idea. They're going to show up in a few hours, all bright-eyed and ready to hold the baby, and they'll laugh at us for our six-hour wait."

"It could be worse," Annabelle pointed out. "My mother was in labor with me for thirty-two hours."

"That does not surprise me," Ryan said solemnly. "You went from a difficult infant to a difficult adult."

"Ha ha."

He shifted close again, his tongue darting out to lick her ear. "I have an idea."

"Oh really?"

Planting a kiss on her neck, he said, "Number four."

She coughed in surprise, instantly catching his drift. "At the *hospital?* No way."

"Come on, it'll be fun."

"You really need to stop promising me fun." She gestured around the quiet waiting room. "So far, I'm not having fun."

"But you will." Before she could blink, he was on his feet and pulling her up. "Let's go make some memories, babe."

Holly looked up from her book. "Going to stretch your legs?" she asked, the amusement in her eyes revealing she knew precisely what they were about to do.

"Sure are," Ryan said easily. "Want anything from the vending machine?"

"No, thanks." Holly winked at Annabelle as Ryan linked his arm loosely through hers as if they were going on a leisurely stroll.

It was past ten, and the hospital corridor was bustling. Nurses in bright pink scrubs hurried by, doctors stood in the hallway studying patient charts, and they passed several family members with either pink or blue balloons going into rooms to visit the new moms. They walked past the nursery, and at the sound of a newborn wailing, Annabelle glared at Ryan. "I refuse to have sex near babies."

He mulled it over, then sighed. "Me too. Let's go downstairs."

This was crazy. Annabelle wanted to object as she followed him to the stairwell. When she'd written that list, she hadn't planned on actually doing any of the things on it. Fantasized about them, sure, but doing them? Again, crazy.

Yet her heart was pounding wildly as Ryan dragged her down the fluorescent-lit corridor of the respiratory ward, and her knees shook when he discovered an empty closet and ushered her inside. Darkness instantly engulfed them, but she could make out a metal rack stacked with boxes of…she squinted…latex gloves.

Ryan followed her gaze and laughed. "Can I please, please fuck you while wearing latex gloves?"

"You are a sick man."

He encircled her waist with hands and bent down to nip at her neck. "Think about how cold and slimy it would feel."

"I'm a firm believer that sex should *not* be cold and slimy."

His mouth moved from her neck to her jaw, his morning stubble tickling her chin. They both froze at the sound of muffled footsteps, but whoever it was walked right past the closet. "Are we really going to do this?" she whispered.

He took one of her hands and placed it directly over his crotch, which sported a thick ridge of arousal. "Hell yeah."

She sighed. "Fine, do your worst."

"My best, you mean." He slid his hand between her legs.

He stroked her gently, as if he had all the time in the world, but Annabelle was very much aware of their surroundings. "If we do this, we do it fast," she murmured.

"If you say so."

Before she could blink, he spun her around so that she was facing the wall, and ground his lower body against her ass. She moaned, the delicious friction causing a ribbon of pleasure to uncurl through her body and settle in her aching core.

Ryan reached around to cup her breasts, his breath warm against her neck. "Hey, I just thought of something," he said, sounding delighted.

"Yeah, what's that?"

"We can cross off numbers two, four and eight, all at once. It's the trifecta...the perfect storm."

It was hard to concentrate on his words when his hands were fondling her boobs. He meant the list, obviously. She strained to remember the items. Sex in public, sex standing up, and...her face heated up. Oh right. From behind.

"I've gotta tell you, babe, I'm loving this list of yours," he rasped, sliding his hands down her belly to unbutton her jeans.

He didn't take them off, just let them fall to her ankles, and then his hand was between her legs. Annabelle's entire body was on fire. The dark closet, the sound of footsteps out in the hall, Ryan's talented fingers poking underneath her panties to rub her clit...it all excited the hell out of her.

"Close your eyes," he whispered.

She obliged, listening to the sound of plastic tearing—he'd remembered to bring a condom—and then a zipper hissing open. A moment later, she felt his cock pressing between her ass cheeks, teasing her puckered hole. Her heart did a somersault. For a second she thought he would venture into the forbidden, but he moved aside the crotch of her panties and pushed into her wet core with one smooth thrust.

God, it felt good. She tried to think about the last time she'd made love to Bryce, tried to remember if it had felt as good as this, but her brain promptly stopped functioning when Ryan began to move.

It didn't last long at all. Four, maybe five strokes, and then she was coming, a fast, pounding orgasm that surfaced out of nowhere. Annabelle gasped as pleasure rocketed through her. She ground her ass against Ryan, milking him, taking everything she could get, and his husky groans heightened her pleasure.

His fingers dug into her waist as he pistoned his hips, fucking her hard, his balls slapping against her ass with each deep thrust.

"Fuck," he wheezed, and then he released a harsh cry and shuddered inside her.

She loved feeling him come, loved the guttural sounds he made, the way he nuzzled her neck, heating her skin with his ragged breaths. She wanted to cry out in disappointment when he finally withdrew, leaving her empty and sated and wanting more. So much more.

It had never been this way with Bryce. Never.

Her legs were still shaking as she bent to pull up her jeans. She buttoned them, turning to face Ryan. His blue eyes glimmered in the darkness, satisfaction etched into his handsome features. He removed the condom, tossed it in the metal garbage can near the door, then zipped up his pants and stepped toward her.

"So...was *that* fun?" he teased.

A breathy laugh exited her mouth. "Oh yeah."

Chapter Six

"What do you want to watch tonight?" Ryan asked, holding up two Blu-Ray cases.

From her spot on the couch, Annabelle snorted. "Rambo one or Rambo two? Seriously, those are my options?"

"It's my pick, remember?" he said defensively. "Last night I sat through that horrible rom com. I think my sperm count dropped in half."

"Don't worry, you looked very manly when you teared up."

"I did not tear up——"

"You did!" she chortled. "Right after the fiancé died. It was like ten minutes into the movie."

"You were imagining it. So which Rambo do you want?"

"Neither. You choose, and I'll just go to the bathroom and slit my wrists."

As usual, her sarcasm never failed to make him laugh. They'd spent an entire week together, and each time she unleashed one of her biting remarks, Ryan liked her even more.

He was used to women treating him like he was some sort of god, especially when they found out he was a SEAL, but Annabelle remained completely indifferent to what he did. She didn't take any crap, from him, or anyone, he suspected, and he loved that. His friends loved her too, even Shelby, who'd given birth to an eight-pound girl. He and Annabelle had gone in to see the baby, and when they were leaving, a sleepy and relaxed Shelby had pulled him aside and said, "She's a keeper."

Shelby might be right. Ryan had never felt this way about anyone, except maybe Jane, but he was trying very hard to banish those inappropriate thoughts. He and Jane would never be together. He knew that. His heart simply needed to get the memo.

Annabelle was helping, though. He loved being with her, and Jane was never on his mind when Annabelle was around.

He smiled as he watched her stretch her legs out. She looked so cute sprawled there on the couch, wearing a pair of tiny black shorts and a yellow halter top. Her long brown hair was tied up in a high ponytail, which made her look like a schoolgirl. Except there was nothing girlish about her body. All curves, all sex appeal.

His cock stirred in his loose shorts. But just as he was about to toss the movies aside and suggest they have hot sex instead, the door to the apartment swung open and Matt walked in.

"Thank the Lord that's over," Matt announced with a groan. He dropped his blue duffel bag and it landed on the floor with a thud. "I swear, I love my mother to death but sometimes I could just strangle—oh, hello there," he drawled, noticing Annabelle on the couch.

She sat up awkwardly. "Um. Hi."

Ryan wasn't surprised to see her eyes widen at the sight of his roommate. O'Connor usually evoked that wide-eyed response from females. Probably the shaved head. It made him look all tough and lethal. Most chicks totally dug it, and it looked like Annabelle wasn't the exception. Her gaze slid up and down Matt's tall, muscular body.

Ryan didn't mind, though. He'd never been the jealous type, and he and Matt had indulged in enough threesomes that he was used to sharing the attention.

"Annabelle, Matt, Matt, Annabelle," Ryan introduced.

Matt flashed a grin. "It's nice to meet you, darlin'."

Ryan rolled his eyes. "Oh no, he darlin'ed you. That means he likes you."

"Where are you from?" Annabelle asked curiously. "The South, I assume."

"Nashville," Matt confirmed. He looked from her to Ryan. "Mind if I hang out with you guys for a while? I need to be around people my own age."

Ryan laughed. "I take it Nana O'Connor drove you nuts."

"As usual." Matt drifted toward the kitchen, calling over his shoulder, "Anyone want a beer?"

"Me," Ryan called back. He glanced at Annabelle. "You?"

She sighed. "What the hell."

Matt came back with three bottles, gave two away, and flopped down on one of the comfortable leather recliners flanking the couch. Ryan took the other chair, while Annabelle stayed on the couch, leaning forward to take a sip of the beer Matt handed her.

It didn't take long for Matt and Annabelle to hit it off, though Ryan wasn't surprised. Matt was the most laidback guy Ryan had ever met, and Annabelle, well, she was thoroughly entertaining. By the time the next round of beers was polished off, the three of them were laughing like old friends. Matt regaled them with stories about his trip home, and Annabelle told them about one of the worst weddings her company had ever planned, something involving feathers and swans and a very drunk uncle.

Her cheeks were flushed from the alcohol, but Ryan knew she wasn't drunk. Tipsy, maybe, but not drunk. Neither was he, and he'd noticed Annabelle checking out Matt several times in the past hour. Again, he wasn't concerned. He was, however, curious to see how far she was willing to go. He'd meant what he said in the hospital—he was having fun acting out all the fantasies on her list. And he knew she was having fun too. Except that she kept insisting the list didn't mean anything.

Which he knew was a total lie.

When Matt left the room to take a quick shower, claiming he was grimy from his trip and now sweaty from the three beers he'd consumed, Ryan joined Annabelle on the sofa and said, "Do you think he's attractive?"

She set down her beer bottle, furrowing her eyebrows. "Matt? Well, sure. Why are you asking?"

He slid closer and placed his hand on her thigh. "I thought maybe he'd be a good candidate for number three."

His remark got him a pair of wide brown eyes. "Are you crazy? That's... just wrong."

He offered a wry look. "Why's that wrong?"

She squirmed a little, and he wondered if she was squirming from discomfort or arousal. Probably the latter, though she'd never admit it. "Threesomes are sleazy. No?"

"Technically, what you want isn't a threesome." He bent close to her ear and teased, "You said you wanted to get fucked by another man while I watch."

"I didn't say I wanted that… I just…" She glanced away.

Ryan grasped her chin with one hand and made her look at him. "Why did you write the list, Annabelle?"

"I told you already." Her cheeks turned pink. "I wanted to show Bryce all the things I'd be willing to do."

"Willing to do, or *dying* to do?"

Her blush deepened.

"There's nothing wrong with wanting to do dirty things."

"Okay, yeah, maybe *some* dirty things, like sex in the hospital, or on the floor, but having sex with another guy…that's so slutty." Embarrassment flickered in her eyes.

"Says who? Who decides what's slutty, what's right or wrong when it comes to sex?" Ryan shook his head. "As long as all the parties involved are consenting adults, why should it matter?"

She visibly gulped. "Have you…and Matt…done stuff together before? With a woman?"

"Yes," he said honestly. "Does that bother you?"

ANNABELLE'S HEART WAS POUNDING HARD. HOW DID RYAN ALWAYS manage to catch her off-guard? She hadn't doubted he was a ladies man and that he'd probably slept with dozens of women, but she hadn't envisioned him in any threeways.

"No. I mean, I don't think so." She froze for a moment. "Wait — did you and Matt and *Christina*…?"

"Yeah."

She bit the inside of her cheek. Wow. She couldn't picture Christina with Ryan and Matt. Christina didn't seem like the type. But along with surprise, Annabelle experienced a wave of envy. Jeez, was she actually jealous that her friend had been fucked by two guys at once?

Annabelle glanced at Ryan, then Matt, who'd just strolled back into the living room wearing a pair of faded jeans and no shirt. No, it wasn't just two guys that appealed to her. It was *these* two in particular.

"It turns you on, doesn't it?" Ryan said in a low voice.

But not low enough. "What turns you on?" Matt asked instantly, swiveling his head toward Annabelle as he sank into his chair.

To her horror, Ryan answered for her. "Doing you while I watch," he told his roommate.

Matt's jaw fell open. Then a faint smile lifted the corners of his mouth. "For real?"

Annabelle met his deep green eyes. She found herself nodding.

He looked intrigued. "Huh. Okay then. Let's do it."

Her breath jammed in her throat like a wad of chewing gum. Oh God. She couldn't believe he'd just said that. And she couldn't believe how quickly her body responded. Her nipples hardened into two tight buds, straining against her halter top. Both men immediately zeroed in on the sight, which only made the tingling worse. She wished she'd worn a bra. She wished Ryan had never seen that list.

"Well?" Ryan prompted. "What do you think?"

Think? Her head wasn't capable of producing thoughts right now. She'd turned into a pile of mush, her pussy aching so badly she squeezed her legs together. What was happening to her? Ever since she'd met Ryan, she'd become a total sex addict. And Matt wasn't helping her condition. He was as gorgeous as Ryan, and...yep, just as well-endowed, she noted when she saw the impressive hard-on pushing against his jeans.

"I...this is crazy," she blurted out.

"What's wrong with crazy?" Matt said in that charming Southern accent.

"Um...nothing, I guess?"

Laughing, he got off his chair and moved to the couch. He sat right beside her, his hard thigh touching her bare one. "I just spent the entire week in Nashville listening to my mother nag me about why I'm not married yet and following my grandmother to every fabric store in the city so she could pick out wool to crochet me a sweater I will never wear." He placed his hand on her knee. "I could use some crazy right now, darlin'."

"You're as bad as he is," she grumbled, hooking a thumb at Ryan.

"Yeah, but I think you want to be bad with us," Matt said with grin.

He was right. She *did* want to be bad. She was twenty-five years old and she'd only had sex with one other man, Bryce, who she'd lost her virginity to. Now that she'd been with Ryan, her eyes had opened to all the sexual possibilities out there. Sex didn't have to be planned, it didn't have to be a three-times-a-week routine and last for ten minutes before Bryce rolled himself off her. This kind of sex was *way* more exciting.

Taking a breath, she looked over at Ryan, who was watching them with amused blue eyes. "Come on, Annie, kiss him. Be bad for a while."

She stared at Matt's mouth. She wanted to. God, she wanted to kiss him and touch him and sleep with him. As if a magnet was pulling her toward him, she leaned into his waiting mouth, gasping when his lips closed over hers. His mouth was firmer than Ryan's, his tongue more insistent, and she was breathless by the time the kiss ended. Little sparks of heat danced along her skin, growing hotter when she noticed the desire glimmering in Matt's green eyes.

"Undo my pants," he said gruffly, locking his gaze with hers.

She found it hard to breathe as she followed his instructions. Her fingers trembled over the button at his jeans. She undid it, pulled the zipper down, and her entire body burned up when his long, thick cock sprang up into her waiting hand. No boxers. God, that was hot.

Annabelle felt Ryan's eyes on her as she stroked his roommate's erection. She turned her head to meet his gaze, and the fire she saw in his eyes stole her breath. It was good fire, aroused not angry, and when she glanced south she noticed he was hard too. Licking his bottom lip, he undid his jeans and pulled out his own cock, stroking himself while she stroked his friend. She looked down at the thick erection in her hand, her heart pounding so fast she feared it would explode.

"What are you waiting for?" Ryan asked in a low, slightly mocking voice. "Take him in your mouth."

As her pulse shrieked in her ears, she slid off the couch onto her knees and did as Ryan asked. Matt groaned softly when she wrapped her lips around his tip, dragging her tongue over the velvety flesh. He fisted her hair, guiding her along his shaft, thrusting impossibly deep. She relaxed her throat and took him in, all the while feeling Ryan's gaze burning into the back of her head.

"Fuck, darlin', that's so good." Matt's husky voice made her shiver. She loved his faint accent, loved the way he moved his hips as she sucked him.

She was just getting into the blowjob when he withdrew from her mouth and hauled her up into his lap. Warm hands snaked underneath her shirt, tugging it up and over her head. Matt's gaze glittered with appreciation at the sight of her bare breasts.

"You're beautiful," he said roughly.

He dipped his head and covered one nipple with his hot mouth, kissing it gently. Annabelle tilted her head to the side, watching Ryan as he watched them. She saw his pulse throbbing in his throat, his lips parted slightly as he moved his fist up and down his cock.

Matt flicked his tongue over her aching nipple, then looked up at her from under unbelievably long eyelashes. "Do you like having him watch?"

She swallowed. "Yes."

Smiling, he turned his attention to her other breast, while moving one hand between her legs to cup her. She moaned, rubbed herself against him. Her skin was scorching hot, her mouth desert-dry. Matt gently pushed her onto her back, his big hands sliding her shorts down her legs. He tossed them aside, spread her thighs, and then his tongue was on her clit. He licked her, eagerly, relentlessly, until her mind fragmented and she climaxed with a loud cry. Her eyes were wide open, locked with Ryan's as she came from Matt's talented tongue.

"Is he good?" Ryan murmured, still working his own erection.

She offered a breathless *yes*, which turned into a deep moan when Matt pushed two fingers into her and started working on her clit again.

"Do you want him to fuck you?" Ryan asked.

Another breathy *yes*.

"Did you hear that, O'Connor? She wants you to fuck her."

Matt raised his head from her pussy, his eyes gleaming with amusement. "Five more minutes. I'm having way too much fun down here."

Annabelle choked out a laugh as he continued to tease her into oblivion. He sucked on her clit, his fingers plunging in and out of her, and she came again, less than two minutes into the allocated five.

Groaning, Matt lapped at her pussy, then gave her one last kiss before climbing up her body. He was bigger than Ryan, his chest massive, his thighs rock-hard as he straddled her. There wasn't an ounce of fat anywhere on his body. He was incredible.

So was Ryan, who, from the corner of her eye, she saw rise from the easy chair. A pang of disappointment, along with a spark of panic, filled her stomach. Was he leaving? He'd made such a big deal about this stupid list and — nope, he was only gone for a few seconds. He strode back into the living room, his jeans undone, his dick at full-salute, and tossed a small packet in Matt's direction.

Matt caught the condom skillfully, unwrapped it, and had the thing on before Annabelle could blink. Ryan resettled in his chair, staring at her as she spread her legs, as she let his friend enter her.

Annabelle gasped as Matt filled her to the hilt. This entire experience was surreal. Surreal but unbelievably hot. Made hotter by the fact that Ryan sat a few feet away, watching her with another guy on top of her, listening to her moans and the sound of Matt's flesh slapping against hers.

"How do you like it?" Matt asked, brushing his lips over hers in a fleeting kiss. "Slow, fast, rough…I'm yours to please."

She swallowed, aimlessly rocking beneath him. "Anything. Do anything."

He grinned and latched his mouth on hers, kissing her senseless as he pounded into her. She wrapped her arms around his strong, corded neck, holding on to him while he drove into her, again and again. But she kept her eyes open. Kept her eyes on Ryan. Pleasure began to rise in her belly, ripples of climax gathering and coiling tight, waiting to be released.

"More," she begged, lifting her ass to take him in deeper.

"Like this," Matt rasped, slamming into her harder.

"God…yes…like that…"

Each word was a struggle. Every muscle in her body burned with anticipation. Matt reached for her legs, lifting them up to his shoulders, and suddenly he was hitting a spot so deep it made her cry out in delight. And through it all, Ryan just watched. His blue eyes glimmering with heat, his fist tight around his cock.

Annabelle couldn't take it anymore. It felt too good, too…good… the tension in her body snapped, a powerful orgasm sizzling each and every nerve ending.

"That's it, darlin', come for me," Matt said hoarsely, moving even faster. His features tightened, his green eyes a bottomless pool of pleasure, and then he let go too, his groans matching Annabelle's as they came together.

When she finally crashed down to Earth, she found both Matt and

Ryan grinning at her. And Ryan was wiping his stomach up with a tissue, she noticed with an odd burst of giddiness. He saw her watching, and laughed softly. "Couldn't help myself," he confessed.

She returned the laugh, though hers was kind of shaky. She was still stunned by what just happened. Matt gently climbed off her, his impressive chest glossy with perspiration, his mouth sporting a crooked grin. "That was…unexpected," he finally said, starting to laugh.

Annabelle felt strangely modest as she found her shorts and top and hurriedly got dressed. "Um, yeah…so…" Her voice trailed off. What did one say in these situations anyway? *Thanks for doing me, Matt? It was nice to meet you?*

Fortunately, Ryan knew exactly what to say. "So, Rambo one or Rambo two?"

"I can't believe I did that," Annabelle murmured several hours later, after the two of them settled under the covers of Christina's bed.

Ryan hid a smile. From the moment he'd met her, he'd known Annabelle possessed a wild side. What did surprise him was the way he'd felt while watching his best friend screw her brains out. It hadn't been jealousy, per se. More like…protectiveness. Matt had the tendency to be rough, and Annabelle had looked so small and vulnerable lying there. For a moment Ryan had been tempted to whisk her in his arms and tell Matt to back off, but in the end he let it happen. Annabelle needed to have fun, to let loose and realize that sex didn't have to be so boring. He wanted to show her how good it could be when you let go. He suspected her ex didn't let go much. The guy sounded like a total douchebag.

"You had fun, no?" he teased.

She snuggled closer, making a contented sound. "Yeah, but this is more fun. I like sleeping with you."

"Me too," he said, amazed by how much he meant those words. He *did* like it, though, holding her in his arms, listening to her soft breathing, feeling her warm breath on his bare chest.

"Can I ask you something?"

"Sure."

"Why did you join the Navy?" She nestled her head against his shoulder. "I mean, you're obviously in awesome shape, but you're so impulsive and kind of wild, and the military is so strict. I can't picture you taking orders and following the rules."

"Why did I join the Navy…" he echoed. "Honestly? I just wanted to get the fuck away from my parents."

"Bad childhood?" she said, sounding sympathetic.

"You could say that." He let out a heavy breath. "Neither of them wanted me. I was a total accident, and the two of them hated each other. I don't even know why they're still married."

"I'm sure they love you," she said softly.

"Sometimes I wonder." He swallowed. "My mother never said a nice word to me my entire life. She's stuck in her own miserable world, constantly whining about how terrible her life ended up. My dad just yells a lot. He never beat either of us, but I swear, sometimes I could see him thinking about it, just kicking the shit out of her so she'd stop complaining."

Annabelle sounded horrified. "That's awful, Ryan."

He shrugged, and the movement sent a strand of her hair onto his chin. He grasped the lock between his fingers, twining it gently. "It wasn't that bad. I was your typical troublemaker as a kid, and I tried to be out of the house whenever I could. And when I was there, I learned to ignore all the yelling and bitching and drinking. We were dirt-poor, too, and kids at school constantly made fun of me for showing up in clothes with holes in them or not bringing a lunch."

"Aww."

"Don't worry, I used to beat them up whenever they started up, and eventually they knew better." A sigh slipped out of his throat. "My grades weren't that great, so college wasn't an option—not that we had the money for it anyway—so when I turned eighteen, I enlisted." He grinned in the darkness. "I'd always loved the water, so I figured the Navy would be the most fun of all the military branches."

"And you became a SEAL," she finished. "And now you're sent all over the world on dangerous assignments and risk getting killed."

"Pretty much, yeah."

She lifted her head. "So how does it work? You get a call telling you to pack up and then you leave the country?"

"Pretty much. I'm on leave for three weeks, though, all of us are, so I don't expect any late night calls."

"Unless another one of your friends is having a baby," she said dryly.

"Jane and Mackenzie are only in their first trimester, so I think we're safe."

"I like Jane. She was really cool."

A wave of discomfort swelled in his gut. Shit. Why had he said Jane's name? Just the sound of it made him cringe a little, mostly because he hated himself for the ridiculous feelings he had for the woman.

"Is something going on with you two?" Annabelle asked warily.

"Me and Jane? Of course not," he replied. "She's marrying my lieutenant."

Annabelle was quiet for a moment. Then, sounding very perceptive, she said, "You have a thing for her, don't you? I kind of suspected at the hospital when I saw you talking to her, but I wasn't sure, not until now anyway."

"I don't have a thing for her," he said quietly. "I *had* a thing for her."

She propped herself up on her elbow. "I knew it. Tell me the details."

He avoided her intrigued eyes. "There aren't any. I met her when she and Becker first started hooking up, and the two of us went out for drinks when they were kind of broken up. Nothing happened," he added quickly.

"But you wanted it to happen." Again, she had that thoughtful look on her face.

"Maybe. But it didn't. And I got over it." He kept his voice firm, hoping he sounded sincere. He and Annabelle were only having a fling, but he didn't want to hurt her feelings by admitting he might still have a tiny, teeny thing for a woman who was off-limits.

"Honestly? You're really over it?"

He met her inquisitive gaze head-on. "Yes."

She offered a faint smile. "Good."

He smiled back, enjoying the possessive note in her voice. He shifted onto his side so they were face to face, then slowly brought his lips to hers in a long, lazy kiss. Annabelle hooked her leg over his, her warm body curling into him as she kissed him back.

When she slipped her hands between them and encircled his hardening dick, he wasn't thinking about anyone but Annabelle.

Chapter Seven

SHE WAS IN DEEP TROUBLE.

Annabelle sat at the edge of Christina's bed, staring at the phone in her hand. For the past five minutes, she'd been debating calling her parents and telling them she couldn't make it for their anniversary dinner, but she knew her mother would kill her if she didn't show up. But going back to San Francisco was the last thing she wanted to do at the moment.

She didn't want to leave Ryan.

And that's why she was in trouble.

When they first started seeing each other, she'd told herself it was just temporary, that they were simply acting out a few fantasies, having some really great sex, and eventually she'd head home, go back to her job and look back on her time with him as a fun vacation fling. But deep in her heart she knew it was far from a fling.

They'd spent two weeks together, and each day that passed, she only liked him more. He made her laugh. Treated her like she was the most beautiful woman in the world. Put up with her endless sarcasm. Bryce hated her sense of humor — he constantly told her she was too negative. And he hardly ever complimented her. In front of parents, sure. Alone, he often acted like Annabelle was there simply to cater to his needs.

What kind of relationship was that?

Truth of the matter was, she had no desire to see Bryce again. She didn't want to rekindle their relationship, not after the way he'd dumped her so callously. But she knew she'd have to see him when she went home. Her parents were hosting a small but formal dinner party in honor of their thirtieth anniversary, and Bryce would surely be there. He was the CEO of her father's company.

She didn't want to face him. What if he was an asshole and brought a date to the dinner? She quickly pushed away the thought. No, Bryce was smart. If he wanted to remain in her father's good graces, he would be on his best behavior tomorrow night.

"Annabelle?"

Ryan's playful voice sounded from the living room. Her heart immediately skipped a beat. He and Matt had gone to see Shelby's baby girl, but Annabelle had opted to stay home. She hadn't wanted to intrude on Shelby and her husband, even though Ryan insisted they wouldn't have minded.

Besides, she still felt kind of awkward around Matt. For a while she thought he'd act all weird around her, or maybe try to sleep with her again, but he treated her like a good pal and nothing more. She wondered if Ryan had spoken with him and told him it was a one-time deal. Because for her, it *was* a one-time thing. As great as the sex had been and as attractive as she found Matt, the only man she wanted was Ryan.

Again, trouble.

"I'm in here," she called in response to his shout.

He poked his head in the doorway a moment later, beaming. "Penny smiled at me today!"

Annabelle rolled her eyes. "She's a week old—it takes like a month for that to happen. It was probably gas."

Ryan looked offended. "Why does everyone keep saying that? I told Garrett he needs to accept it—his baby likes me more than him."

She laughed. "Uh-huh, sure thing."

Ryan plopped down beside her on the bed. "So what do you want to do tonight?" He wiggled his eyebrows. "We only have two more items on the list left."

"And they'll have to wait," she said with a sigh. "I'm flying to San Francisco this afternoon. Remember the anniversary party I told you about?"

"You're leaving?"

His dismayed expression brought a smile to her lips. "Yes, but I'll be back tomorrow night, and then I'll stay here for another week or two until Christina gets back."

He relaxed. "Right, I forgot about that. Are you excited to see your folks?"

"Uh, no."

He shot her a curious look. "You don't talk about them much. What are they like?"

"Come with me and see for yourself." The request flew out before she could stop it, surprising them both.

What was she thinking? She couldn't bring Ryan home with her. Her parents would flip out. And it would pretty much be like waving a big sign that said "Bryce and I are over!" But they *were* over, and her parents had to accept it sooner or later.

And it might be nice having Ryan along for moral support. Her parents drove her nuts most of the time.

"Are you serious?" he said, raising one brow.

"Yeah, I guess I am." She shifted, lying down next to him and resting her head on his chest. "Sometimes I hate going home. My parents can be really difficult."

"They can't be as difficult as mine. Unless they're both raging alcoholics too," Ryan said dryly.

"No, not alcoholics. Just rich snobs."

"How rich?"

Discomfort rose up her chest. "My dad owns the largest shipping company in the country." She sighed. "Last year for my mother's birthday, he bought her an island in the Mediterranean."

"Liar."

"I wish I was lying."

Ryan whistled softly. "Wow. So that rich, huh?"

"Yep." She hesitated, then decided to tell him. "And for the sake of full disclosure here, you should know that my ex runs my dad's company, and my parents still think we're getting married."

His chest rumbled beneath her ear as he laughed. "Gee, I can't wait to go home with you, Annie. Sounds like it'll be a blast."

"You don't have to go," she said quickly. "I'll manage."

He rolled her over, so that she was on her back and he was leaning above her. His blue eyes searched her face. "Do you want me to go home with you, Annabelle?"

She swallowed. "Yes," she admitted.

"Then let's call the airline."

He was in deep trouble.

Ryan tried not to react as he slid into the plush leather backseat of the limousine Annabelle's parents had sent for them. She'd called them with their flight information, and although she insisted they could take a cab, Gregory and Sandra Holmes refused to be talked out of sending a car. Yeah, some car.

He barely noticed the scenery whizzing past them outside — he was too busy staring at all the ridiculous luxuries in the back of the limo, like the two separate phone lines, the small plasma TV screen, oh, and the mini fridge. He'd been to the Bay Area a few times in his life — once to visit his grandmother, who'd lived there for a few years before moving to Florida, and once with some of the guys in his training class when he'd first joined the Navy. But he had a feeling Annabelle's San Francisco was a lot different than the one he'd experienced.

He still wasn't certain why he'd agreed to come with her. Never in his life had he met a girl's family. Never. And Annabelle had already warned him that one, her parents wouldn't be thrilled to see him, and two, her ex-fiancé would be there. Yet for some stupid reason, he'd come along anyway.

Okay, maybe not for a stupid reason. He'd come for Annabelle. Because she'd looked so panicked at the thought of going home alone and facing Bryce, and Ryan hated seeing her in any kind of distress.

Which meant he was in trouble.

Usually, when he started caring too much about a woman, he cut and ran. He didn't want a relationship — he'd seen firsthand how relationships destroyed people. His parents hated each other, they both drank themselves into a stupor just to tolerate each other's company. Why would he ever want to put himself in that position? Yeah, maybe all relationships didn't end up like his parents', but why take the risk?

And now here he was, sitting in a limo on the way to Annabelle's parents' home, which was a total relationship move.

"We're almost there," Annabelle said, sounding unenthused as she gestured out the window.

Ryan followed her pointed finger, his eyes widening as the limo entered a gorgeous neighborhood overlooking the bay. Annabelle's folks lived in Pacific Heights, an area filled with ritzy shops and stately homes that had survived the earthquake and fire of 1906. The entire area screamed *money*, and as the limo slowed in front of an enormous mansion that looked like a museum, Ryan knew he was officially out of his element.

Annabelle thanked the driver, while a speechless Ryan grabbed his overnight bag and followed her out of the limo. She hadn't bothered to pack, saying all her "fancy" clothes were here at the house she'd grown up in. Now, Ryan looked at that house, unable to fathom the colossal palace before him. It was made of white limestone and resembled a French chateau, with a pillared entrance and a million gleaming windows.

"Holy shit," he muttered under his breath.

"Don't let the house intimidate you," Annabelle said. She made a face. "My parents are the ones you should be scared of."

A housekeeper in a black dress and white apron let them in at the massive front doors, and as they stepped onto the marble floor in the foyer, a tall brunette wearing a cocktail dress and pearls floated down a winding staircase.

She was obviously Annabelle's mother; the resemblance was uncanny. Only, while her daughter's eyes were full of fire and mischief, Sandra Holmes' gaze was cool and appraising.

"Thank heavens you're here," Sandra said in a shrill voice, making no move to hug or kiss her daughter. "Dinner starts in an hour. You need to—" She wrinkled her nose in distaste, noticing Ryan. "And who might this be?"

"Mom, this is Ryan Evans, a friend of mine from San Diego." Annabelle's voice was sugary-sweet as she added, "I hope you don't mind, but I invited him to dinner."

It was amazing—although Sandra's expression never changed, Ryan could practically feel an ice-cold wave pour out of the woman and slam into him. Oh, she totally minded, and he suddenly wished he could disappear into a puff of smoke. Damn it. Why the hell had he offered to come here?

"Oh, how nice." Sandra's voice was polite, but the fury under the surface was unmistakable. She flicked her gaze to the maid hovering discreetly nearby. "Magdalena, why don't you show Mr. Evans up to one of the guest rooms so he can freshen up and get ready for dinner. I'd like a word with my daughter."

Ryan reluctantly followed the dark-haired maid upstairs, forcing his jaw to stay closed as he stared at his surroundings. Pieces of art, mostly oil paintings, hung on the cream-colored walls in the hallway, and he could have sworn he saw one that looked a hell of a lot like one of the Monets he'd seen in a book once.

They passed nearly a dozen doors before the maid paused in front of one and opened it for him. "Right this way, sir," she said politely.

"How many rooms does this place have?" he asked curiously.

"Twenty-eight," she said in a brisk voice. "And fifteen bathrooms." Magdalena pointed to a door a few feet away. "The restroom is in there. Enjoy your visit, sir."

After the maid left, Ryan looked around the guest room in wonder. It was twice the size of his and Matt's living room, with a huge bed, a gleaming hardwood floor and a large armoire near the window that looked like it belonged in Queen Elizabeth's bedroom. *It's just a fucking house,* a little voice said. *Relax.*

Okay, he could relax. Taking a breath, Ryan headed into the bathroom and splashed some water on his face. He wished Annabelle would hurry the hell up and come find him, because he had no clue how to find his way back downstairs. The second floor was a freaking maze.

Fortunately, Annabelle bounded in the room a few minutes later, looking extremely frustrated. "Let me guess," Ryan quipped. "She's not happy."

"Not happy at all," Annabelle confirmed. "But she's also the best actress on the planet, so don't worry, she'll pretend to adore you during dinner."

He laughed. "I can't wait."

Annabelle stepped closer and wrapped her arms around his neck. "Seriously, though, don't worry," she said softly. "My parents are all bark and no bite. And I'm so happy you came here with me. My mom just told me Bryce and his parents will be here in an hour."

"Do your families know you broke up yet?"

She nodded. "Apparently Bryce told them last week. My mother didn't even call me to find out what happened."

"Maybe she thinks it won't last."

"Well, she'll be wrong." Annabelle stood up on her tiptoes and brushed her lips over his. "I have no interest in getting back together with that jerk."

Ryan kissed her back, rubbing the small of her back and pulling her closer. His groin tightened, desire rising inside him, and he forced himself to break the kiss. He needed to bring his A-game tonight, to stay alert, and Annabelle was too damn distracting sometimes.

"I wish you'd told them I was coming," he said ruefully. "I feel like a party crasher."

"You're my date," she said firmly. "And they're just going to have to deal with the fact that I want to be with you."

His heart nearly stopped, then sped up in sharp beats. "You want to be with me?" he echoed.

A pang of discomfort filled his body, along with a strange jolt of pleasure. He didn't know how to react to her confession. He should've been scared shitless. He didn't do relationships, never had. So why wasn't he scared? And why were the words *I want to be with you too* biting at his tongue?

"I haven't left your side in two weeks," she said, oblivious to his distress. "Doesn't that say something?"

"It says...a lot." He swallowed, then took a step backwards. "I think that suit you made me pack isn't fancy enough, babe."

"It's fine," she assured him. Her eyes twinkled. "I'll just rip it off you tonight anyway."

He looked around the extravagant room. "I won't have to sleep here alone, will I?"

"Nah, I'll sneak in here later to keep you company." She headed for the door. "I'm going to get dressed. So should you. I'll come back and get you in twenty minutes?"

He watched her go, suddenly longing for his bachelor pad in San Diego. Fuck. This was so not his scene. He'd grown up in the slums of LA, in a seedy two-bedroom apartment across the street from a liquor store that got robbed at least twice a week. His parents were pathetic excuses for human beings, and his childhood was one he wanted nothing more than to forget. Sure, his life was great now. He'd joined the Navy, found a family with the guys on his team, had his own place. But that didn't mean he belonged here with Annabelle's wealthy-ass parents in their wealthy-ass castle.

Shit, would there be ten kinds of silverware at the dinner table tonight? He suddenly felt like throwing up.

It was a relief when Annabelle returned a half an hour later, taking his breath away in a long, emerald-green dress. The neckline was modest, but the skirt had a slit that revealed a lot of thigh. Her hair was swept up in a complicated-looking updo, she wore very little make-up, and her only piece of jewelry was a sparkling diamond pendant nestled in her cleavage.

"You look like a princess," he said hoarsely.

She grinned. "Does that make you my prince?"

He glanced down at his two-hundred-dollar suit, a suit that would probably make most women all mushy and hot but would in no way impress Annabelle's parents. "A prince I am not," he sighed.

"Cheer up. It's just dinner, and tomorrow we can explore the city before we fly back to San Diego." She mimicked the words he constantly tossed her way. "It'll be fun."

"Whatever you say," he said noncommittally, all the while knowing that what awaited them downstairs would not, in any way, shape or form, be fun.

And he wasn't wrong. Annabelle's parents met them in the sitting room, which looked exactly like a living room but rich people were funny that way. Annabelle's dad was a commanding man with a head of salt-and-pepper hair and deep wrinkles around his mouth, probably because all he did was frown. He frowned when Annabelle introduced them, frowned when Ryan shook his hand, frowned when he offered Ryan a drink. Neither Sandra or Gregory spoke to him during the fifteen minutes the four of them spent in the sitting room, so when Gregory pulled him aside after Sandra announced it was time to congregate in the dining room, Ryan was thoroughly surprised.

"I'd like a word with you, if you don't mind," Gregory said cordially.

Ryan glanced at Annabelle, who offered a tiny shrug. So he said, "Yes, sir" and followed the older man while the two women headed off, Annabelle's mom chattering on about the new silverware she'd ordered from Paris.

Gregory led him into a large study with oak-paneled walls and an expensive burgundy carpet. There was a huge stone fireplace on one side of the room, and two plush chairs in front of it. "Have a seat," Mr. Holmes said graciously.

Ryan didn't want to sit, but he did. Annabelle's dad took the seat across from him. The older man unbuttoned his pristine navy-blue suit jacket, then clasped his hands in his lap and said, "How did you meet my daughter?"

Ryan gulped. "Annabelle told you in the other room, sir. She's staying in my building."

Gregory frowned. "And what exactly is the nature of your relationship?"

Fuck. He felt like he was in an interrogation room. "We're, uh, seeing each other, I guess." He swallowed again, his mouth too dry to work.

Jeez, why the hell was he so intimidated by this man? He was a Navy SEAL, for fuck's sake. He was good under pressure, and more than used to getting yelled at. Yet despite his training and background, he found himself extremely uneasy around Annabelle's dad.

"Are you aware that my daughter is engaged to be married?" Gregory asked coolly.

"I was under the impression the engagement is off, sir."

"For the moment, perhaps, but there's no doubt in my mind that my daughter will marry Bryce Worthington." Another frown, this one deeper. "He's a worthy match for her."

Ryan bristled. All right, he saw where this was going. Bryce was worthy, Ryan was not. Well, fuck that.

"I have to disagree," he said politely. "Annabelle was unhappy with Bryce."

"And she's happy with you?"

"Yes, sir, she is."

"What is it you do again?" Gregory asked, as if Ryan hadn't just told him five minutes ago in the sitting room.

"I'm in the Navy," he answered through clenched teeth.

"Right, the Navy. I take that to mean you travel frequently, sometimes at a moment's notice?"

"Sometimes," he said warily.

"Then how do you expect to provide my daughter with a stable, comfortable life?"

"With all due respect, Mr. Holmes, I've only known your daughter two weeks. We're not really at the point where we're discussing our future."

Frown number three made an appearance. "Well, you see, I *am* thinking about the future. My daughter deserves a man who can support her, who can provide her with the life to which she's accustomed, and I don't believe that man is you. Frankly, I don't believe you're good enough for her." Gregory leaned forward, a calculated glint in his brown eyes, the same shade of brown as his daughter's. "So, with that said, let's get down to business. How much?"

Ryan faltered. "What?"

"*How much*, Mr. Evans?"

Was this some kind of code? He had no fucking idea what this man was talking about, and he was tempted to unleash a right hook in the older man's jaw. Nobody had ever spoken to Ryan this way, in such a chilly, disgusted voice, as if he were nothing more than dog shit under the guy's shoe. Even his drill sergeant during Hell Week had been nicer than this, and that guy had been a total dick.

"How much will it cost me for you to say goodbye to my daughter and walk out the door right now?"

It finally dawned on Ryan. The son of a bitch was trying to bribe him. *Bribe* him. Who the hell did this man think he was, the Godfather?

"Nothing." His jaw was so stiff he could barely spit out the word. "It will cost you nothing, because I'm not going anywhere."

Gregory's eyes narrowed. "Don't be difficult, son. I'm sure we can work something out."

"I'm not your son," Ryan said coldly. He slowly rose to his feet. His hands were icy with rage, and he pressed them to his sides. "I think we're done here."

As if on cue, a soft knock sounded on the door.

"Come in," Gregory barked.

Magdalena the maid appeared in the doorway. "Mr. Holmes, the Worthingtons have arrived, along with Mr. Kildaire and his guest."

"Make sure everyone is seated correctly," Gregory said briskly. "And send young Mr. Worthington in here, please." He glanced at Ryan. "Mr. Evans was just leaving. Take him to the dining room."

Ryan shot Annabelle's dad an overly bright smile. "Great chat, sir.

Thanks so much for inviting me to dinner." He made for the door. "Oh, and happy anniversary, by the way."

The moment he was out of the study, Ryan released the breath he'd been holding, forcing his body to relax. The fucking nerve of that man. Did Annabelle know what a bastard her father was? Should he tell her?

The sound of voices drifted from the dining room, and he heard Annabelle laugh, not quite genuine but still melodic. He slowly unclenched his fists and tried to paste on a smile. He had to get through this dinner. He had to do it for her.

"Did Dad give you a hard time?" Annabelle asked quietly when he approached her.

"No, just the usual 'what-are-your-intentions' chat," he said in a light tone.

She slipped her hand into his, stroking his fingers. "I'm sorry."

So was he. He wished he could tell her what her father had just tried to do, but now was neither the time nor the place. The dining room was as enormous as every other room in the house, boasting a table that could easily seat fifty. Tonight it was a small party, only the Holmes family, the Worthingtons, who looked like complete pricks, and Joe Kildaire, a wealthy investment something-or-other whose date looked like she'd had at least thirty-five plastic surgeries.

Fuck, what was he *doing* here?

He snuck a sidelong glance at Annabelle, admiring her gorgeous profile, but not even the sight of her could dim his panic. He looked around the room, from the gleaming crystal chandelier to the perfectly set table with an endless amount of silverware and wine glasses.

It didn't take a genius to figure out he didn't belong here.

And he never would.

Chapter Eight

RYAN LOOKED MISERABLE. ANNABELLE FELT TERRIBLE AS SHE WATCHED him pick at the filet mignon on his plate, his dark head bent slightly. He'd barely said a word since his talk with her dad, and she could tell he felt like an outsider as the guests chatted with her parents at the dinner table. He'd only raised his head a few times since sitting down, each time to send a scowl in Bryce's direction.

Annabelle wanted to scowl too. Bryce had strolled into the dining room with her father, pulling her into his arms for a warm hug as if nothing had happened between them. She had to admit, he did look good in his pinstriped black suit, blond hair perfectly cut. His chiseled features focused on her every few seconds, and he kept shooting her endearing little smiles. She had no idea what he was up to, but she didn't like it, whatever it was.

"So, are you enjoying your vacation, Annabelle?" Bryce asked, lifting his wine glass to his lips and taking a long sip.

"Yes, San Diego is beautiful," she replied in a polite voice.

"Not as beautiful as you look tonight, I'm sure," he teased.

She noticed her parents exchange a pleased look. She stifled a sigh. Why was Bryce acting like Mr. Charming all of a sudden? He'd dumped her, for Pete's sake.

The dinner dragged on. Bryce continued to flirt with her, Ryan continued to sulk, and Annabelle's parents chatted with the Worthingtons and Kildaires as if nothing was out of sorts. By the time the small catering staff cleared the dinner plates and brought dessert out, Annabelle was ready to tear her hair out. She tried to draw Ryan out of his shell, but he barely paid any attention to her.

His blue eyes became alert, though, when Bryce suddenly cleared his throat and stood up. "All right, I think it's time to put an end to all the tension," he said cheerfully, holding the stem of his wine glass.

The adults at the table looked intrigued.

"Sandra, Greg, I know you were both upset to hear that Annabelle and I broke up, but I want you both to know that Annabelle and I have seen the error of our ways."

Huh?

Beaming, Bryce went on. "I'm happy to announce that the wedding is back on."

As Annabelle's mother clapped her hands together in delight, Bryce walked around the table to where Annabelle was sitting and reached for her hand. A sick feeling rose up her chest, settling into a lump in the back of her throat. What the *hell* was he doing?

"Stand up, sweetheart," Bryce urged. "Let's toast to our happiness."

"What? No, Bryce, this is not—"

Without letting her finish, he took her arm and forced her to her feet. Annabelle's gaze sought out Ryan's, but he refused to meet her eyes. His broad shoulders were as stiff as a board and she noticed a muscle in his jaw twitching. Oh God. This was a disaster.

She opened her mouth to object again, but Bryce broke out in a long, bullshit toast about happiness and marriage, and everyone at the table raised their glasses, clinking them together in celebration. Annabelle had never seen her parents look happier, and she could've sworn she saw a flicker of satisfaction in her father's eyes, as if he'd known this was coming. Bryce's parents got up and hugged her, expressing their joy that the two "children" were still getting married.

Bryce smiled warmly, then whispered close to her ear. "You forgive me for all those things I said, right, sweetheart? You know I didn't mean them."

Her lips tightened. Trying to control her anger, she whispered back, "I don't know what the hell you're up to, Bryce, but I am *not* going to—"

The words died in her throat when she heard Ryan's chair scrape against the floor. Without a word or a look in her direction, he walked out of the dining room.

Panic filled her body. "Ryan—" she called, but Bryce tightened his grip on her hand.

"Let him go. This is obviously very awkward for him, us getting back together," Bryce said smoothly.

"We are *not* getting back together," she hissed out. Then she shrugged his hand off her arm and ran out of the dining room after Ryan.

She caught up to him just as he reached the front door. "Wait," she said breathlessly. "Please, don't go."

Very slowly, he turned to face her, his blue eyes utterly expressionless. "Do you seriously think I'm going to stay?"

"Bryce and I aren't back together," she insisted. "I don't know what the hell he's up to, but I promise you, Ryan, I am not marrying that jerk."

He didn't answer.

She stepped toward him, cupping his chin with her hands. "Please don't go. Or at least wait for me to change and I'll go with you, okay?"

Weariness etched into his features. Sighing, he covered her hands with his and very gently removed them from his face. "You can't go with me," he finally said, his voice rough.

She wrinkled her nose. "Why not? Trust me, the last place I want to be right now is here. I just want to throttle Bryce for what he did back there. He knows damn well we're not back together."

"Look, it doesn't matter." There was a chord of frustration in his voice.

"What do you mean, it doesn't matter?"

He let out a heavy breath. "You should probably go back to Bryce anyway."

Ice hardened her veins. "Pardon me?"

"This isn't really my scene, babe." He reached up to loosen his tie. "It's a little too much for me, actually."

"What exactly are you saying?"

"I'm saying I don't belong here." He tore off the tie and shoved it in the pocket of his black trousers. His voice was suddenly cool, careless. "We were just having some fun, Annabelle. I didn't sign up for family weekends and drama and all that crap."

Her hands trembled. "You offered to come home with me."

"Yeah, and it was a big fucking mistake, okay?" He raked one hand through his dark hair. "Let's just make this easy, babe. We spent a couple of weeks together, had a good time, but now it's time to end it."

"End it," she repeated dully.

"Yes. Because honestly? The fun's over for me."

The cruelty of that comment hit her hard. Her chest felt like someone had sliced it open, and in that moment she realized just how much she cared about this man. Damn it, she'd fallen in love with him. Her heart squeezed in pain and humiliation. God, she was so stupid.

"Can I ask you something?" she asked shakily, forcing herself to meet his eyes. "Do you even feel *anything* for me?"

He hesitated, and her heart ached again.

"Do you?" she demanded.

Ryan's gaze didn't waver as he gave a slight shake of the head. "No," he admitted.

Tears pricked her eyelids. She quickly blinked them back. Anger joined the sorrow swimming in her gut. She narrowed her eyes, unable to accept what he'd just said. "You're lying. You do have feelings for me."

"You turn me on, sure," he said callously. "But I don't love you, if that's what you're getting at." He grimaced. "Fuck, we both know I'm in love with someone else."

The knife in her heart twisted several more times, leaving her chest raw and empty. "Jane," she said weakly.

"Yes." He averted his eyes. "It's always been her, all right?"

"Were you using me to try to get over her?"

He nodded.

The tears returned, this time doing more than stinging her eyes. They streamed down her cheeks and she viciously swiped at them with the back of her hand. She took a deep breath. "Go, then. You obviously don't want to be here, and frankly, I don't want you here either, so just go."

His blue eyes flickered with regret. "I'm sorry, Annabelle."

"Yeah, me too," she said bitterly.

He started to reach for her, then seemed to change his mind. "It was fun at least, no?"

"Yeah, loads of fun," she answered darkly. "Now do me a favor, Ryan, and get the hell out of my house."

Chapter Nine

IT WAS PAST MIDNIGHT WHEN RYAN LET HIMSELF INTO HIS APARTMENT, his suit rumpled from the flight and his heart battered from everything he'd put it through tonight. *You did the right thing*, the voice in his head said, but he didn't feel reassured. Had he done the right thing? He couldn't get the image of Annabelle's tears out of his mind, and it killed him knowing he had hurt her.

But she would be better off in the long run, right? He didn't belong in her world, and he would never fit in with that wealthy lifestyle of hers. Her father had made that pretty damn clear. Annabelle would be fine. She'd probably get back together with that asshole Bryce, move into a big mansion, and live a luxurious life. He was sparing her the embarrassment of being with some military bum who made in a year what her father probably earned in a week.

You are not good enough for my daughter.

Gregory's harsh words continued to buzz in his brain. He groaned softly, then pulled his tie from his pocket and hurled it across the room. He stalked into his bedroom, where he tore off his suit and slid into bed, naked and pissed off.

The moment his head hit the pillow, the scent of orange blossoms filled his nostrils, which only made him angrier. Damn Annabelle and her snobby parents and her sexy orange blossom smell. He groaned again, the sound muffled by the pillow, and then in an uncharacteristic burst of anger, he threw the pillow across the room. The damn thing hit the stack of books atop his dresser, sending the pile crashing to the floor.

With the instincts of a well-trained SEAL, Matt suddenly appeared in the doorway. "What happened?" he demanded.

Ryan let out a hysterical laugh. "Nothing. Books fell, that's all. Sorry if I woke you."

Matt studied him, a worried expression filling his face. "What the hell happened to you?"

"Nothing," he said again.

"You have crazy eyes, man. The same look you had on your face during that last gig in Afghanistan." Matt furrowed his brows. "Weren't you supposed to come back from San Francisco tomorrow night?"

"I left early." Then he thought, to hell with it, and added, "I broke up with Annabelle."

Matt's eyes widened. "What? Why the hell did you do that? We both know you're crazy about her."

He smothered a sigh. "I'm crazy about Jane," he corrected.

His friend went silent for a moment. "No, you're not." A shrewd glint entered Matt's eyes. "You don't have that lovelorn little boy look on your face anymore when you say her name."

"Fuck. Just mind your own business, O'Connor. Annabelle and I are over, and that's that." Sarcasm dripped from his tone. "If you want her around that badly, you date her."

Matt raised both eyebrows. "Wow."

"Wow what?" he grumbled.

"You're in love with her."

Ryan gritted his teeth. "Would you go back to your room already? I'm trying to sleep."

"No, you're not. You're trying to sulk."

"Fuck off, Matt. Just leave this alone."

Matt shook his head, but rather than pressing the subject, he simply walked away. A moment later, Ryan heard Matt's bedroom door shut with a soft click.

Damn it. Matt was wrong. He wasn't in love with Annabelle. He couldn't be. Two weeks, that's all they'd spent together. Had some sex, shared some laughs—that wasn't love.

Was it?

He settled back in bed, staring up at the ceiling in dismay. No, he couldn't love her. And he just prayed that Matt really would leave it alone. He didn't need his friend harassing him about this break-up, if you could even call it that, and he certainly didn't want to think about Annabelle anymore. It was over. Done. Better off forgotten.

But apparently the words *leave it alone* weren't in his best friend's vocabulary.

When Ryan walked into the kitchen the next morning after a sleepless night of tossing and turning, he found Jane sitting on one of the stools in front of the narrow counter. She wore a turquoise sundress, her red hair hung in a loose braid down her back, and for the first time in a long time, he didn't feel a burst of longing when he saw her.

"So how'd you fuck it up?" she asked when she saw him, cutting right to the chase.

He ignored the question, heading for the fridge. He pulled out a carton of orange juice, then leaned against the sink as he took a deep swig of juice. "Don't you have better things to do than bug me at—" he glanced at the clock on the microwave, "—seven o'clock in the morning?"

"Nope," she said breezily.

"Did O'Connor call you?"

"Yep." Her blue eyes searched his face. "He said you dumped Annabelle and he asked me to come over to slap some sense into you."

"Trust me, ending it made perfect sense," he muttered under his breath.

"I don't believe you." Her chin jutted in its usual stubborn pose. "Annabelle is awesome. She's funny and smart and it was obvious you two really hit it off. So how on earth does it make sense to just dump her like a piece of—"

"Her father tried to bribe me to get out of her life," he cut in, his voice hard.

Jane's jaw fell open. For once in her life, she was actually speechless, and Ryan could see her brain working overtime, trying to figure that one out.

"No way," she finally breathed, sounding horrified.

"Yes way."

Hopping off the stool, Jane marched over and dragged him into the living room, where she made him sit on the couch. She plopped down beside him and ordered, "Tell me everything."

So he did. He told her about the trip to San Francisco, about the goddamn palace Annabelle's parents lived in. The way her mother had looked down her nose at him, the fun chat with Annabelle's dad. He even threw in Bryce's surprise the-wedding-is-back-on announcement, just for kicks. When he finished, Jane looked utterly amazed.

"That sounds…terrible."

"It was," he confirmed. "Really awkwardly terrible. Now do you see why I ended it?"

She looked at him in disbelief. "No, I don't, actually. When in the hell did you become a coward?"

His skin prickled with offense. "I'm not a coward."

"Yes, you are. You felt out of your league, got all insecure, and took off like a scared little bunny rabbit." She softened her tone. "Look, I know you didn't have the most luxurious of upbringings, and I'm sure being around all those rich people was overwhelming, but come on, Ry, you're better than that. You're better than *them*, and you should have fought for her instead of letting her father scare you off."

He suddenly regretted ever telling Jane about his childhood. He should've known she wouldn't understand. She came from a great family, and even if she hadn't, she fit in wherever she went. He could see Jane getting along splendidly with Annabelle's snotty parents, that was just the kind of person she was. But him? He would never fit in with those snobs.

"I just don't get how Annabelle didn't see through your bullshit break-up speech." Jane shook her head in bewilderment. "She seemed pretty sharp when I met her at the hospital."

Guilt swarmed his gut as he remembered what he'd said to Annabelle. *It's always been her.* He quickly averted his eyes, scared she might read his mind, which of course she did.

"There's more, isn't there?" she said with a sigh.

"No," he lied.

"What did you tell her to get her to believe your crap?"

He stared at some random point behind her head, determined not to meet those keen blue eyes. "Nothing."

"Ryan."

"Jane."

He nearly jumped when he felt her hands on his chin. She forced him to look at her, her palms warm against his jaw. "What did you say to her?" she asked sternly.

Swallowing, he met her gaze head-on. "I told her I was in love with you."

She let out a startled expletive. "For God's sake, Ryan, why the *hell* would you—" She stopped abruptly, searching his expression. "Oh fuck, you actually believe you meant it."

Irritation climbed up his chest. "Maybe I did mean it."

Jane shook her head, the sympathy in her eyes making him wince. Great, she felt sorry for him. How fucking wonderful. "I know we had a little flirtation going when Beck and I broke up all those months ago, but come on, Ry, you're not in love with me."

"Maybe I am," he said roughly.

"No," she disagreed. "Maybe you think you are, because I'm the first woman you've ever opened up to, but we're best friends and nothing more. Deep down, you have to know that—"

He kissed her.

He hadn't planned on doing it, didn't think about the consequences either. One second he was looking into her gorgeous blue eyes and the next he was covering her mouth with his. He'd fantasized about this moment for months, wondered how it would feel, how she would taste, but the moment his lips met hers, reality crashed into him like a tidal wave.

"Fuck," he muttered, quickly breaking the lip contact. He avoided her eyes again, ashamed of what he'd done. He wanted to slap himself, not just for forcing a lip-lock on his best friend, but because he knew now, with total certainty, that he'd just kissed a woman who was the equivalent of a sister.

A woman who rewarded the unwanted contact with an angry scowl. "What. The. Fuck," she snapped.

"I'm sorry." He sucked in a breath, cringing when she scooted to the other end of the couch. "I thought—shit, Jane. That was a crappy thing to do."

"Beyond crappy," she grumbled. Then, to his surprise, she started to laugh. "That totally felt incestuous, no?"

He laughed too. "Um, yeah, to say the least. I'm sorry," he repeated.

Jane's laughter died, replaced by a heavy sigh. "I forgive you." She paused. "But now that you've gotten that out of your system, can you please get on a plane to San Francisco and win back the woman you *actually* love?"

He hesitated. "No," he finally said.

"Why not?" She sounded frazzled.

"Because this doesn't change anything. Maybe I misunderstood my feelings for you, but I know exactly where I stand with Annabelle's family. Her dad tried to pay me off, for fuck's sake."

"Well, screw him," Jane retorted. "You love Annabelle, not her dad."

"I don't belong in her life," he said softly.

She slowly slid back toward him. This time when she touched his cheek, her fingers were gentle. "Then you know what that makes you, Ry?"

"What?" he asked hoarsely.

She dropped her hand, the disappointment on her face unmistakable. "It makes you a goddamn fool."

Chapter Ten

ANNABELLE SPENT THE MORNING IN HER CHILDHOOD BEDROOM, TRYING to figure out what the heck to do. Her heart felt like someone had smashed it with a hammer, and she still couldn't believe what a fool she'd been, actually believing that she and Ryan had more than a fling going. Somehow, during their two weeks together, she'd fallen for him.

But he hadn't fallen for her.

She sat down at the edge of the four-poster bed, looking around the bedroom in dismay. Decorated in shades of cream and yellow, the room boasted an antique dresser, a huge desk built into the wall, and a walk-in closet that was bigger than Christina's bedroom back in San Diego. Everything was neat and pristine—her mother didn't allow clutter. Growing up, Annabelle had hated this perfect, impersonal room.

She was probably going to have to move back in here until she found a place of her own, and she wasn't looking forward to being under the same roof as her parents again. But what choice did she have? No matter what Bryce said, she wasn't going to marry him. Because despite how things had ended with Ryan, her time with him had shown her that she didn't want to be with Bryce. She wanted a man who gave a damn about her, who made her feel beautiful and special, who made her laugh and appreciated her.

Bryce Worthington was not that man.

She still didn't know why he'd dropped that bomb at the dinner table last night without even speaking to her about it first. After Ryan left, she'd gone up to her room and locked the door, refusing to talk to anyone. She'd heard Bryce and his parents leaving, heard him assure everyone that his fiancée was just a little "overwhelmed". Overwhelmed, her ass. Who did he think he was, telling everyone they were back together?

A sharp knock rapped on her door, and she lifted her head in irritation. "Yes?" she called.

"Miss Holmes," came Magdalena's polite voice, "Mr. Worthington is here to see you."

She stifled a groan. Great. Bryce was back, no doubt to try and talk her into marrying him. For a moment she wanted to tell the housekeeper to kick him out, but then she realized this was the perfect opportunity to set things straight.

"Thanks, Magdalena. Have him wait in the den," she replied. "I'll be down in a minute."

As Magdalena's footsteps retreated down the hall, Annabelle walked into her private bath and checked her reflection in the mirror. Her eyes looked a little red, probably from all the crying she'd done after Ryan left. She pinched her cheeks to give them some color. When she saw Bryce, she didn't want to look like a gaunt, pathetic girl who'd been dumped — twice.

He was standing at the bay window when she strode into the spacious den. She joined him, frowning when he tried to draw her into an embrace. "No, Bryce," she said stiffly, shrugging his hands off her.

His pale-blue eyes flickered with annoyance. "I can't hug you now?"

"No, you can't." She crossed her arms. "What the hell was last night about? We're not back together and you know it."

He looked sheepish. "I know, it might have been a little presumptuous of me, but I thought you'd be happy."

"Happy?" she echoed in disbelief. "You broke up with me because you wanted to *take a walk on the wild side*, and all of a sudden you want to marry me again?"

He shifted, discomfort lining his face. "I made a mistake," he said in a vague tone. "I realized right after I ended it just how much I missed you."

She snorted. "Is that why you were making out with some girl at the Sheppard party?"

His eyes flashed. "Who told you that?" Before she could reply, the anger in his eyes was replaced with regret. "I messed up, okay? But I'm willing to make it up to you, sweetheart. I really want to marry you."

She rolled her eyes. "Well, I don't want to marry you."

He faltered. "You don't?"

Was he seriously surprised? She let out a harsh laugh. "Of course not. Why would I want to marry a guy who dumped me like a piece of trash?"

His jaw tensed. He turned his head and focused on the sparkling water of the bay a hundred yards away. When he finally turned back to her, suspicion hardened his face. "Is this about that guy you brought home last night?" His voice went cold. "I'm willing to forgive you for that, so why can't you forgive me?"

"This isn't some forgiveness contest," she retorted. "And me not wanting to marry you has nothing to do with Ryan. Not that it's any of your business, but we're not seeing each other anymore."

Relief filled his eyes. "Then there's no reason for us not to get back together."

She released a frustrated sigh. "Why are you so eager to marry me? Is someone holding a gun to your head, for Pete's sake?"

Something about his expression gave her pause. It wasn't so much guilt as it was...fear? She uncrossed her arms, letting them dangle to her sides. She suddenly felt weary. "What's going on, Bryce?"

He mumbled something.

"I can't hear you," she snapped.

"Your father," he said, raising his voice.

"What about my father?"

"He threatened to fire me, okay?" Bryce spat out, sounding livid. "He said if I didn't stop screwing around and do right by you, I'd lose my job."

Horror swarmed her body. He couldn't possibly be serious. Her dad was controlling, sure, but not cruel. Right?

"If you're lying to me, I swear to God, Bryce, I'll kick your ass," she warned.

"I'm not lying, Annabelle. He pulled me into his study before dinner last night and laid it all out."

She stared at Bryce, a vine of disgust twining around her spine. "So you were willing to marry me to keep your job? That's pathetic."

His face turned red. He opened his mouth to say something, but she was through listening. She held up her hand to silence him. "We are not getting married, Bryce. I don't care what threats my dad made against you, but if it makes you feel better, I'm going to talk to him right now and tell him to stop interfering in our lives." She sighed. "I'll make sure you keep your job, okay?"

Surprise filled his gaze. "You will?"

"Yes, so long as you understand that we are *not* getting back together. I don't want to." She paused. "And I don't think you do either. So please, Bryce, just leave."

With a nod, he stepped away from the window. "I am sorry, you know." He met her eyes, shamefaced. "I know I was an ass to you, but I think we can both agree our relationship wasn't working."

She couldn't help laugh. "Yeah, I think you're right about that."

Her chest felt surprisingly light as she walked Bryce to the front door. They didn't hug or kiss goodbye; he just slid out the door, and the past five years they'd spent together simply floated away in the warm morning breeze.

Annabelle closed the door after him, then leaned against it, collecting her thoughts. A minute later, she straightened her shoulders in determination and made her way to her father's study.

RYAN RAISED HIS BEER TO HIS LIPS, STARING GLUMLY AT THE TV. THANK fuck Matt was out. It spared him the humiliation of being horribly belittled for his current viewing choice. But this was the last movie he'd watched with Annabelle, and he'd always been a sucker for self-torture. He drained the rest of his beer, the cold alcohol sliding down his throat but doing nothing to soothe the ache in his gut.

He missed Annabelle. He'd known her for only two weeks, and yet it felt like so much longer. And now that she was no longer in his life, it was like there was a big gaping hole in his chest. It was stupid, really. Things between them would have ended anyway—she had a job, a life, in San Francisco. Wasn't like she would've moved to San Diego to be with him.

Quit thinking about her, he ordered himself. *She's gone, it's over. Go out and get laid.*

But the idea of having sex with some random chick at a club or bar held no appeal for him. He didn't want random. He wanted Annabelle.

It was funny—for months he'd thought he was in love with Jane, and in the end he'd been totally blindsided by his love for Annabelle.

The click of the door opening jolted him from his thoughts. Shit. Matt was back.

Ryan set down his empty bottle and looked around for the remote control so he could turn off the movie before he got caught watching it. Damn, where the hell was the—

He froze when Annabelle strode into his living room.

She wore a pair of baggy cargo shorts, a snug blue tank top, and red flip-flops. His pulse immediately sped up, getting faster when she crossed her arms over her chest, emphasizing her full cleavage.

"Hi," she said casually.

He swallowed. "Hi."

One delicate eyebrow lifted. "Why didn't you tell me my father tried to pay you off?"

A wave of surprise crashed into him, along with a flash of regret. He hadn't wanted her to find out about that. Her father might be an ass, but he was still her father. And Ryan hated the pain he saw swimming in her eyes.

"I didn't want to ruin your relationship with the guy," he admitted.

She uncrossed her arms, perching one hand on her hip. "Out of curiosity, how much did he offer?"

He made a wry face. "We never got that far, to tell you the truth. I told him to screw off long before we made it there."

Something that resembled satisfaction flickered on her face. "Good." Her eyes darkened. "But then you told *me* to screw off, too."

Regret rose in his chest. He wanted to apologize, but she lifted her hand to silence him.

"I get why," she said quietly. "You told me about the way you grew up, how awful it was. And then my dad goes and tells you that you don't belong. I can see why it freaked you out."

He slowly held her gaze. "You do?"

"Everyone gets insecure sometimes, Ryan. I just wish you'd talked to me about it instead of—O-M-G, are you watching *Second Time Around?*" she suddenly demanded, noticing for the first time what was on the screen.

His cheeks heated up. Fuck. This was goddamn mortifying. "Uh, it's on TV," he lied.

"No, it's not. I can see the player counting the minutes going by." Annabelle let out a delighted laugh. "You miss me!"

He tried to tamp down his amusement, but it came out in the form of a sheepish smile. "Yeah, maybe a little."

Before he could react, she bounded toward him and launched herself into his arms. He held her close, breathing in the sweet scent of orange blossoms, rubbing his chin against the silky-smooth flesh of her neck. God, it felt good holding her again.

"I miss you too," she said. "I know it's only been a day since you left, but it feels like forever."

"I know," he confessed.

She searched his face. "I just...what you said at the house...you didn't mean any of it, did you?"

"None of it," he said gruffly.

Relief flooded her face. "I thought so. Not at the time, but after I confronted my dad and found out what he tried to do, I figured you said all that stuff because you were...I don't know, scared?"

As a rule, he hated to admit fear, but at the moment, he knew he had no choice. If he wanted this woman back—and God, he did—then he had to be completely honest with her. "I felt like a loser," he mumbled. "I thought I wasn't good enough for you, so I said whatever I could to convince you I didn't want you."

"And the thing about...um...Jane?"

He touched her cheek. "I don't love her. I thought I did, a while ago, but I was wrong." He swallowed hard. "But you...I'm in love with you, Annabelle, and I know I'm not wrong about that."

A smile tugged at her lips. "You're in love with me?"

He nodded earnestly.

The smile widened. "Good. Because I'm in love with you too."

Pleasure soared in his chest. "You are?"

It was her turn to nod. "And I already decided I won't do the long-distance thing. Those relationships never work out."

He moistened his dry lips. "I can't move to San Francisco, babe. I need to stay close to the base so—"

She interrupted with a laugh. "Duh. I'm going to talk to my boss about transferring me to our San Diego office. She's always talking about how that location is understaffed, so I think she might really go for it."

Emotion clogged his throat. "You want to move here?"

"Why not? I like it here."

"What about your family?"

"I think it might be a good idea to be away from them for a while. God, I'm so furious at my dad. I can't believe he did that to you, and then he tried to do the same thing to Bryce."

Ryan frowned. "What?"

"He threatened to fire him if he didn't get back together with me," Annabelle said darkly. "But I convinced him to let Bryce keep his job."

"I hate that I might have done something to ruin your relationship with your father," Ryan said roughly.

She sighed. "I'll forgive him eventually. I hate staying mad at people. But like I said, I think some space from him and my mom will be for the best."

He drew her into his arms, dipping his head to kiss her. "So do you want to move in here?"

She looked startled. "Here?"

"Duh," he mimicked. "Eventually we'll get a place alone if you want, but I can't abandon Matt just yet. We signed a one-year lease."

She laughed. "Way to get ahead of yourself, Roger. I was thinking more along the lines of staying at Christina's. She and Joe might end up finding a place together anyway, which means I could stay upstairs for good."

Ryan couldn't help but smile. For good. He liked the sound of that. "Well, my door's always open, if you change your mind."

She leaned in to kiss him again. "Okay, now that we've settled that… can we have make-up sex?"

He rolled his eyes. "Like that's even up for debate."

"We still have two more items on the list to check off," she reminded him, arching one eyebrow.

He struggled to remember the elusive two items, then grinned when he did. "Number ten," he said with a decisive nod. "Let's start with that one."

Annabelle shook her head. "No way. I took a shower before I boarded the flight. I'll get all sticky if we do number ten."

But he was already on his feet, heading for the kitchen to get a bottle of maple syrup.

Glancing at her over his shoulder, he flashed a brilliant smile and said, "Trust me, it'll be fun."

The End

Up next: Matt's story! Keep reading for The Heat is On...

The Heat is On

An Out of Uniform Novella

Elle Kennedy

Chapter One

"EVERYONE DOWN ON THE FLOOR!"

Matt O'Connor always knew there was a reason he hated banks, but it wasn't until this exact moment that he figured out why: money made people go insane. And a building full of it? Well, apparently that turned people into idiots.

Yup, idiots. That was the only word to describe the three morons who bounded into the lobby of San Diego Savings and Loans with pantyhose covering their faces. They wore ill-fitting camo outfits that they'd probably picked up at a discount army surplus store, and the way two of them held their handguns revealed that handling weapons wasn't their strong suit. The third guy, whose long black hair stuck out from beneath his ridiculous hose mask, held his 9mm with ease, but aside from the fact that he knew how to grip a gun, he was as inept as the others.

Several female patrons in the brightly lit lobby shrieked at the sight of the robbers, immediately face-planting themselves on the tiled floor. An older gentleman took his time lowering himself down, while a couple of others just stood frozen in place as if they couldn't figure out if this was for real or if they were being pranked.

"This is a bank robbery!" Black Hair shouted.

Matt rolled his eyes. First of all, no shit. Secondly, didn't robbers say something like "This is a hold-up!"? Who used the words *bank robbery* during a bank robbery?

"You! Yeah, you, shaved head!"

Huh. They were talking to him, Matt realized. He turned slowly to find the barrel of a gun pointed at his face, this one wielded by a guy with a huge hooked nose that the hose couldn't hide. "I said down on the ground."

With a sigh, Matt got to his knees. Then, when the gun waved in front of his eyes, he reluctantly lay on his stomach. He could've probably taken down this trio of morons in less than ten seconds, but he didn't want to do anything rash, not until he got a better feel for these guys. Chances were, their weapons weren't even loaded, but he still decided to let it play out. Plus, he was tired from the grueling workout he'd just put his body through on the SEAL obstacle course back on base, and besides, he was kinda curious to see how these robbers planned to carry out their heist.

Hook Nose moved away and situated himself at the door, pointing his gun at the overweight security guard whose only attempt at stopping the robbery had been squeaking "I'm a security guard!" when the three men barreled into the bank. The robber in the bright red sneakers paced the lobby, watching the patrons lying on the floor, while Black Hair headed for the nearest teller and said, "Where's the manager?"

Matt heard tentative footsteps from behind the counter and then a woman with a faint Indian accent said, "I'm the manager."

"Listen here," Black Hair yelled.

"Okay, we can all hear you," an annoyed female voice mumbled to Matt's immediate left. "No need to keep yelling."

He shifted his head, surprised when he noticed the blonde hottie lying on her stomach a couple of feet from him. He hadn't noticed her when he'd come in, and since he could describe each and every last detail about each and every last person in this bank, he deduced that Blondie must've come in when he was talking to the teller.

Because he definitely would've remembered seeing her.

She was tall, judging by the long, lithe body stretched out on the floor, and her hair was the palest shade of yellow, falling into a pair of big gray eyes. The most distinct thing about her, though, was that she didn't seem frightened, upset or panicked in the least. If anything, she looked bored by this entire situation.

Spotting him peeking over at her, Blondie rolled her eyes and whispered, "Do you think they bought *Bank Robbing for Dummies* to prepare for this caper?"

"Nobody is going to get hurt!" Black Hair was shouting at the bank manager. "We just want the money."

There was the sound of paper crumpling, and when Matt tilted his head, he saw Black Hair handing the teller a brown paper bag. Oh for chrissake.

"They couldn't even spring for a duffel bag?" he muttered under his breath.

Beside him, Blondie coughed to smother a snort.

A register dinged open, followed by four others, as Black Hair moved to each teller's wicket to collect his hard-earned cash. When he finished, he tossed the bag over to Red Shoes, then turned back to the manager. "Now we go to the big safe."

A beat of silence. "You mean the vault?" the woman asked cautiously.

"Yes, the vault, *bitch*."

"Oooh, someone's getting upset," Blondie whispered.

Matt choked back a laugh.

"Nobody here has the combination to the safe," the manager said. "Only the branch manager can access it."

"You said you were the manager," Black Hair snapped.

"I'm the assistant manager," came the meek reply.

Silence.

"Uh-oh," Matt's new favorite person muttered. "This sure is a conundrum."

"How will they ever open the big safe now?" he whispered back.

"*Shut up!*"

The sharp yell came from Red Shoes, whose pacing had brought him to their vicinity.

Matt didn't even flinch as the gun barrel jammed into the nape of his neck. Right, because this idiot was really going to shoot him. These guys couldn't be older than twenty, twenty-one tops, and they obviously had no clue what they were doing.

Matt's shoulders tensed as he debated whether to wrench the gun from this imbecile's hands. His muscles relaxed. Nah, no point causing trouble. His interference might make these guys trigger-happy and he had no desire to see anyone get hurt. This heist couldn't last much longer, and no doubt these losers would be arrested the second they exited the bank.

And anyway, it was just starting to get fun.

As Matt and the blonde fell silent, Red Shoes clucked his tongue in approval, lifted his gun, and paced off. At the counter, Black Hair was forcing the manager to dial the branch manager's home phone number.

"Speakerphone!" he barked.

Matt really wished he could see what was going on above him, but he had to settle for just hearing it. The assistant manager's landline resonated a loud busy tone.

"I guess the branch manager is too cheap to invest in call waiting," Blondie murmured.

"Maybe he can't multi-task when it comes to communication," Matt pointed out, fighting a grin.

"Quiet!" Red Shoes barked at them.

"Call his cell phone," Black Hair ordered.

This time they got a dial tone, only to be replaced with a booming male voice that announced, "Lewis Templeton, San Diego Savings and Loans. Leave a message."

More silence.

Obviously Black Hair and his crew of misfits had no idea what to do now that they'd been barred access to the big safe. Across the room, a woman whimpered.

"You're lying," Black Hair finally accused. "You do know the combination to the vault, don't you?"

"I really don't," the manager protested.

"Liar!"

"I changed my mind," Blondie whispered. "I thought they had the IQ of first-graders, but I've demoted them to kindergarten."

Matt laughed, only to receive another harsh reprimand from Red Shoes, who was beginning to look frazzled by this entire mess. He kept glancing at the enormous window, then at the confused people standing outside the bank doors wondering why they couldn't get in.

"Someone's using their iPhone out there!" Red Shoes blurted out, sounding frantic. "I think they're calling the cops, Billy! We should split!"

Billy, the robber formerly known as Black Hair, spun around angrily. "What did I tell you about using our real names, you fucking idiot? Stick to the codes."

"I bet one of them is *eagle*," Matt murmured.

"Sorry, Eagle." Red Shoes sounded humbled. "But we need to split, like, *now!*"

From the corner of his eye, Matt saw the red sneakers making their way to the wicket. The two robbers huddled together, mumbling to each other about their next move.

A streak of impatience shot through him, and a little alarm went off in his head. All right. This had gone too far. The guys were panicking now, and idiots plus panic plus guns could only equal trouble. Someone could actually get hurt.

He glanced at Blondie. "Stay down," he said in a low voice.

Her gray eyes widened, mouth parting to protest, but he was already on his feet and springing to action. It took two seconds to disarm Billy and Red Shoes, and two more to land an uppercut on Billy's jaw that sent the guy slumping unconscious onto the floor. Without even breaking a sweat, Matt wrenched Red Shoes' arms behind his skinny back, locking him in an iron hold that had the guy gasping in pain. Then he raised one of the guns he'd confiscated from the robbers and pointed it at Hook Nose, who looked like a deer caught in headlights over by the door.

"Drop your weapon, or this idiot dies," Matt called cheerfully.

Hook Nose hesitated for all of a second, and then his handgun clattered to the floor and landed next to the foot of the security guard. "Now get on the ground, hands on your head," Matt ordered.

The guy dropped down like a bowling pin, just as the wail of sirens filled the air.

Matt glanced over at the guard, who was staring at him with shocked eyes, and said, "You're welcome."

Chapter Two

THE COPS DIDN'T KEEP THE PATRONS IN THE BANK FOR LONG. AFTER slapping cuffs on the idiot robbers and carting them into the waiting police cruisers out front, the three officers gathered everyone's statements and collected contact information should they be called in as witnesses for the moronic trio's trials.

The officer who questioned Matt looked about nineteen, and listened in awe as Matt described how he'd taken out the robbers. He explained he was a Navy SEAL, which got him another dose of awe and a bunch of questions, but Matt was only half paying attention to the conversation. Ten feet away, Blondie was speaking to a female police officer who was scrawling things down in a little black notebook.

Now that he had a better view, he realized Blondie was even hotter than he'd thought. Tall, as he'd suspected, but with the figure of a centerfold. Tiny hips, big tits, and the roundest, perkiest ass he'd ever seen. His mouth watered just from looking at her, and a burst of irritation went off inside him when he noticed the officer close her notebook and gesture that Blondie could leave.

Interrupting his own officer mid-sentence, he said, "Can I go now? I've kind of got somewhere to be."

The young cop looked down at the notes he'd made. "Yeah, you're free to go. We'll contact you if there's anything further."

"Good. Great." Matt was already heading toward the double doors.

He caught up to her just as she reached the small parking lot next to the bank.

"Hey!" he called.

She stopped, glanced over her shoulder, and a wide smile spread across her lips. "Oh, it's you. The big hero."

"Don't bother hiding it. We both know you were impressed with what I did back there," he said with a cocky grin.

Her gray eyes twinkled. "Yeah. I guess that was pretty impressive. What are you, a superhero?"

He shrugged. "I'm a Navy SEAL."

"Oooh, a soldier," she teased, running a manicured hand through her long, blonde hair. "I guess I'm lucky I decided to cash my check today. And to think we never would've met if I did it yesterday." She tilted her head. "Then again, if I did it yesterday, I wouldn't be late for work right now. Good thing I'm my own boss, because I don't think 'I was caught in a bank hold-up' would fly as an excuse for being late."

He grinned at the sarcastic note to her voice. "Yeah, I don't think my commander would accept it either." He paused. "I'm Matt, by the way."

"Savannah," she replied, sticking out her hand.

He shook it, and a tremor of heat went through him the moment their palms touched. This woman was extremely hot, and definitely amusing. He had a date tonight with a waitress he'd met last night at a club, but suddenly he had no desire to hook up with the voluptuous brunette. He was far more interested in this leggy blonde in front of him.

"Savannah," he echoed, hearing his southern drawl rear its head. Damn accent always seemed to get stronger when he was flirting. "Your parents like the South or something?"

"No, they like eco-systems."

He blinked. "Huh?"

"My dad is a geography professor at Stanford. He's a big fan of grasslands."

For the life of him, Matt couldn't figure out if she was joking.

"I'm not joking," she said, as if reading his mind. "He teaches an entire unit on the tropical savannahs of Northern Australia."

"Oh. Wow. I honestly don't know what to say to that."

"Yeah, most people don't." She tossed her hair over her shoulder, then clicked her key fob. Two sharp honks came from a shiny red Toyota parked a few spots away. Savannah took a step toward it. "Okay, gotta run. Thanks for saving us from the bank robbers."

"Wait," he cut in.

She stopped. "What?"

He suddenly felt awkward. He wasn't used to women being completely indifferent to his charms. Though in his defense, he hadn't been giving her his A-game. That eco-system thing had thrown him off.

"Do you want to get together sometime?"

She seemed to think it over.

To *think* it over.

Since when did women need to mull over the idea of a date with him? The other members of his SEAL team, including his best friend Ryan, were either married, engaged or in serious relationships, but Matt was still carrying on the tradition of hot hook-ups and no-strings flings. He loved women, and he had no desire to settle down with just one. Where was the fun in that? There were so many gorgeous females out there, and he'd spent the better part of ten years sampling each and every one. He was twenty-eight years old and he always got what he wanted in the sex department—and right now, he wanted Savannah.

"Nah, I think I'll pass," she finally replied, then had the nerve to give him a sympathetic smile.

He returned the smile, but his was loaded with heat. "Are you sure? You were just caught up in a very dangerous situation—I think you might need some comforting."

She gave an unladylike snort. "Comfort sex? Seriously, you're offering me comfort sex?"

Matt faltered. Again. This woman was totally throwing him off his game.

He pushed aside the disconcerting thought, gathering up every ounce of charm and confidence he possessed. "I think you might need it," he said solemnly.

She just raised one dark-blonde eyebrow. "I think I need to get to work, actually." She took off walking again.

Matt hurried after her, catching up as she reached for the door handle of the Toyota.

Ah, a challenge. Okay. If she wanted to play hard to get, he was all for it. But he knew this attraction definitely wasn't one-sided. He had plenty of experience with the ladies, and he *knew* when one liked him.

Didn't he?

"Take it easy, Matt," she added as she opened the door and slid into the driver's seat.

"I know a great Italian place," he persisted. "Just me, you, a bottle of wine..."

"Yeah, Italian's not really my thing," she said, cutting him off. Then she leaned out of the car and pointed to the sky. "Hey, I think the Bat-signal's calling you."

He fell for it. And when he turned back, she had reversed out of her parking space, giving him a sassy wave before she peeled off.

SAVANNAH HARTE WAS SMILING AS SHE DROVE AWAY FROM THE BANK AND headed toward Market Street. Despite herself, her body was still reacting from the encounter with Matt. Her heart was doing little flips, and her palms were actually a bit damp. Weird. She flirted with sexy men all the time, but something about Matt the Navy SEAL aka Bank Savior had totally and instantly turned her on. Maybe it was the shaved head. Or that unbelievably hard and appealing body. Even his awkward pick-up lines had succeeded in making her hot.

But as appealing as he was, she wasn't about to blow off Jake for a total stranger. She didn't play by many rules in her life—rules just sucked the fun right out of things—but there was one strict guideline she followed: one man at a time.

She wasn't the kind of girl who dated a whole bunch of guys at once. That just seemed tacky and insensitive to her. And at the moment, she was seeing Jake, the tall sexy surfer she'd met on the beach last week.

Not that she'd be dating him for long. She had no interest in committed relationships. Commitment only led to ruts, and she didn't want to be falling into any ruts. Like her parents. Jeez, talk about boring. She loved them both to death, but growing up she'd decided she wanted nothing more than to *not* follow in their footsteps. Their life was so monotonous it made her want to shake them by the shoulders and say, *This? This is what you always wanted for your lives?* Sitting on the couch every night taking turns with the remote. Weekly bridge games with their neighbors. The same old Sunday brunch at Applebee's.

Nope. Definitely not for her. She lived for the thrill of first kisses and whirlwind romances, and once any hint of comfortable domesticity entered the equation, Savannah Harte was outta there. No thank you.

But she did have some code of ethics, and seeing two or more guys at once was where she drew the line.

Too bad, though. That Matt... He really was cute. And the way he'd taken down those three idiots at the bank—she'd actually felt a streak of arousal watching him do that. Rare these days, finding a man capable of kicking total ass.

"Ah well," she murmured to herself, steering the car toward the end of the street, where her corner flower shop was located.

She pulled in around back and parked in the miniscule lot, then grabbed her purse and headed into the shop from the rear door.

Fortunately, when she walked into the bright main room, it was devoid of customers. Savannah's new assistant, Chad, stood behind the narrow red counter, and his brown eyes filled with relief when he spotted her. He'd only been working with her for a couple of weeks, not long enough to leave him in charge of the store, which got busy this time of year. No comparison to Valentine's Day or Mother's Day, of course, but September was also a peak time. For some reason, parents liked to buy their college kids flowers to celebrate the new school year, or the *new life journey*, as many of her customers liked to harp.

"I'm sorry," she said as she reached the counter. "I swear I didn't abandon you. Some people decided to rob the bank while I was there."

"For serious? Are you okay?"

She appreciated Chad's concern. She liked the guy, in spite of his tendency to say things like "for serious". "I'm fine," she assured him. "Was everything okay while I was gone?"

He pushed his sagging wire-rim glasses up the bridge of his nose. "It was fine. I sold a wreath, and three dozen roses."

"Any problematic customers?"

"No. They were all pretty nice. Oh, but you did get a phone call." Chad rummaged in the drawer underneath the counter and removed a pink message slip. He handed it to Savannah. "It was an event planner. She's planning a wedding and was interested in a quote."

Savannah glanced down at Chad's neat block writing. *Annabelle*

Holmes, Prestige Events. She'd never heard of either Holmes or the company name, but Savannah liked the idea of doing flowers for a big event. She'd only recently started handling parties and weddings, and the money they brought in was pretty appealing. She didn't have another wedding scheduled until the end of the month, so hopefully she could squeeze this event in for some extra cash flow.

"I'll give her a call," she said absently, tucking the message into her pocket. She glanced at Chad with a grin. "So, are you ready to learn how to arrange centerpieces?"

Her new assistant brightened. For a twenty-year-old man, he was oddly interested in flowers. Not that she blamed him. Flowers were her livelihood. There was nothing that brightened her day more than a bouquet of pretty, colorful blooms.

Well, that and sex. But she'd have to wait for tonight to experience that particular joy. She had a date with Jake later and was already imagining all the naughty things he would do to her body. For a second, though, the image of Jake's dark eyes and dimpled cheeks was replaced with the one of Matt's green eyes and chiseled features, but she quickly banished the thought.

Matt had been cute, sure, but, in Savannah's life, cute guys were always in constant supply.

Chapter Three

"WOULD YOU QUIT SULKING?" ANNABELLE HOLMES GRUMBLED AS SHE steered the olive-green Jeep down a street littered with little boutiques and a vast number of coffee shops. "So you got rejected. Big deal. Actually, it's about time. I feel comforted knowing that even sluts like you strike out every now and then."

Matt just glared at her. Normally he enjoyed Annabelle's endless sarcasm, but he wasn't in the mood for it today. It had been almost two weeks since the encounter with Savannah at the bank, and he still couldn't fight his disappointment that she'd turned him down. He'd even gone so far as to try and track her down, but all he had to go on was her name. He'd typed Savannah into Google, hoping maybe he'd get lucky, but he got over six million results. He'd tried Facebook too, but there was a ridiculous amount of Savannahs on the site and he'd given up after scrolling through the first ten pages of profiles.

So yeah, Annabelle was right. He did have to quit sulking. Obviously he was never going to see Savannah again. He knew that. But Annabelle didn't have to gloat about it.

"You're being very insensitive about this whole thing," he grumbled back. "And I'm not a slut."

Annabelle hooted, her big brown eyes lighting up in delight. "Yeah freaking right. You are *so* a slut. You had sex with me less than an hour after we'd met."

"You wrote up a sex list," he shot back. "So who's the slut, hmmm?"

"I was exploring my sexuality," she said in her defense. "You, on the other hand, finished exploring years ago. Now you're just a manwhore. Wait, I think this is it." She squinted. "Yeah, it's here."

A two-story corner shop came into view. Hanging on the storefront was a big purple sign that read *Harte to Harte Flowers*. He rolled his eyes. How cute.

"Besides," Annabelle said as she executed an unbelievably impressive parallel parking job across the street from the shop, "you don't know, maybe you'll run into her again. If you're meant to, you will. Fate makes things happen."

"I don't believe in fate."

"You should. I mean, look at me and Ryan. He slid into my bed in the middle of the night thinking I was someone else, and now we're in love. Fate."

"Luck," he corrected.

"Stop being such a Negative Nancy." She killed the engine and yanked on the parking brake. "All you have to do is snap your fingers and you can get laid. Why don't you call up your new BFF Aidan and set up a pub crawl or something, you know, have a three-way or fourgy or whatever it is you guys do."

"He's not my BFF," Matt grumbled. "We just hang out sometimes."

Because all my friends are in love, he wanted to add, but didn't because he knew Annabelle would just accuse him of being jealous. He wasn't, though. He was happy for his friends, he truly was, but their no-longer-single status made it hard for Matt to find a wingman for a night out on the town. A few months ago he'd gone for beers with Aidan Rhodes, who worked in Naval Intelligence out on the base, and the two men had instantly hit it off. Aidan was a couple of years younger, and, like Matt, always up for a good time.

And though he wasn't going to admit it to Annabelle, he and Aidan did have a threesome last month, with a hot redhead visiting from Kansas.

"I don't want a fourgy," he added with a frown. "I want some good, old-fashioned, one-on-one with the hot blonde I met. Is that too much to ask for?"

"Stop whining. It's unattractive."

"That's not what you said the night I rocked your world."

Annabelle didn't even have the decency to blush. Instead, she laughed again. "You rocked my body. There's a difference."

Was there? He always felt oddly uncomfortable when Annabelle, or any of his friends, for that matter, tried to explain what love felt like.

Sure, he loved people—his mom, Nana O'Connor, his four older sisters. But *love* love? He had no clue how that felt. If he weren't constantly surrounded by happy couples, he wouldn't even believe it existed.

He and Annabelle got out of the car and headed for the flower shop. He walked ahead, opening the door for his friend's girlfriend like the Southern gentleman he was. A bell chimed as they entered the store. Almost immediately, the heady and powerful scent of flowers filled his nostrils. He breathed it in, reminded of the yard in his mom's Nashville house. The O'Connor women loved to garden.

His gaze took in the elaborate arrangements and baskets of fresh-smelling flowers practically overflowing the shop's small space.

"So pretty," Annabelle murmured as she admired a vase containing bright yellow tulips intermingled with curly white willow and white shasta daisies. That he knew the kind of daisies they were boggled the mind. Apparently he'd picked up some gardening knowledge over the years without knowing it.

Footsteps sounded from behind a green curtain separating another doorway from the main room. "I'll be right with you!" a muffled feminine voice chirped.

"I like this place," Annabelle whispered to him. "It's the perfect combination of charm and elegance. Think Holly will like it?"

"How the hell would I know?" he mumbled. "This is why you should have brought *Holly* and not me."

"Holly was busy. And you're my friend. Friends do this kind of stuff for each other."

He pretended to brood, but he wasn't annoyed that Annabelle had dragged him along on her errands. He liked spending time with her, and he was actually proud of her for what she was trying to accomplish. She'd left behind a successful job at one of the top event planning firms in San Francisco just so she could be with Ryan, and Matt fully supported this new venture. Annabelle and Carson Scott's wife, Holly, had started an event planning business of their own, and the two women had already planned and catered some seriously ritzy parties. Matt had helped out at one of their wedding receptions and was floored by the results.

The footsteps from the back room grew louder. He swung his head toward the curtain in time to see a very familiar face.

Recognition dawned in her gray eyes at the same moment.

"Seriously?" Savannah said with a sigh.

"I know what you're thinking," he blurted out, "but I'm not stalking you."

"Uh, I *wasn't* thinking that. But *now* I am."

A flush crept into his cheeks. His peripheral vision caught Annabelle giving him a perplexed look. Well, no kidding. He was usually way smoother than this, but yet again, Savannah brought out his inner stammer.

An awkward silence descended, which Savannah ended with an impatient frown. "Usually when someone comes into a store, they have some sort of purpose. To buy something, to ask about an item... In this case, it would be flowers." She gestured to a vase on the counter. "Are you here to buy flowers?"

Matt was tongue-tied. Fortunately, Annabelle took pity on him and flashed Savannah a big smile. "I'm Annabelle Holmes from Prestige Events. We spoke on the phone this morning?"

Savannah's face relaxed. "Oh. Right." She stuck out her hand, which Annabelle shook firmly. "It's nice to meet you."

Matt finally found his voice, feeling the weird urge to clarify why he was there. "I don't work for Annabelle."

Both women shot him a strange glance.

"And we're not dating either. I'm here as a friend. We're friends. Me and Annabelle... We're..."

"Friends," Savannah finished. She furrowed her brows. "Uh, yeah, so should we talk about what Harte to Harte Flowers can do for you?"

The question was directed at Annabelle, who was now staring at Matt as if he'd grown a bushy mustache. "Matt, why don't you...browse or something?"

In other words, *go away.*

As much as he didn't like being banished, he desperately needed to regroup. Drifting over to a display case filled with intricate wreaths, he took a calming breath and tried not to kick himself in the shin. Okay, this was getting fucking ridiculous. Somehow he ended up turning into a blubbering imbecile when Savannah was around. But he'd just been thrown for a total loop.

Annabelle's comment about fate blazed through his mind. Was she right? Had fate actually placed Savannah in his path again? And if so, how could he make sure she didn't go sprinting in the other direction? As far as first impressions went, he'd blown it. His second impression wasn't much better, either. What he needed to do now was channel his innate hotness, will up some confidence, which he usually possessed in spades, and get Savannah to agree to go out with him.

After he convinced her he wasn't a total loser.

SAVANNAH SHOOK HANDS WITH ANNABELLE AGAIN, PLEASED WITH THE agreement they'd reached. Apparently Annabelle and her partner were in search of a florist they could use on a regular basis. Annabelle had agreed to hire Savannah for an upcoming wedding, and Savannah was determined to impress her. This was a test of sorts, which, if she passed, could lead to a possible stream of income she would totally benefit from. She'd been thinking about opening a second location for almost a year now, and working with an up-and-coming event company would be good for business.

"So the bride and I will come by on Wednesday to discuss what she's looking for," Annabelle said. "You can come up with some ideas and designs, and we'll go from there."

"Sounds good," Savannah answered. "Thanks for thinking of my shop."

Annabelle smiled. "I had a good feeling about it when I browsed your website. I really think—"

A loud clatter interrupted her sentence. Savannah turned to see Matt bending down to retrieve an empty plastic bucket he'd knocked off a stool near the rose display. The sight of his taut ass sent a rush of warmth to her body. Lord, the man filled out a pair of jeans really, really nicely. She'd been trying to ignore him during the entire discussion with Annabelle, but her gaze had floated in his direction every few moments, admiring the view.

He was just as sexy as she remembered. And still equally adorable.

She got the feeling he was usually pretty smooth when it came to chatting up girls, yet he blushed and stammered whenever she was around. Kind of a turn-on, watching this big, gorgeous man get all tongue-tied around her. Definitely a nice ego boost.

And now that Jake was out of the picture…

"He's not usually so pathetic," Annabelle said in a low voice, snapping Savannah from her thoughts.

She glanced at Matt again, who now stood near the door with his arms crossed, as if he was afraid to touch anything else.

"I think you make him nervous." Annabelle's laugh held a note of admiration. "To be honest, I've never seen him all blushy and weird around a girl."

Savannah shrugged. "I tend to have that effect on men," she joked.

That got her another laugh. "Well, put him out of his misery, will you?" Before Savannah could object, Annabelle called Matt over. "Savannah wants to talk to you, stud. I'll wait in the car."

Just like that, Annabelle hurried off, her brown hair bouncing over her shoulders as she left the store. The bell over the door chimed, then tinned away into silence.

Matt walked over to her, a rueful grin on his face. "Annabelle's not very subtle," he remarked.

"Not really."

He rested an elbow on the counter, an action that drew her gaze to his impressive biceps. He instantly noticed where her eyes had landed, and his grin widened. "You think I'm hot," he said, sounding delighted.

Savannah rolled her eyes. "Sounds like *you* think you're hot."

A pained look flitted across his face. "Show some mercy already. For some reason I act like a total moron when I'm around you. The least you can do is admit this attraction isn't one-sided."

A smile lifted the corner of her mouth. He had a point. Maybe he did deserve some leniency. Besides, she really had no reason not to see him again, now that she'd ended things with Jake. Alas, her sexy surfer ended up being kind of boring and a bit of a jerk.

Matt, however, didn't seem at all boring.

"Fine," she said. "I find you attractive."

"Thank Jesus. Now will you agree to go out with me or what?"

The words were gruff, completely unpolished, but he seemed pleased with himself that he'd finally said something right.

"I'm not looking for a relationship," she admitted. "And now that I'm doing the flowers for that wedding, I won't have much time to date anyway."

"You can make time for one drink." His green eyes glittered playfully. "I promise, I'll make it worth your while."

"Do people still use that line?"

"Yup. So what do you say?"

Another smile tickled her lips. "I guess I can squeeze in one drink after work."

His entire face lit up like a little kid's on Christmas morning. "What time should I pick you up?"

FOR THE FIRST TIME IN HIS LIFE, MATT WAS ACTUALLY NERVOUS ABOUT a date. As he stepped out of the shower, dripping water all over the bathroom mat, he wondered if he should ask Annabelle to come downstairs so he could ask for clothing advice.

Jeez. What the hell was wrong with him? He could seduce the panties off a nun, for fuck's sake. Women freaking loved him. If he was the kind of guy who ticked off notches in his belt...well, he'd be on his tenth belt by now.

But Savannah made him feel like an anxious teenager again. It wasn't just her looks that captivated him, though her smokin' body did make his mouth water. She was just so...self-assured. She seemed to know exactly who she was, completely comfortable in her own skin, and her easygoing attitude and sharp wit were a total turn-on. He didn't usually think beyond the first date, but with Savannah he already wanted more and they hadn't even gone out yet.

Which was why he couldn't have sex with her tonight. As much as he wanted to, as much as his body throbbed at the mere thought of her, he needed to force himself to keep his hands off her this evening. It was messed up, but he feared that if he slept with her so soon, this fascination would disappear, and he wasn't ready for that to happen yet.

Another first—he wanted to get to know a woman before he screwed her.

God help him.

Deciding to forgo calling Annabelle—he wasn't in the mood to be ridiculed—he strode into his bedroom and threw open the closet door. As he dressed, he marveled at the silence in the apartment. Ever since Ryan moved upstairs into Annabelle's place, Matt was living solo. Made it easier to bring chicks back here without worrying about keeping Ryan up, though he didn't do it often. He didn't like having women over. They always wanted to stay when he only wanted them to leave.

Clad in a pair of jeans, a black T-shirt and an open blue button-down, he grabbed his keys from the basket on the hall table and left his second-floor apartment. He took the stairs two at a time, suddenly eager to get going and see Savannah again. The black SUV he'd just signed the lease on had decent speed, so he made it to Savannah's shop in less than fifteen minutes.

Shutting off the engine, he took a deep breath and hopped out of the SUV. There was a separate entrance to Savannah's upstairs apartment, with a small intercom mounted on the wall. He buzzed. A few seconds later, her chirpy voice said, "Come up."

Uh-oh.

She wanted him to come upstairs?

That wasn't part of the plan. He'd hoped to wait down here for her, then drive her to the classy bar he'd researched on the web. He was kinda scared to be alone with her. At least with other people around, he wouldn't be able to rip her clothes off and devour her body the way he so desperately wanted to.

Gulping, he opened the door and climbed the narrow staircase up to the second floor. Savannah's door was painted a bright yellow, and it swung open the moment he reached the landing. She appeared in the doorway, wearing a pair of tight black yoga pants and a loose red T-shirt that didn't hide the fullness of the breasts beneath it.

"Hey," she said with an easy smile. "I figured we'd stay in, if that's cool with you?"

Another gulp. Crap. Looked like he needed to conjure up some willpower. Pronto.

In a strained voice, he said, "Sure."

Savannah gestured for him to come inside, and when he stepped into the apartment, he immediately saw her personality splashed all over the place. Mismatched furniture, some modern, some antique, filled the spacious living room. Colorful abstract paintings hung on the walls, with the occasional breathtaking landscape sandwiched between them. A small kitchen was tucked off to one side, and the living area was separated from the sleeping area with a see-through Japanese screen that featured bright pink cherry blossom trees. He caught a glimpse of a large futon with a bright magenta bedspread, but tore his gaze away.

He couldn't focus on the bed. Beds meant sex. And he was determined not to sleep with Savannah until he figured out why he liked her so much.

"I like your place," he said, turning to meet her silver-gray eyes.

"Thanks," she said simply.

"Have you lived here long?"

"About eight years now." She headed to the kitchen and opened the fridge, reappearing a moment later with a six-pack in her hands. "I moved in when I bought the shop."

They headed over to the plump brown sofa. Savannah flopped down, removed two beer bottles from the case and held one out to him. After a second of hesitation, he joined her on the couch. At least three feet of space separated them, but it was still too damn close for comfort. Her sweet scent wafted over, surrounding him in a lust-crazed cloud. Of course she smelled like flowers. Roses and lavender, with a hint of minty soap thrown in.

He unscrewed the cap of the bottle and took a long swallow of beer, hoping the cold liquid would ease the burn in his groin. But then Savannah reached up to untie her ponytail, letting her pale blonde hair fall loose, and the burn deepened. Fuck, he wanted to run his fingers through that silky hair, feel it tickling his pecs as she straddled his naked body, riding him…

No sex, a little voice ordered.

Right, no sex. He took another sip, then set the bottle down on the coffee table.

"So," he started. "Your dad teaches at Stanford… Does that mean you're from Palo Alto?"

"Yeah, I grew up there. I moved here after I dropped out of college."

He grinned. "You're a college dropout?"

"Sure am. I was never a school person. I wanted to work with flowers, so I moved down here to work at a nursery one of my mom's friends owns. When this store came up for sale, she went in on the deal with me. We were partners until about three years ago, and then I bought her out."

Matt was impressed. Savannah couldn't be older than twenty-seven, twenty-eight, and she already owned her own business. A successful one, judging by the fact that she'd been able to buy out her partner.

"Where are you from?" she asked him.

"Nashville. Well, just outside of it. My family owns a cattle ranch."

She laughed. "You're a cowboy, huh?"

"Nah, I wasn't cut out for cowboy life. I left home at eighteen, joined the Navy, and now I live here full-time."

"Too bad." Her gray eyes darkened to smoky silver. "Cowboys are extremely sexy."

He swallowed. Fuck, why did she have to look at him like that? Like she wanted to lick him up. He was normally the one dropping the loaded remarks while his date steered the conversation to more wholesome topics. He found this role reversal totally disconcerting.

Savannah slid closer and rested her hand on his thigh.

Matt nearly jumped off the couch. Her hand was warm, her fingers teasing as she ran them along the denim seam of his jeans.

"How do you like owning your own business?" he blurted out, desperate to ignore the searing bolts of heat moving from the tips of her fingers to his suddenly throbbing thigh.

Savannah let out a sigh. "Are we really going to do this?"

"Do what?"

"Carry on with the idle chitchat when we both know what we *really* want to do?"

His cock jerked, strained against his zipper. She instantly noticed the reaction, a small smile spreading across her lush pink lips.

"Look, I don't like relationships," she said bluntly. "They don't interest me. But I am interested in flings. Fun, casual flings, no strings, no promises, just a good time and great sex."

He wanted to ask *why*. Why did she hate relationships so much? But his vocal cords had gone numb. She was using his own lines on him.

Fun, casual, good time, great sex. He couldn't even count how many times he'd uttered those exact phrases.

And as much as he wasn't sure he liked being the recipient of his own speech, the moment the word *sex* slipped from her luscious mouth, all he could think about was shoving his cock deep inside her.

"So if you want me—" her gaze moved to the bulge of his crotch, "—and I think you do, what do you say we just skip the tell-me-about-yourself and get to the fun part?"

Chapter Four

SAVANNAH KNEW SHE WAS COMING ON STRONG, BUT BLUNT HAD ALWAYS been her style. From the moment Matt had walked into her apartment, she'd wanted to tear his clothes off. So why shouldn't she? Life was too short, wasting time pointless. If you wanted something you might as well take it. Well, some things. She wasn't about to rob a bank to score some extra cash, but when it came to men, why not take what was right in front of you?

She slid closer to Matt's suddenly tense body, noting the reluctance in his piercing green eyes. Since he didn't strike her as the kind of man who did the whole romantic dates and chaste kisses thing, his hesitation confused her.

It also made her all the more determined to seduce him.

Running her fingers up his thigh, she leaned toward him and murmured, "Kiss me."

Desire flooded his gaze, but the reluctance didn't dissipate completely. "Don't you want to get to know each other better first?"

"Not really." She moved her hand up his chest, her heart doing a little flip at the feel of his rippled abdominal muscles. Jeez, he was rock-hard. Not an ounce of fat on the guy.

She grasped the sides of his open button-down and slowly pushed it off his broad shoulders. After a beat, he helped her out, sliding his arms out of the sleeves and tossing the shirt aside. She saw his throat working as he visibly swallowed, but he didn't protest when she reached for the hem of his T-shirt and peeled it off his chest.

Her breath caught. Man oh man. His bare chest was spectacular. Almost completely hairless, save for a dusty line of dark hair that arrowed down to the waistband of his jeans. His pecs were huge, stomach flat with a delicious-looking six-pack. She couldn't help herself—she had to touch it. The moment her fingers grazed the tight muscles of his belly, he sucked in a breath, then cursed loudly.

"Fine," he said with a groan.

She grinned. "Fine, what?"

"I'll have sex with you. Is that what you want to hear?"

"Yep." She narrowed her eyes. "You're not going to cry rape afterwards, are you?"

A laugh burst from his chest. "No. Are you?"

"No." She paused. "Now take off your pants."

He raised an arrogant brow. "Do it for me."

Savannah fought another grin. A challenge. She liked it. Scooting closer, she found the button at his waistband and undid it, then dragged his zipper down. She tugged, but when the material didn't budge, she hopped off the couch and knelt before him, getting a good grip on his jeans and pulling them down a pair of long, muscular legs that made her pulse race. His boxers came off with the jeans, leaving him gloriously naked on her couch.

Savannah's entire mouth went dry as a desert. Clothed, this man was gorgeous. Naked? Out of this freaking world. His skin was golden brown, hard and sleek, and his erection was enormous, jutting upward and nearly reaching his navel.

Her previously arid mouth filled with moisture. Her gaze zeroed in on his impressive erection, her head dipping forward as if drawn in by a magnet. Her lips hovered over his tip.

"Are you just going to kneel there and do nothing?" he ground out.

"What do you want me to do?" she teased.

"What the hell do you think?"

Her tongue darted out for a quick taste, a fleeting swipe across his engorged head. "That?" she asked, pasting on an innocent look.

His features looked tortured. "Among other things."

"Oooh, intriguing. What kind of other things?" Before he could respond, she took him deep in her mouth and sucked hard. Then she moved her mouth away and offered a tiny smile. "Something like that?"

He groaned in reply.

"Or maybe this?" she said helpfully, wrapping her fingers around the hard length of him and pumping slowly.

His hand lowered to cup her head, long fingers threading through her hair and guiding her back to his groin. "All of it," he choked out. "Do it all and quit teasing me."

A laugh bubbled in the back of her throat, only to be cut off when he thrust his cock between her parted lips, stealing the breath from her lungs. Deciding she'd teased him enough, she went to work on him, sucking softly, then dragging her tongue up and down his shaft. His hand fisted her hair, and a ragged moan echoed in the room. She relaxed her jaw and took him deeper, alternating between long sucks and the sharp pump of her hand.

When she felt his tip throb against her tongue, she lifted her head and grinned up at him. "You're not allowed to come yet."

His voice came out rough, but she heard the teasing note to it. "Says who?"

"Me." Standing up, she quickly removed her pants, shirt and panties, pleased when she noticed his eyes smoldering at the sight of her naked body.

"You're incredible," he hissed out. "I want to eat you up, Savannah."

"Yeah? Get started, then."

It was meant to be a joking remark, but he immediately slid off the couch, sank to his knees and brought her to his waiting mouth. Sparks of pleasure ignited inside her, heating her skin and making her sag against him. He took advantage of the loosening of her legs, spreading them wider as his mouth homed in on his intended destination. She moaned at the first brush of his tongue over her clit, the raspy feel of his stubble against her inner thighs, the warmth of his breath against her core.

He licked her again, once, twice, and then her legs were yanked out from under her and she found her butt colliding with the couch. Matt dove back in, proceeding to bestow her with the most mind-blowing oral sex she'd ever experienced. He captured her clit between his lips and suckled, then licked the swollen bud over and over again, until pleasure gathered in her belly and sizzled in her bloodstream like a drug. At the feel of his finger prodding her opening, she lost complete and total control.

The orgasm ripped through her like wildfire. She lifted her pussy to Matt's mouth, taking everything he had to offer. When the climax finally ebbed, she felt exhausted. Winded. She couldn't recall ever coming that hard.

Her heart still thudding erratically, she slid off the couch and fumbled with the purse she'd left nearby. She came back with a condom that she swiftly rolled onto his massive erection, and then she lay on her back and pulled his big body on top of her.

"Fuck me," she begged. "Now."

"Fast or slow?" he rasped. "What'll make you come again?"

"Fast," she ordered, her pussy throbbing in anticipation. God, she wanted him in there.

He swiftly obliged, driving his cock into her soaking-wet channel and sending her body into another tailspin. His hips pistoned as he moved inside her, the muscles of his gorgeous chest tight with arousal. Savannah clung to him, her fingernails digging into his back as she raised her hips to meet each frenzied thrust.

They exploded at the same time, letting out matching groans. Tingles spread through her as she felt Matt shudder inside her, as he buried his face in the crook of her neck and kissed her fevered skin. Finally they both grew still, just lying there for several long moments, as Savannah tried to catch her breath and waited for her heartbeat to steady.

When she met Matt's eyes, they were glimmering with residual heat. Even though he'd just pulled out and removed the condom, she could see his cock beginning to harden. Wow. Apparently he wasn't just Superman, he was the Energizer Bunny too. But it wasn't the new dose of lust in his gaze that worried her; it was the flicker of amazement she saw there.

Fine, so the sex had been much better than average, but she could already see his handsome brain working, classifying this wild sweaty encounter as something unbelievably special.

Normally she ended things when the men in her life got that look on their faces, but she wasn't ready to say goodbye to Matt just yet.

Still, she needed to make sure they were on the same page.

"Just a fling, right?" she said warily.

Matt slid closer and nibbled on her bare shoulder. "Nothing more," he assured her. "I just want to see you again after tonight."

"No strings?"

"No strings. Just fun." He solemnly brought his hand to his heart. "I promise."

"Fine." She jumped off the couch, reached for his hand, and tugged him to his feet. "Let's move to the bed. If we're going to see each other, we might as well have sex again."

His shoulders shook with laughter. "Might as well," he agreed.

Savannah's head was bent over a yellow legal pad when Matt strode into the flower shop two days later. They'd gone through several more rounds of out-of-this-world sex last night, but today he was determined to launch what he'd dubbed Operation Wholesome. Yes, Savannah drove him wild in bed, but the brief moments of laughter and conversation they'd shared in between hot naked time were equally addictive. He might have promised to keep it casual, but deep down he knew he wouldn't live up to that promise.

He wanted to get to know Savannah Harte, and damned if he'd let her stop him from doing that.

As he headed for the counter, he tried not to question his actions. This need to spend time with Savannah outside the bedroom was weird enough already. He was living the dream, after all. Hooking up with a woman who wanted nothing more than some fun between the sheets? Normally his idea of heaven. The fact that he wanted more was too perplexing to examine deeper at the moment.

"Hey," Savannah said absently. "I don't have time to get jiggy right now, Superman. I'm going over this list Annabelle emailed me about the wedding."

He grinned at the nickname, which she'd come up with after he'd described some of the rescue missions he'd been involved in. He couldn't discuss most assignments or offer many details, but Savannah had been curious about the life of a SEAL. Since she hadn't been displaying much interest in him aside from the sexual kind, he'd jumped on the opportunity to bond. And now his heart did a dumb little flip each time she called him Superman.

"I'm not here to get jiggy," he replied cheerfully. "I'm here to take you to lunch."

She lifted her head from the notepad, pale yellow tresses falling into her eyes. "I can't. I'm busy."

"Tough." He crossed his arms over his chest. "You need to eat. And you can bring your work with you if you want. I can help you come up with ideas for the centerpieces."

She gave a throaty laugh. "Oh, really? You're going to talk centerpieces with me?"

"Why not? Every female in the O'Connor family has a green thumb. It's in my genes."

Although she looked dubious, she still pushed back her stool and hopped off. Pleasure jolted through him as he realized she'd accepted the invite. As much as he enjoyed seeing her naked, the thought of having lunch with her—with both of them fully clothed—held a huge amount of appeal.

Again, the reaction troubled him. What the hell was going on? Normally he wholeheartedly agreed with Savannah's views on relationships—who needed 'em? Yet here he was, nearly coming in his pants because this sassy woman was going to eat lunch with him.

"We need to go somewhere nearby," she said as she grabbed an oversized green canvas purse and slung it over her shoulder. "I want to come back and finalize the orders for the centerpieces."

"No problem," he said easily.

He waited for Savannah to summon Chad from the back and ask him to watch the store, then walked ahead to hold the door open for her, admiring the way her filmy floral-print skirt swirled around her knees. He'd scouted the area on the way over and noticed a small pizza café with an outdoor patio, which he now suggested. Savannah nodded in agreement, and they made their way down the sidewalk.

Ten minutes later, they were seated on the cobblestone patio. After ordering beers and a pizza to share, Savannah pulled her notepad from her purse and said, "Okay, let's see your flower expertise."

"Hit me," he said, leaning back in the wrought-iron chair.

"The bride wants, and I quote, 'something blue and white and sparkly, but natural looking'."

Matt burst out laughing, and was rewarded with a frown from Savannah.

"Do you see why I'm so frazzled?" she said with a sigh. "I mean, can you get any *less* articulate than that?"

Sensing her frustration, he went serious. "So what are you thinking?"

Her straight white teeth sank into her bottom lip, an action that sent a rush of heat straight down to his cock. The memory of those teeth nibbling on his own lips was still fresh in his mind. Quickly, he forced the thought aside.

"Blue orchids," she finally said. "Natural birch branches, crystal bowtie vases, and something white… Calla lilies?"

He shook his head. "No way. Too fancy. Lilies will draw the attention away from the orchids. Go with white hydrangea."

Surprise filled her eyes. Then she started to laugh. "Jeez, you really do know flowers."

He smirked. "Told you."

"That's a good idea," she admitted. "I didn't think of hydrangea." She paused in thought. "Yeah, it's really good actually. I'll get started on that today."

"See how easy that was?" He flashed a charming grin. "Centerpieces, done. What's next?"

"Backdrops for the head table. The bride wants blue and white again, feminine and elegant."

"Easy," he replied. "Blue and white silk panels with floral accents."

That got him another laugh. "Will you marry me?"

He knew she meant it as a joke, but something inside him shifted. If any other woman had said that to him, joking or otherwise, he'd be running out the door right about now. Marriage was not something you kidded about, not in his life. As much as he loved his family, he couldn't stand the constant smothering. Not just toward him, but to their partners. His parents' marriage had been so overly loving it'd made him uncomfortable, and all four of his sisters were happily married, constantly gushing about their husbands. Ever since he was a kid, he'd felt uneasy around the constant shows of affection. Couldn't really explain it, or put his finger on it, but he'd known even back then that he didn't want that much love in his life.

Having another person know him inside and out, digging into his psyche, finishing his sentences?

It was too damn intimate, and for Matt, intimacy ended with sex.

So why didn't Savannah's off-hand remark scare him to death, the way it should?

The waitress arrived with their pizza before he could analyze the strange reaction. He and Savannah quickly dug in, polishing off the entire pie in no time. Afterwards, they leaned back in their chairs, quietly sipping on their respective beers. He didn't feel the need to fill the silence, and she didn't seem to either. It was nice.

When she finally spoke, she caught him off-guard. "Why are you single?" she asked curiously.

He shrugged. "Why are you?"

"I asked first."

Setting down his beer bottle, he clasped his hands together on the table. "Relationships seem like too much trouble."

"How so?"

"I don't like the idea of sharing my entire being with another person."

She cast him a mischievous grin. "Commitment-phobic. I get it."

"And you're not scared of commitment?" he shot back.

"Nope. It just bores me." Her gray eyes took on a faraway glint. "You know that feeling you get when you kiss someone, when you sleep with them, for the first time? That...*thrill*."

"Yeah..."

"I think I'm addicted to it," she confessed. "I'm addicted to firsts."

"Seconds can be just a good," he pointed out.

"Sure, but eventually the thrill goes away. So that's when I go away."

Matt opened his mouth to ask her if that's what would happen with them — would she simply go away? But before he could speak, a male voice interrupted their discussion.

"Savannah?"

A thirty-something guy with messy blond hair stopped by the railing separating the patio from the sidewalk. He wore a pair of long orange shorts and a white muscle shirt, and he was staring at Savannah as if she were his long-lost love.

"Hank," she said in surprise. "It's good to see you again."

At her casual, impersonal words, Hank's entire face fell. "Where've you been?" he asked, a plaintive note entering his voice. "I haven't seen you in months."

She shrugged. "I told you, I'm busy with the store."

Hank's dark eyes shifted to Matt, and a suspicious cloud floated across his face. "You don't look busy."

Savannah held up her legal pad. "This is a working lunch."

"Oh." The guy brightened, slightly. "Do you have time for dinner this week?"

"Sorry, I can't. I'm doing the flowers for a huge wedding so I'll be working non-stop until then."

That got her another "Oh". Hank fidgeted with his hands. "Okay, then. Give me a call when you're done with the job?"

"Sure."

Her noncommittal tone was unmistakable. Despite himself, Matt felt a pang of sympathy for the dude. He also experienced a wave of unease, watching the expression on Hank's face. Was that how *he* looked when he was around Savannah? All lovelorn and pathetic?

Fuck, who was this woman? It was like a scene out of *There's Something About Mary.* Did every man who met her fall head over heels for her?

"Well…I gotta go," Hank mumbled. With an awkward wave, he strode off.

Matt offered a rueful look. "You could've let him down more gently."

Irritation flickered in her eyes. "I did let him down gently. Four months ago. We went out a few times, and sure, he's cute, but he's not exactly the sharpest tool in the shed. Holding a conversation with the guy was painful. I told him about a dozen times that I wasn't interested in continuing it."

"Did you sleep with him?" Matt couldn't help but ask, then cringed at the possessive note in his voice.

"Yeah, I did." She studied his face. "Oh brother. You're jealous."

"I'm not jealous," he protested.

She laughed. "Oh yes you are." Her annoyance returned, only this time it was directed at him. "Don't go all crazy on me, Matt. I'm sure you've slept with dozens of women, and I'm not the least bit jealous about it."

Which bothered him almost as much as *his* sudden encounter with the green-eyed monster. He got the feeling Savannah wouldn't even bat an eyelash if he ended things between them right here and now. He wasn't sure if her borderline-scary casual attitude was legit, or simply a cover for serious commitment issues she refused to admit to. He decided to believe the latter—only way to preserve his ego, after all.

Still, the jealousy coursing through his blood at the appearance of Hank only grew stronger when he imagined Savannah in bed with the guy. Damn it.

"Let's get out of here," he said gruffly, reaching into his back pocket for his wallet.

She must've seen the fiery look in his eyes, because hers widened slightly, and then a slow smile curved her mouth. Matt dropped a few bills on the table, reached for her hand, and practically dragged her back to the shop. At the sight of her scrawny assistant behind the counter, he hooked a thumb at the door and barked, "Take a break, Chad."

The kid gulped, nodded, and took off.

"I'm thinking I might like jealous Matt," Savannah laughed as he flipped the sign on the door from "open" to "closed".

He locked up and moved toward her with predatory strides. Took her hand again and pulled her behind the curtain into the back room. Before she could say another word, he covered her mouth with his and kissed the hell out of her.

Savannah gasped against his lips, her hands reaching up to twine around his neck. Matt had no idea what had come over him. Something hot and primal spiraled down his body and grabbed hold of his dick, hardening it to a level he hadn't thought possible. It was almost painful, the throbbing erection straining against his zipper.

Coming up for air, Savannah murmured, "He really didn't mean anything to me. You don't need to go all caveman, Superman."

"Let's not talk about Hank," he ordered, his hand seeking the hem of her skirt and bunching it between his fingers.

He shoved the material up to her hips, tore off her bikini panties, and placed his palm on her pussy, rubbing it slowly.

Savannah let out a little sigh. "God, that's good."

He kept stroking, running his finger up and down her damp slit, then dipping them into her opening and plunging deep. She sagged against his chest, moving her hips to meet each lazy thrust of his finger. Matt's entire body went taut with lust. Fuck, he wanted this woman. He could probably come just from the feel of her slick wetness coating his finger.

As a red haze of desire fogged his vision, he hurriedly undid his jeans, covered his dick with the condom he'd tucked in his pocket, and angled himself between Savannah's firm thighs.

"You sure it doesn't make you jealous?" he found himself taunting. "The thought of me doing this to someone else." He teased her clit with the tip of his cock.

Her gray eyes went glazed. "Nope. Doesn't make me jealous at all."

"You sure about that?" He slid one hand underneath her shirt, shoved it under the left cup of her lacy bra and squeezed her breast.

She gasped.

"It really doesn't drive you crazy, knowing I've done this to countless other women?" He found her nipple and pinched it between his fingers.

Savannah gave a soft moan. "How many is countless?"

"*Countless,*" he emphasized in a cocky tone.

He could've sworn he saw a flash of something in her eyes — actual jealousy? — but it disappeared quickly.

"No, doesn't bother me," she muttered.

She tried to reach down to encircle his shaft, but he sidestepped, letting his hand drop from her breast. Taking a step back, he fought a grin at the sight of her flushed cheeks, parted lips and lust-filled eyes. Oh yeah. No matter how unaffected she tried to act, she was totally into him. She fucking craved him.

"Okay," he said with a shrug. "Then I guess I've got nothing to prove."

Her face flooded with shocked disappointment as he removed the condom and tucked his cock back into his boxers. "What the hell are you doing?" she complained.

"Not being childish." He smothered a laugh. "You're right, seeing one of your exes got me a little crazy. I figured if I brought you back here and had my way with you, I'd prove to myself I don't give a damn about that loser you slept with, because he could never fuck you the way I do. But you've shown me the light."

"Huh?"

Poor woman looked so dismayed he almost kissed her again. "You obviously don't care about my past, so I shouldn't care about yours. Which means there's no need to play macho games with you."

Savannah bit her bottom lip. "So you're just going to…*go?*"

"Uh-huh."

"But…" she sputtered.

"You said you had work to do," he said innocently.

"I do…but…"

He hid a grin as he zipped up his pants. Heading to the wastebasket by the door, he dropped the almost-used condom into it and glanced at Savannah over his shoulder. "Call me when you have time," he said cheerfully.

He waltzed through the curtain, though walking was an impressive feat considering the enormous boner poking into his jeans. His cock ached so badly he almost marched back to Savannah and screwed her brains out. But he forced himself to keep walking.

Operation Wholesome was in full gear. If he gave in now, everything he'd accomplished today would've been a waste. She'd agreed to a lunch date. She'd displayed a real, non-casual reaction to his taunt about his past girlfriends. And he'd left her wanting more. Wanting *him.*

All in all, a successful afternoon.

Chapter Five

MATT'S ARMS BURNED AS HE HAULED HIMSELF UP THE CARGO NET OF THE base's obstacle course, one of the toughest in the country. He was nearly forty feet off the ground, clinging to a net that consisted of vertical and horizontal ropes strung along a frame, and he still had to get to the other side. No big deal, though. He and the others had trained hours upon hours on this thing back in the day. He could do this course in his sleep.

Ryan Evans, his best friend and former roommate, had already climbed the net and was nearly off the frame, prompting Matt to pick up speed. When his feet finally collided with the hard ground, he let out a breath and grinned, knowing without being told that he and the guys had completed the course in record speed.

Today's exercise was meant to show the new trainees that finishing the course with a decent time wasn't something that would happen overnight. Apparently a cocky recruit had passed out from exhaustion yesterday trying to conquer the course, after being ordered to call it a day. The commander had asked Matt and some of the other members of SEAL Team Fifteen to put on a little demo for the newbies this morning, show them what they could look forward to after they completed their BUD/S training.

The small group of young men broke out in polite applause when the demo ended, but Matt could see several faces gleaming with determination. Those were the ones who'd end up making it through the program. He'd worn that same expression when he'd first joined up. The others...well, most of them would burn out, or quit long before their training ended.

"You were slacking," Ryan said as he tossed him a bottle of water.

Matt unscrewed the cap, took a couple of swigs, and then poured water on his face and neck. "Yeah, I know. Sorry, man. I was a bit distracted."

"Nice time," another voice remarked.

Matt turned and greeted his buddy Aidan Rhodes with a grin. "Hey, man, didn't realize you were allowed to leave the desk."

"Hey, I might have a desk job now, but I can still kick your ass on that course," Aidan shot back. "I had the best time in my class." As the two men bumped fists, Aidan asked, "Want to a hit a club this weekend?"

Matt hesitated. "Not sure yet. I might have plans. But I'll shoot you a text and let you know at the end of the week."

"Cool." Aidan ran a hand through his close-cropped brown hair. "I should head in. Keep in touch, bro."

As Aidan strode off, Carson Scott and John Garrett approached, using towels to wipe the sweat from their faces. "Beers?" Carson suggested.

Matt grinned. "It's eleven thirty in the morning."

"Shit, you're right. Better make that coffees then."

The four of them left the base and drove over to Shelby Garrett's bakery, which also doubled as a coffee shop. They planted their asses on the chairs out on the small patio, while the part-timer, Amy, brought over some coffees.

"Shel's not working today?" Matt said, watching as the young employee headed back inside.

Garrett shook his head. "Penny's colicky. Little bugger kept us up all night, so I ordered Shel to stay home and relax."

Matt smiled at the mention of Garrett's six-month-old daughter. The squirt was pretty damn adorable, with her father's dark hair and mother's sparkling blue eyes. All the guys on the team had instantly fallen in love with the kid, though Will Charleston's new baby, Lucas, was pretty freaking cute too. It seemed like everyone around him was popping out babies. Jane, the wife of their lieutenant Thomas Becker, was due to deliver next month, and he'd even overheard Carson's wife, Holly, mention to Annabelle that she wanted to try for a baby soon.

"Tell them the other news," Carson spoke up, sounding edgy.

Matt and Ryan eyed Garrett uneasily. "What other news?" Ryan asked.

After taking a long sip of his coffee, Garrett set down the mug and said, "I'm going off active duty next month."

Silence.

It took a few seconds for the words to register in Matt's head, and when he realized he'd indeed heard them right, he shook his head in shock. "You're off the team?"

Garrett nodded. "I took a position with a security firm in San Diego. I'll still be in the reserves, but no more missions for me."

Ryan looked flabbergasted. "Why the hell not?"

"Because I've got a wife and kid to worry about now. Look, guys, I've done a hell of a lot to serve my country. Now it's time to focus on my family."

The second silence that followed dragged on for longer. Matt couldn't believe what he was hearing. He'd figured John Garrett would be career navy. Guy had enlisted at the age of eighteen, went to officer school, worked to make it to junior grade lieutenant. And now he was getting out?

"It's time," Garrett repeated, his voice quiet.

Matt was the first to snap out of his surprised trance. "Are you sure about this, man?"

"Oh yeah. Trust me, when you get married, you'll understand. My two girls come first now."

Carson smirked. "Oh, I think Matt understands. Rumor has it he's found the woman of his dreams."

Matt's eyebrows shot up. "Where the hell did you hear that?"

"Holly and Annabelle were gossiping about it yesterday." Carson wiggled his eyebrows. "According to Annabelle, you're in love with a woman named Georgia who has really nice tits."

"First, her name is Savannah," Matt said coldly, "and second, her tits are none of your business."

Both Carson and Ryan hooted, while Garrett's mouth lifted in a wry smile.

"Shit, it's actually true," Ryan said gleefully. "I figured Annie was exaggerating when she mentioned it, but that possessive look on your face...fuck, you really are into this girl."

"How big are her tits exactly?" Carson asked with a curious tilt of the head.

Matt jabbed a finger in the other man's direction. "Like I said, none of your business." He glanced at Ryan. "And Annabelle *is* exaggerating. I'm not in love with anyone. Savannah and I are just having a little fling."

"If it's just a fling, then you should have no problem sharing the juicy details," Ryan pointed out, a wide smile on his face.

Matt faltered. His friend had a point. In the past he'd had no qualms discussing the measurements of the current female in his bed. But he felt guilty objectifying Savannah in that way. Sure, she was a knockout, but that wasn't the only reason he liked her. She was smart, funny, sarcastic... stubborn. Yeah, definitely stubborn. He'd left the ball in her court after their encounter in the shop two days ago, and she still hadn't called. A part of him feared his taunting had only annoyed her and that she'd washed her hands of him and went after some other dude. Like Hank.

"Still want to convince us it's just a fling?" Carson said when Matt hadn't answered for more than a minute.

"It is," he finally muttered. "She's fun to be with. And she has no interest in anything serious, so it's, you know, perfect for me."

Had they heard the tremor in his voice during those last three words?

Shit, they had. All three men were staring at him as if he'd slathered on lipstick or something.

"You want more," Carson accused.

"No," he said quickly. "No way."

"Fuck, you totally do. I know the feeling, man," Carson added with a sigh. "When Holly and I first hooked up, she insisted she didn't want a relationship. It took me weeks to convince her to give us a chance."

"I don't want to convince Savannah of anything," he objected. "Like I said, it's just a casual thing. I don't plan on—" His cell phone, which he'd placed on the table, vibrated. Matt's heart did an involuntary lurch when he noticed the caller ID. "Hold on. I gotta take this."

He was out of his seat and moving to the other end of the patio in nanoseconds, while Carson and Ryan busted out laughing. "Say hi to Georgia!" Carson the five-year-old called.

Matt hit the *talk* button. "Hello?"

"You're playing hard to get," was the greeting he received. "I don't know how I feel about that."

He grinned at the petulant note to her voice. "I'm doing no such thing."

"I don't like games, Superman."

"Neither do I." He paused. "Except Scrabble. I'm pretty good at that one."

A heavy sigh echoed in his ear. "Are you waiting for me to beg, is that it? Because I don't like begging. I've always thought I'd be a terrible beggar, sitting there on the sidewalk, holding out a tin can. I think eventually I'd get bored and go look for a job."

Laughter rolled out of his chest. "I'm not sure, but that comment might have been politically incorrect."

"I don't like politics either," she said breezily. "Now, what'll it take to get you to come over?"

"Who says I want to? Maybe I've grown bored of having sex with you." He smiled to himself, proud that he was finally back on track. All the charm he'd perfected over the years had dissolved during those first few encounters with Savannah, but he was slowly regaining ground, and the outrage in her voice confirmed it.

"You have not. I am unbelievably good at sex."

"You're okay."

"Uh-uh, no way. I'm awesome. So level with me, what do I have to do to get you to see me again?"

"For sex?" he clarified.

"Well, duh."

He pretended to think it over, then said, "A date."

She balked. "I told you how I feel about that."

"Those are my terms, take them or leave them. One date for every round of sex."

"You're an awful person."

"Is that a no?"

There was a long pause, followed by a soft curse. "No, it's not a no."

"Then it's a yes?" he prompted in amusement.

"Yes, it's a yes." Another pause. "Where are you now? The store's pretty empty so I can leave Chad in charge for the rest of the day."

"I'm in Coronado. We were doing a training demo at the base." An idea entered his mind. "Why don't we go to the beach? You mind driving over here?"

He expected another protest, but to his surprise, she sounded enthused. "Sure, I'll head over to you."

They arranged to meet in an hour, and Matt was smiling as he hung up the phone and wandered back to the table. Of course, his friends immediately noticed the smile and proceeded to harass him.

"Was that Georgia?"

"Is her ass as nice as her boobs? Annabelle didn't mention."

"Wanna babysit Penny to prepare for the baby you'll have with your future bride?"

"Ha ha," he said, rolling his eyes as he reached for his coffee. It had grown cold, but he still swallowed a mouthful of the lukewarm liquid so he wouldn't have to dignify any of their stupid questions with a response.

SAVANNAH'S HEART SKIPPED A BEAT WHEN SHE GOT OUT OF HER CAR AND found Matt sitting on the hood of his SUV. They'd arranged to meet in a gravel lot near the beach, and the entire drive over she'd tried convincing herself she was pissed off at Matt for sex-blackmailing her into a date.

But the moment she laid eyes on him, she realized just how glad she was to see him, and how *un*-pissed she was.

He wore a pair of camo pants, a tight green T-shirt and aviator sunglasses, looking like the hot military man he was. She'd been thinking about him nonstop since he'd strolled out of her shop the other day. She wasn't sure if there was an equivalent for blue balls when it came to women, but after he'd teased her into oblivion and then left her in the lurch, her body had ached so badly she'd had to go upstairs to her apartment and make herself come to stop the throbbing pain.

"Where are your swim trunks?" she asked as she headed over to him.

He jumped off the hood. "Got some in the back." He planted a quick kiss on her lips and then popped the trunk of his car and bent forward.

Savannah couldn't help but check out his sinewy back and firm ass. Heat seeped into her cheeks when she heard him pull down his zipper. "You're getting changed out here?" she said in surprise.

"There's no one around. I'll only be a sec."

He kept his back to her, and her gaze was glued to him as he dropped his pants and boxers in one swift motion. And then there he was, in all his bare-assed glory. Cotton lodged into every corner of her mouth. She could barely swallow as she stared at his taut behind. How was he *this* sexy?

She forced herself to look away. She couldn't jump the guy in public, no matter how badly she wanted to.

He turned a moment later, a pair of sky-blue swim trunks hugging his trim hips. Two beach towels were tucked under his arm and a smile graced his sensual mouth. "Ready?"

She gulped. "Uh-huh."

They descended the concrete staircase and made their way to the beach. Savannah instantly kicked off her flip-flops and dug her bare toes into the warm, white sand. In the distance, she spotted the commanding shape of Coronado's Naval Base. "What kind of demo were you doing over there today?" she asked curiously.

"Obstacle course." He cast her a cocky smile. "We were showing some of the new recruits what we've got."

"Your arrogance makes my heart go a-flutter," she said sweetly.

"What about my ass? Does that make your heart flutter too?"

"No," she lied.

He just laughed.

The beach was completely deserted, so they had their pick of spots to spread out their towels. Once they were settled, Savannah peeled off her green sundress and shoved it inside the oversized beach bag she'd brought. She pulled out a tube of sunblock and innocently held it out. "Do my back?"

"No."

"What do you mean, no?" She couldn't help but feel a little insulted.

"I'm not putting my hands on you," Matt said cheerfully, plopping down on his towel. "I know exactly what you're trying to do. You're tempting me with your goddess body in the hopes that I'll be so overwhelmed with lust that I'll cut the date short so we can fuck like bunnies."

"I am not."

Okay, so maybe she was trying to tempt him. Truth was, she hadn't hung out with a guy in ages. A dinner or two before getting naked, sure, but once sex entered the equation, she made sure to keep it that way. For some reason, though, Matt was determined to spend time with her.

What was wrong with him?

She unscrewed the cap and squirted a glop of sunblock into her palms, proceeding to slap it across her skin in frustration. Really, what *was* the matter with him? Here she was, offering him wild, no-strings sex, something most men dreamed of, and he wanted to *get to know her*. Didn't he realize — she sucked in a breath. Oh Lord, he'd taken off his shirt.

Her body went into sexual overdrive at the sight of his sleek, golden muscles.

"So tell me about your parents."

The awareness sizzling through her veins fizzled with a *pop*. "Why do you want to know about them?" she demanded.

He chuckled. "Relax, darlin', I'm not going to track them down and murder them. I just want to know what they're like."

"Okay, you want to know what they're like? They're perfect," she said with a sigh. "And boring."

"With you as a daughter, I doubt they're boring."

Savannah fixed her gaze on the calm waves lapping against the shoreline. She breathed in the clean scent of salt, suddenly wishing she'd tried harder to seduce him right out of this "date".

"They're just so predictable," she finally admitted. "They finish each other's sentences, laugh at all the same jokes, do all the same things. It's…well, like I said, boring."

She felt Matt's gaze burning into her skin. When she glanced over, his green eyes revealed a perceptive glint. "What's the real reason?"

She swallowed. "What real reason?"

"Why you're so bothered by their relationship."

"I'm not…I'm not bothered by it."

"Sure you are. So why?"

Uneasiness swirled in the pit of her stomach. "I don't know."

"Of course you know." He tilted his head. "What is it about them that bugs you so badly?"

She grew silent.

"Come on, tell me. I'll even make you a deal. If you tell me, I'll tell why I'm bothered by *my* family."

His offer sparked her interest. Despite her reluctance, she found herself trying to put her feelings into words. "I guess it's… They're just…still so in love. After twenty years, they still act like newlyweds. Their relationship is so solid I can't make sense of it."

Matt's forehead creased. "Why not?"

"Because every relationship I've ever had has died a fiery death. I just don't get how they're still together. How they made it work." She was momentarily puzzled, despite the fact that she'd wondered about this for years. "Seeing them just makes me glaringly aware that I'm different."

"Why did your previous relationships fail?" he asked curiously.

She shook her head in confusion. "I honestly don't know. One minute everything was great, and the next they just ended. First with my high school boyfriend Rick, then in college with this guy Kevin, then Greg. Either I get bored, or they get bored, or both of us do — no matter what, it always ends."

"So you've decided to prematurely end things instead?"

She shrugged. "Why not? Obviously I'm not cut out for relationships. Which I'm totally fine with." She changed the subject before he could question her again. "Okay, your turn. Tell me why your family bugs you."

"They express their emotions so easily," he said without hesitation. "I don't get it."

Savannah had to laugh. "Uh, you express your feelings pretty easily too. You've made it more than clear you're interested in me."

Now he seemed to falter. "That's different. I'm talking about…love, I guess. They're so quick to gush about how much they love each other. For me, it's always been more difficult, telling people how I feel about them."

A short silence stretched between them. Discomfort roiled inside her. This was the most honest, disturbing conversation she'd ever had with a man, and the need to flee rose in her chest, tingled in her legs. Abruptly, she jumped to her feet and said, "I'm going to take a quick dip."

Without waiting for a reply, she nearly sprinted across the flour-soft sand. The water that swirled around her ankles was warm, soothing. Taking a breath, she dove in, submerging herself in the ocean and swimming out a dozen yards. When she finally came up for air, she glanced at the beach and saw Matt still lying on the towel, propped up on his elbows. She couldn't see his expression but she imagined he looked as confused as she felt. What on earth was she thinking, telling him about her parents' marriage, her past relationships?

She was treading in dangerous territory here. Having honest heart-to-hearts with a guy? She hadn't done that in years, not since she'd decided to focus on the thrill of firsts and avoid the pain and heartache that came from messy break-ups. Evidently she needed to regain her footing, remind herself that her time with Matt was temporary, the way it always was in her life.

Collecting her composure, she took another deep breath, then smoothed her wet hair away from her forehead. She kicked off in a leisurely stroke, and by the time she emerged on shore, she felt calm and centered and determined to lead this affair with Matt back in the direction it belonged.

To the bedroom.

Chapter Six

MATT GROANED SOFTLY AS SAVANNAH'S HEAD BOBBED UP AND DOWN his hard length, her tongue gliding across the sensitive underside of his shaft. Savannah's blowjobs continued to amaze him. She gave them a hundred and ten percent, focusing all her delicious attention on the task at hand. She used her hands and tongue and mouth and even teeth, until he could barely remember his own name.

She sucked his tip gently before taking him nearly to the back of her throat. Groaning again, he cupped her head and gave an upward thrust. She moaned, the sound vibrating through his cock. She'd had his clothes off the second they'd stepped into her apartment, and as irritated as he'd been then, he felt none of that irritation now. Instead, he leaned his head against the headboard of her bed and closed his eyes, losing himself in the mind-blowing sensations she produced in his body.

His eyelids popped open when her mouth disappeared, but she didn't leave him in the lurch. She just shimmied up his naked body, rolled a condom on his stiff shaft, and lowered herself onto him. The moment her wet heat clamped over him, he wrapped his arms around her slender form and pulled her toward him.

"I need to taste you," he muttered hoarsely.

Savannah cupped her tits and brought them to his mouth. He devoured one, then the other, licking and sucking her pearly-pink nipples while she rode him in a slow, lazy rhythm. Her skin tasted like saltwater, and the still-damp hair streaming down her shoulders had a slight curl to it. She was the most beautiful fucking woman he'd ever seen, and a fresh dose of arousal flooded his groin.

"See how much better this is," she murmured, bending down to kiss him. "Who needs dating?"

If he weren't on the verge of losing control, he would've been annoyed with the throaty remark, but as it was, he couldn't concentrate on anything but the feel of her tight pussy squeezing the hell out of his dick.

"Faster, darlin'," he said, gripping her hips. "Make yourself come before I explode."

With a sexy little smile, she did what he asked, grinding her lower body against his in a reckless pace. His breathing became labored, a tense knot of impending release coiling in his body. Savannah rode him hard and fast, but still he held back, watching the hazy desire swimming in her gray eyes, waiting for the moment her lips parted to let out a wild cry. Her inner muscles gripped his cock as she lost herself in orgasm, and the knot of tension inside him snapped apart. His climax seared into him, the incredible burn spreading through his body until every muscle, every limb was infused with pleasure.

Savannah collapsed on top of him. Her hair tickled his chin. He could feel her heartbeat hammering against his chest.

"Why does it just seem to get better?" Her breath moistened his shoulder.

He was wondering the same damn thing. As much as he didn't like Savannah's "first thrills" mentality, he understood it. After half a dozen times, he got bored of the woman in his bed. The sex just lost some of its passionate appeal after a while. But not with this woman. With Savannah, each time felt like the first time.

"Maybe it's a sign," he said gruffly.

She lifted her head to peek up at him. "A sign of what?"

"That you should be more open-minded to this dating thing."

Her hand slid between their sweat-coated bodies to squeeze his condom-covered dick. "I'm more open-minded to *this* thing."

Making a disapproving sound with his tongue, he reached down and firmly moved her hand. "No way. You don't get the little soldier again until after the next date."

She burst out in gales of laughter. "You have a nickname for your penis?"

"No," he lied.

Her laughter died, replaced by a groan of frustration. "You're seriously sticking to this ridiculous plan?"

"Yep. One round of sex for every date."

"You're a sadist."

"Yeah, but you still like me."

She sat up with a thoughtful look. Pink splotches covered her breasts, chafed from his stubble. He liked the sight, liked knowing he'd marked her this way.

"If we order Chinese food, does that count as a date?" she inquired.

He mulled it over. "Sure."

"And then afterwards we can do this again?"

"That's the rule."

"Fine." Her arm shot out to the phone on the bedside table. "Let's have some dinner so I can play with the little soldier."

"THIS IS *PERFECT*," ANNABELLE EXCLAIMED, MARVELING OVER THE SAMPLE centerpiece Savannah had created. They'd agreed for Annabelle to come by the shop at ten in the morning in order to approve or ask for a redo of Savannah's work. Approval seemed to be the conclusion. So far, Annabelle loved everything, including the sketches Savannah had done of the orchids twining around the delicate white birch archway that would serve as the altar.

Annabelle pulled out her phone and snapped a few photos of the centerpiece. "I'm sending these to Jeannine. She was happy with the description I gave her, but I'd like to give her a visual so she can suggest changes if she wants."

Luckily, the bride agreed with Annabelle's assessment, quickly texting back *PERFECT*.

Savannah experienced a burst of pride. She'd worked hard on the arrangement, and she was glad her efforts had been successful. She'd dreaded having to redo the centerpiece, particularly because of the vague details the bride had described. Now she wouldn't have to.

"Did you order the silk for the head table panels?" Annabelle asked.

She nodded. "I'm holding on to all the receipts and invoices like you asked."

"Thanks." With a faint smile, Annabelle leaned against the counter. "So how are things with Matt?"

Her guard instantly shot up. She knew Annabelle was dating Matt's best friend, so a part of her wondered if Matt had put Annabelle up to this. Was he fishing for information? After his whole date-for-sex trade, she wouldn't put it past him.

But although she wouldn't admit it to him, she really was starting to enjoy their dates. Yesterday they'd gone for lunch at a fish and chips place near the harbor, and when he picked her up after work that evening, they'd seen a new horror movie playing at the Royal, an old-style cinema house near San Diego's East Village.

The talking wasn't bad either. She loved hearing about his family and he never ran out of stories to tell about his four older sisters. Apparently they fussed over their baby brother like mother hens. His mother and grandmother sounded sweet as hell, though she could understand why he felt smothered by them sometimes. Who wouldn't, when your mother insisted on sewing nametags with bright red fabric hearts into every piece of clothing you owned?

But she knew she couldn't keep letting it happen. All the dates, the long talks…way too close to relationship territory here, and she knew from past experience just how bad she was at those. Back when she'd actually cared to find someone to share her life with, she'd only ended up broken-hearted. Now she knew better, and no matter how much she liked Matt O'Connor, she needed to put some distance between them before anything got too serious.

Sensing Savannah's hesitation, Annabelle's smile widened. "He didn't ask me to ask, I swear. It's just that we haven't seen him around the building the past week, so I figured he was hanging out at your place."

"Yeah, we've been hanging out," she said carefully.

"Does he make you melt in bed every time he calls you *darlin*?" Annabelle mimicked Matt's faint drawl, then laughed. "I just about did."

Savannah's eyebrows shot up. "You slept with Matt?"

Annabelle looked sheepish. "Yeah. I figured he'd tell you."

"Oh. He didn't."

The icy jealousy coursing through her veins came out of nowhere. For some reason, her claws came out at the revelation that Matt and Annabelle had slept together. She tried to stop the annoying reaction, but it only intensified when she unwittingly pictured them naked together.

"It was just a one-night thing," Annabelle added. "Ryan was there too."

Savannah pasted a bright smile on her face, but she suspected Annabelle could see right through it. The other woman's cautious tone had spoken volumes. "I'm sure it was fun," she said, cringing at her overly cheerful voice.

Annabelle let out a laugh. "You're jealous."

"And you're laughing about it," she grumbled. "Aren't you nice."

"I'm not laughing at *you*. Well, I guess I am, a little, but that's just because you're totally busted." Annabelle's brown eyes shone with delight. "You keep acting like you don't care about Matt one way or the other, but this proves that you do."

Savannah eyed her suspiciously. "Did you...you purposely told me about having sex with Matt, didn't you? You wanted to see my reaction."

"Yep," Annabelle said, making no move to apologize. "I just know he's really into you, and I wanted to make sure you felt the same way. Obviously you like him more than you're willing to admit."

She wanted to protest, but couldn't bring herself to do it. Annabelle probably wouldn't believe her anyway, if she insisted she didn't have deep feelings for Matt.

But she *didn't* have deep feelings for him. She liked him. She loved having sex with him. That was as deep as her feelings ran.

Surrrre, said the mocking voice in her head.

Gritting her teeth, she ignored the internal taunt. Even her own consciousness was trying to convince her she was in love with the guy. Well, she wasn't. She didn't do pesky emotions like love. Apparently she liked Matt enough to experience a spark of jealousy at the thought of him with another woman, but that did not mean she liked him enough to have a relationship with him.

She suddenly realized she needed to make it clear to him where she stood. Matt and Annabelle believed there was some love connection happening between them, and who could blame them? Here she was, going to movies and lunch dates with the guy, listening to his funny family anecdotes. No wonder Matt and his friends thought the fling was turning into something more.

Maybe it was time to set them straight.

MATT KNEW SOMETHING WAS UP WHEN SAVANNAH SUGGESTED THEY GO to one of the busiest bars in town for their next date. The past week, they'd gotten closer than ever, and he'd started looking forward to their non-sex moments. He usually did most of the talking, but eventually he'd gotten Savannah to open up and tell him more about her life. She even confessed about her cheerleading days, which he teased her about mercilessly. He couldn't imagine her doing cartwheels and shouting "B-E aggressive!" to a crowd of high school football fans.

Each time she revealed something personal, though, she immediately pulled back, and this morning when they'd made plans to meet up tonight, he'd heard the unmistakable distance in her voice. He knew Annabelle had been at the shop earlier to go over some wedding details, and he wondered if she'd done or said something to upset Savannah. But he couldn't imagine that happening. In fact, he was pretty sure he knew exactly why Savannah was acting the way she was.

They were getting too close for her comfort.

Pushing the thought aside, he focused on Savannah, who was sipping on a vodka-cranberry and laughing at the antics of a few younger guys arguing over by the pool table. He knew why she'd suggested the Sand Bar for tonight's date. The place was loud and always filled to capacity, offering pretty much the opposite of an intimate atmosphere. This bar was one of his favorite dives — he came here often with the guys — but it wasn't the place to have a real conversation, which was something he'd been looking forward to all day. But this was Savannah's way of distancing herself. She'd been doing it ever since the beach. The sex was still as hot and passionate as before, but the emotional barriers Savannah kept in front of her heart only seemed to grow higher.

"I'm in the mood for something different tonight," she announced, a wicked smile curving her mouth.

His guard shot up. "What kind of different?" He had to raise his voice over the din.

Her gaze swept over the throng of bodies in the room. She lingered for a moment on a tall, blond-haired guy wearing a football jersey. "Him, maybe? What do you think, is he good in bed?"

Uneasiness washed through him. "What are you suggesting, darlin'?"

She shrugged, and the loose wide-necked shirt she wore slid down, revealing her bare shoulder. "Might be fun to have some company tonight."

A threesome. Christ, she was actually suggesting a threesome?

His first instinct was to shout "hell no". Not that he was a prude or anything. He and Ryan had indulged in plenty of threesomes. So had he and Aidan. But Savannah's proposition absolutely floored him. Especially since he knew it was just another part of her plan to push him away. She probably expected him to balk at the idea, storm out in disgust.

Or...maybe she was actually serious.

He couldn't deny that he'd met his match in the form of Savannah Harte. She loved sex just as much as he did, and she was always quick to initiate a fun way to spice things up. Like the other night, when they'd ordered that Chinese food and she proceeded to lick low mein noodles off his stomach. She definitely knew how to have a good time.

So did he. Usually. But right now...shit, was she serious or should he call her bluff?

He decided to test the waters first.

"You want some random guy to join us tonight?" There was a sharp edge to his voice.

Her gray eyes twinkled. "Why not? According to Annabelle, you're no stranger to threesomes."

"Annabelle told you about that night?"

"Yup. And she also said it wasn't an isolated incident, for you, anyway." Savannah leaned forward, and the neckline of her shirt sagged lower, revealing her creamy-white cleavage.

Trying not to look at those mouthwatering tits, Matt kept his gaze on her face, studying her. "Threesomes can be entertaining," he said neutrally.

"Exactly. So let's do it."

Before he could respond, a familiar voice sounded from behind them, and then Aidan Rhodes strode up to their table. "O'Connor," he said, raising his beer in greeting. "What's going on, bro?" He noticed Savannah and grinned, the dimples in his cheeks popping out. "Who's your friend?"

Interest flickered across Savannah's face as she appraised Aidan. Matt wondered if she found Rhodes attractive. He wasn't into guys, but even he had to admit that Aidan had it going on. Six feet tall, strong jaw, perpetual stubble, and of course, those dimples. Annabelle had once told Matt that women *loved* dimples.

"This is Savannah. Savannah, this is Aidan," Matt said, then gestured to the empty chair at their table. "Have a seat, man."

Aidan sat down and took a long swallow of beer. "I'm not interrupting anything, am I? I came here with a few other guys from base, but two of them have already hooked up with total strangers and the third might be throwing up in the bathroom."

"Your friends left you all alone?" Savannah mocked, laughing softly.

Aidan's dark eyes swept over her, zeroing in on the cleavage Matt had been trying to avoid. "They sure did. Good thing I found some new friends."

Matt sipped his own beer, watching the casual interplay between Savannah and Rhodes. Nearly an hour passed, and although Matt was an active participant in the conversation, cracking jokes with Aidan, his mind was somewhere else the entire time.

He watched Savannah and Aidan interact, wariness creeping up his spine. Neither one was outright flirting or anything, but he could tell they each found the other attractive. His chest squeezed at the thought, but at the same time, he liked and respected Aidan. He was a good guy, really truly decent, and if they were seriously going to have a three-way tonight, better with Aidan than some stranger.

Matt almost choked mid-sip as he realized where his train of thought had taken him. Fuck, was he actually considering this ménage idea?

"I'll be back in a few." Aidan's voice made Matt lift his head. His friend had stood up and was already heading toward the restrooms.

Matt noticed Savannah's gaze focus on Aidan's ass as he strode off.

"I like him," she remarked. "How come he's not a SEAL like you? He's just as ripped, physique-wise."

"You like his body?" Matt said darkly.

"Sure." She reached out to rub the center of his palm with her fingers. "It's obviously not as super-duper sexy as yours, *darlin'*, but you've got to admit, he's a hottie." She cocked her head. "Have you ever had any threesomes with him?"

Matt gave a reluctant nod.

She raised one eyebrow. "Really. How were they?"

"Pretty damn good," he admitted.

"So what do you think...?" She tilted her head again and flashed him a sexy smile.

He clenched his teeth. "Do you really want to do this or are you trying to..."

"Trying to what?"

"I don't know." He felt frazzled. "Get me to break up with you or something."

"Breaking up implies we're in a relationship. And we're not. I just want to have a good time, Superman. It's all I've wanted from the start. And I like Aidan. He's really cute."

"Cute enough to fuck?"

A brief flash of indignation blazed through her eyes. "Yeah, actually he is. And considering you've seen him naked while the two of you screwed who knows how many chicks, I don't see how you can be upset with me for bringing it up."

She did have a point. Matt hated hypocrisy, yet here he was, getting pissed that she'd suggested something he and Aidan had already done a few times before.

"You *really* want this?" He studied her intently.

Savannah's expression never wavered. "Yes."

"Fine then." From the corner of his eye, Matt spotted Aidan returning from the men's room. Just as Aidan reached the table, Matt stood up and clapped a hand on his friend's arm. "You want to get out of here?" he asked roughly. "Savannah and I were thinking of heading back to her place."

Surprise creased Aidan's features. "You want me to join you?"

He lowered his voice. "My girl's in the mood for some extra company."

Aidan slanted his eyes at Savannah, looking more than a little intrigued. "You want some company, honey?"

Savannah's cheeks turned a shade of pink. "You'd be into that?"

"I'm into a lot of things," Aidan replied with a husky laugh. He glanced at Matt. "You cool with this?"

Matt forced a nod. "Definitely. I'm all about making Savannah happy."

Chapter Seven

SAVANNAH'S APARTMENT WAS DARK WHEN THEY WALKED IN TWENTY minutes later. Aidan had driven over in his own car, while Matt and Savannah took the SUV. The whole ride over, Matt wondered if the gorgeous blonde beside him would call this off, but she didn't say much during the ride, save for a few flirty remarks about how it had been ages since she'd done something this crazy.

So here he was, still calling her bluff, still riddled with doubt that she'd actually go through with this. Not that the idea of a threesome freaked him out or anything. He was a healthy, red-blooded male who never had any inhibitions when it came to sex. Hell, his cock was already semi-hard and nobody was naked yet. If Savannah truly wanted to get it on with two men at once, he had no problem helping her live out the fantasy.

But he *would* have a problem if it turned out this whole three-way thing was simply a ploy to put some more distance between them. He'd never pegged Savannah as the type to play games, and he sincerely hoped that wasn't the case now, but considering her abrupt decision to invite a third player into the mix, he had to wonder. Especially since this bright idea had come days after she'd revealed some personal, emotional details to him, which she evidently hadn't liked sharing.

Savannah Harte was scared of relationships. He had no doubt about that anymore. He just hoped that fear wasn't driving her right now, that it wasn't a way for her to push him away.

When they entered her apartment, however, pushing him away was not at all what she did. Instead, she moved closer and kissed the hell out of him, her tongue sliding into his mouth. He was gasping for air when she finally pulled away, surprised by her take-charge attitude. As he watched, she turned around and stepped toward Aidan, placed her hands on his shoulders, and leaned up to brush her lips over his.

He knew he had no right to be upset, or even angry. He'd agreed to this stupid idea. But somehow he'd expected her to back out at the last moment. Looked like backing out wasn't on her agenda. His stomach clenched as Savannah deepened the kiss with Aidan, who responded without any hesitation.

Despite the aching of his heart, Matt's body reacted the way it always did when the promise of sex hung in the air. His cock hardened, muscles tensed, skin heated. When Aidan's hands slid down to cup Savannah's ass, Matt's erection twitched involuntarily. He hated that seeing another man's hands on Savannah could get him going. He wasn't sure he wanted to share her with anybody else, but at least here, with Aidan, he had some semblance of control. Aidan was a good buddy of his and Matt knew he wouldn't do anything to hurt Savannah.

"We need a bed," Aidan rasped against Savannah's lips, breaking the kiss.

With a smile, she gripped his hand and led him toward the screen separating the living area from her bedroom. She paused to grasp Matt's hand too, her hips swaying as she led the two men toward the bed. She really wanted this, Matt realized, and conflicting emotions warred inside of him.

On one hand, he admired her confidence, how in tune she was with her sexuality. She knew what she wanted, went after it, and had no regrets. She was his perfect match, sexually at least, a rare woman who had zero reservations in the bedroom. She held the same enthusiastic outlook about sex that he normally did.

Funny, how the tables had completely turned on him.

Aidan paused at the foot of the bed, his dark eyes smoldering with heat. Matt noticed his friend's cheeks were slightly flushed and he had that careless swagger that indicated he was probably a little buzzed from the alcohol he'd consumed tonight.

Savannah glanced from one man to the other, shooting them a coy smile. "Come on, boys. Strip."

Aidan grinned at Matt. "I like her."

"So do I," he answered roughly.

Knowing it was too damn late to back out now, Matt bent to unlace his boots and kicked them aside, then unzipped his pants and let them drop to the floor. Shirt, boxers and socks came off, until he stood naked in front of Savannah. His cock jutted out, begging for her attention. Aidan's dick was at full salute too.

Heat suffused Savannah's gray eyes, darkening them to metallic silver. With methodical movements, she pulled her shirt over her head, shimmied out of her jeans and panties, and stepped closer to Aidan, fully naked. Then she slid down to her knees and wrapped both hands around his friend's shaft.

Matt clenched his teeth. When Savannah's lips parted to wrap around Aidan's tip, simultaneous jolts of arousal and jealousy struck him. He didn't want to be turned on watching Savannah blow someone else, but he was.

Lowering his hand to his throbbing erection, he stroked himself slowly while Savannah worked on his friend. Aidan groaned in approval, rocking his hips to meet Savannah's lips. He moved backwards toward the bed, slipped out of her mouth and sank onto the mattress.

Savannah promptly climbed up too and continued to lick at him eagerly. After a few seconds, she lifted her head and turned to Matt. "Are you just going to stand there?" Her voice came out in a teasing drawl.

Still gripping his shaft, he walked over to the bed and stared at her enticing bottom. The way she was bent over Aidan left her fully exposed to him. Matt's mouth went dry as he stared at her pink slit and the puckered ring of her ass. He moved toward her as if pulled by a magnet.

She squeaked in delight when she felt his hands on her cheeks, spreading them wider. Using the tip of his index finger, he stroked her pussy, groaning when moisture coated his fingers.

Savannah thrust her ass out even higher. "*Please.*" The pleading note to her voice made him smile.

"Don't be cruel," Aidan laughed from the bed. "Give her what she wants, bro."

Sinking to his knees, Matt leaned forward and dragged his tongue along her damp flesh, eliciting a desperate whimper from her mouth. It came out muffled, what with Aidan's cock deep in her throat. Forcing every drop of jealousy from his body, Matt focused on pleasing his woman. He licked her up like an ice cream cone, then thrust his tongue deep inside her. As he started suckling on her clit, he pushed two fingers into her and fucked her with them. When he felt her muscles clamp around his fingers, he quickly withdrew. She deserved to be teased a little.

On the bed, Aidan let out a ragged moan and gently moved Savannah's head away. "Not yet," he ground out. "I want to come inside you, honey."

Savannah let Matt give her one more swipe of the tongue, then sat up and turned to meet his eyes. The expression on her face sent a bolt of desire straight to his cock. Her cheeks were pink, her lips wet from sucking Aidan, her eyes glazed and heavy-lidded.

"Are you having fun?" he couldn't help but rasp.

She nodded slightly. Her gaze traveled to his erect cock. "Come here," she ordered.

He stood up and moved toward her. She took him in her mouth and he almost keeled over from the sensation. Aidan slid up so he was sitting behind Savannah, wrapping his muscular arms around her so he could cup her tits with his palms. As Savannah's tongue danced along his shaft, Matt's eyelids fluttered. He forced his eyes to stay open, to watch the way Aidan's fingers played with Savannah's rigid nipples. Fuck, that was hot.

His reluctance was slowly dissolving like a teaspoon of sugar in water. This wasn't as painful as he'd thought it would be. Aidan knew how to please a woman, and judging by Savannah's muffled moans she obviously enjoyed the way the other man fondled her breasts. Matt was as hard as a rock, eager to fill Savannah's ass with his cock at the same time another man penetrated her tight pussy.

Savannah nibbled on his tip and another groan slid from his mouth. No, this encounter wasn't awkward or painful at all. Here he was, with a good friend of his, the woman he loved, and the chemistry between the three of them was out of this—

The woman you love?

It was a miracle his dick didn't go soft at that moment. The appearance of the L-word in his brain shocked the hell out of him. Was he in love with her? How was that possible? His gaze swept over her flushed face, those perfect breasts and tanned skin and tousled blonde hair. He loved seeing her arousal, loved the little sounds of pleasure she made in the back of her throat. He wanted her to feel good. He wanted to make her happy.

Fuck, he was actually in love.

The newfound emotion brought a rush of pleasure to his body. Suddenly he needed to be inside her, some primal urge to claim her taking over. Pulling his dick out of her mouth, he strode over to the bedside table, yanked open the drawer and grabbed the box of condoms he'd stashed in there the other day. He took out a tube of lubrication and set that down on the bed, then removed two square packages from the box, tossed one to Aidan and ripped the other open so he could sheath himself.

"Who do you want in your ass?"

Savannah looked up in surprise at Matt's gruff inquiry. At her obvious hesitation, he shot her a mocking smile. "This is your show, darlin'. Tell us what you want."

Her face pink with excitement, she answered his question with actions rather than words. Straddling Aidan, she lowered herself onto his waiting erection, moaning as she fully seated herself. Matt's chest tightened with pure heat as she bent forward and pushed her ass up in the air in invitation.

He didn't need to be asked twice.

Coming up behind her, he widened his stance, then picked up the lube and squeezed a generous amount into his palm. As Aidan thrust upward to meet Savannah's frenzied movements, Matt got Savannah nice and slick. When his tip rubbed her tender opening, she cried out in delight and wiggled against him.

"Slow down, honey," Aidan murmured, planting his hands on her slender hips to steady her. "Let him work his way in."

Matt's entire body burned with red-hot lust as he eased into that tight rosette. He reined himself in, gritting his teeth to stop from coming right there and then. It felt like an iron fist squeezing his cock. His head lolled to the side. Fuck. So good. No way was he lasting more than a minute.

While Aidan kept Savannah still, Matt moved in and out, slowly going deeper at each lazy drive of his cock. When his entire length was buried inside her, all three of them groaned. And then they started to move.

SAVANNAH WONDERED IF IT WAS POSSIBLE TO DIE FROM ECSTASY. SHE'D been with two men before, but Matt and Aidan were by far better endowed than her previous lovers. She felt unbelievably filled as their cocks slid in and out of her. Her pulse hammered in her ears, her breathing labored as she rode Aidan. Behind her, Matt kept to an excruciatingly slow pace. She knew he was allowing her to get used to the sensations, but his languid movements drove her crazy.

Twisting her head, she met his eyes and issued a breathy command. "Faster. Please."

His features tight with desire, he offered a quick nod, then plunged into her so hard she cried out with pleasure that bordered on pain. Beneath her, Aidan's dark eyes glimmered with unrestrained heat. "That's it, honey, fuck me harder."

It was too much. Every muscle in her body was coiled, like a rattlesnake ready to pounce. She needed to come so badly she could barely breathe, definitely couldn't form any coherent thoughts.

"Rub her clit," came Matt's hoarse demand.

Her vision went hazy as Aidan reached between them and captured her clit between his fingers, rolling it gently. She sagged forward, nearly drowning in the waves of bliss. Aidan's cock stretched her aching core, and Matt was buried so deep in her ass she didn't know where she started and they ended. In the back of her mind, she realized it was not Aidan, but Matt she was more focused on. She was listening to *his* breathing, feeling *his* hands digging into her hips, groaning each time *his* erection slid into her. Aidan's fingers between her legs felt incredible, his hard body beneath hers was amazing, but only when she focused on Matt did she feel the ripples of impending orgasm dance low in her belly.

Since now wasn't the time to question that revelation, she closed her eyes and lost herself in the moment. Her muscles tightened, contracted, coiled again and then seemed to snap apart as release crashed into her. Pleasure sizzled through her veins, infusing into the tips of her nipples, her clit, her core.

As she came apart, she felt more than heard each man lose control. Aidan's cry was huskier, more restrained, while Matt gave a guttural groan that sent shivers through her. She was nearly panting as the two men came, as Matt tenderly caressed her hips and Aidan continued to brush his fingers over her clit.

"Holy shit," Aidan swore when their heavy breathing finally grew quiet. One hand touched Savannah's chin. "That was first-class."

She managed an exhausted smile. "Right back at you."

Her body suddenly felt empty as Matt pulled out of her ass, followed by Aidan's gentle withdrawal. She rolled off him, smiling again when she watched him hop off the bed and fumble on the floor for his clothes. "I should get going," he said absently.

Evidently he wasn't a cuddler. She admired the attitude, though. He'd gotten what he wanted and now he was taking off. Right to the point. She liked that.

"Thanks for coming over," she murmured.

He laughed softly. "I should be thanking you. You were amazing." He glanced over at Matt, who was slipping into his boxers. "Thanks for having me, bro."

Matt just shrugged. "Anytime."

Anytime?

Savannah wondered if that meant he wanted Aidan to play with them again. The thought made her stomach a little unsettled. Aidan was insanely cute and definitely talented in bed, but during those last few moments before her orgasm, Matt had been the only man on her mind, the only one she'd been concentrating on. She wasn't sure why that happened, or how she even felt about it.

"I'll walk you out," Matt said to his buddy.

With another dimpled grin, Aidan offered a cute "Later, Savannah" and followed Matt to the front door. She heard the door open, close, then lock. When Matt appeared at the foot of the bed a moment later, he wore a wry expression on his handsome face.

"You okay?" she teased. "Or did we wear you out?"

"I'm fine." He cleared his throat. "So listen…"

A startling combination of hope and disappointment clamored inside her. He was going to break it off with her. This threesome had evidently been too much for him. He'd only been pretending to enjoy it, but now that his friend was gone, he was going to tell her that he didn't want to be with someone as slutty as her. Awful as it was, it was what she'd been trying to achieve, yet a part of her was upset that it had been so easy, childish as *that* was.

"Savannah, I think I'm falling in love with you."

Even though she was lying down, she almost fell over. "What?"

"You heard me," he said gruffly.

"You...I...of course you're not." She sat up abruptly. "That's silly."

Anger flashed in his eyes. "Why exactly is that silly?"

Panic spiraled through her body. How was this actually happening? This damn threesome was her way to try and put some distance between her and Matt. All those dates and talks and the staggeringly amazing sex... It scared her. After the fierce jealousy she'd experienced when learning that Annabelle had slept with Matt, Savannah had realized just how close she was to developing real feelings for him. It was like she was falling off a cliff and had two landing options — the water, which meant being safe and happy but alone, or the jagged rocks, a relationship that, like all the others, would end in heartbreak.

She didn't want to crash into those rocks. Her first priority had always been herself, and so she'd tried pushing Matt away by bringing another man into their bed.

And he'd liked it!

She'd seen the fire burning in his eyes when both he and Aidan had been fucking her. And now he was telling her he loved her?

"You can't actually mean that," she burst out. "And is this really the time you want to declare your love? After I just slept with your friend?"

"It was just sex," he said with a shrug. "But you and me...that's more than sex. I think you know it but you're too scared to admit it. We get along —"

"So?" she cut in. "I get along with my dentist — that doesn't mean we love each other."

"We laugh together," he went on, ignoring the interruption. "We like the same shitty horror movies, we have mind-blowing sex, we never run out of things to say to each other." Looking aggravated, he put on his T-shirt, then buttoned up his jeans. "So yeah, all those things make me think this is more than a fling."

She bit on her thumbnail, reverting back to an old habit she only turned to when she was seriously panic-stricken. He couldn't really mean any of this. Or at least, the love part of it. They'd known each other two weeks, a month if you counted the first meeting at the bank. That wasn't enough time for him to fall in love with her.

She didn't *want* him to fall in love with her.

Matt released a ragged breath. "Why does it not surprise me that you're reacting this way?"

She bristled. "What's that supposed to mean?"

"It means you're a coward, Savannah. You act all tough and confident, like you don't care about anything but having a good time, but we both know that's a big fat lie. You *want* a relationship — you're just too damn scared."

Her lips tightened in offense. "I told you, I'm not a relationship person. They never last for me."

Matt barked out a humorless laugh. "Because maybe you haven't found the right man, ever thought of that? If you're not meant to be with someone, obviously the relationship will end. But when you find the right person…" He let the comment hang.

"And I suppose you're the right person for me?" She scoffed. "We've known each other a couple of weeks, Matt. It won't work out between us."

He raised one dark eyebrow. "Do you have psychic powers I'm not aware of? How do you know it won't work out?"

She raked her fingers through her hair in an aggravated gesture. "Because it never does. Not for me, anyway. Something always ends up going wrong."

"Maybe it won't this time," he said quietly.

"And maybe it will." She stuck her chin out stubbornly. "I made the decision a long time ago not to take that chance. I don't want any more broken hearts. And I'm tired of the awful sense of boredom and sadness I feel when the thrill dies."

Realizing she was still naked, she scrambled off the bed and angrily rummaged on the floor for her clothes. She shoved on her jeans without bothering with underwear, threw her shirt over her head, and crossed her arms. "Look, I really do like you," she said, softening her tone. "Enough that I don't want to come to the point where I *don't* like you anymore, or where you don't like me."

"And what if we never reach that point?" he challenged.

Her shoulders sagged. "I always get to that point."

Frustration creased his forehead. "So you're just planning on living the rest of your life in fear, avoiding anything good that comes your way? Because damn it, Savannah, *we* are good. And you're a fool to throw it away." His voice hardened. "I told you how difficult it is for me to talk about my emotions, but I was willing to take the risk, to tell you how I feel."

Pain circled her heart. "Matt…"

"Whatever," he muttered. "Obviously you can't take a risk of your own."

"That's not fair," she protested. "I've made it clear from day one what I wanted out of this. I never lied to you or misled you."

He released a heavy sigh. "You're right. You didn't. But things have changed since day one. We have the potential to be really good together and you're too scared to give us a chance."

To her dismay, tears stung her eyelids. But the fact that she was about to cry only brought a spark of anger to her belly. Why was he pushing her? She'd told him her feelings about relationships. Just because he'd suddenly decided he was in love with her didn't mean she was going to launch herself into his arms and profess her undying love.

Unbearable silence hung between them, until Matt finally cursed under his breath and took a step back. "Forget it. I'm not going to beg you to have a relationship with me. I'm not that guy. But I'm not going to pretend this is just a fling either."

She blinked, trying to stop the tears from falling.

"So here you go," he said in a tone lined with resignation. "You've got your wish. A couple of weeks of casual, no-strings sex. Hope you had fun."

Without another word, not even a goodbye, he turned his back on her and left the apartment.

Chapter Eight

"ARE YOU *DRINKING*?"

The outraged female voice jolted Matt from his catnap. Cranking open one eyelid, he saw two pretty faces hovering above him. His fuzzy eyesight recognized Annabelle, but it took a few seconds to register the petite brunette beside her as Holly Scott, Carson's wife. He wasn't used to the haircut yet. Holly had recently chopped her long brown hair into a chin-length bob, which emphasized her emerald green eyes and the delicate angles of her face.

Propping himself up on the couch cushion with his elbow, he glanced at the half-empty beer bottle on the coffee table and mumbled, "It's from last night."

Annabelle planted her hands on her hips. "I can see the condensation dripping down the side. This was just opened."

Holly rolled her eyes. "It's ten in the morning, Matt. That's so pathetic."

No, what was pathetic was telling a woman he loved her for the first time in his life only to be shut down big-time.

But he decided not to say that aloud.

"Since when did you two become my mother?" he grumbled, sitting up with a tired yawn.

"Since you promised you'd let us borrow your SUV for the wedding today," Annabelle snapped. "I texted you about it last night and you texted back *yeppers*. I took that to mean you'd help out."

He straightened up, rolling his shoulders to get the kinks out. He'd been lying on the couch for about three days now, only dragging himself up to get a beer or use the john. Empty pizza boxes were stacked on the floor and he wrinkled his nose at the stale odor of old beer emanating from the empty bottles littered all over the room.

"Shit, I forgot about that," he said, shooting them an apologetic look. "Do you just need the keys or am I driving you over to the banquet hall?"

"There's a ton of stuff to carry in," Holly said, "so it would be cool if you could come and help unload."

"You don't have to stay for the wedding obviously," Annabelle added.

He lifted his arms above his head and stretched. "Okay. Let me hop in the shower and then I'll take you."

Leaving them in the living room, he headed to the bathroom, where he took a quick shower, brushed his teeth, and shaved three days' worth of stubble off his face. Holly was right, he realized as he stared at his tired eyes in the steamy mirror. He *was* pathetic. So things had ended with Savannah. Big fucking deal. It only went to show that his initial decision to stay single had been a smart one. Love made people go nuts. His sisters had turned into mushy, sappy idiots, and so had he, the night he'd told Savannah how he felt about her.

He was better off alone. Better off going back to his old lifestyle, making sure things stayed light, and keeping his damn feelings to himself.

After dressing in jeans and a T-shirt, he reentered the living room to find that it was now spotless. In the ten minutes he'd been gone, Annabelle and Holly had carted off the pizza boxes, gotten rid of the bottles, and even wiped down his coffee table. The flowery scent of air freshener hung in the large space, and both women were sitting on a couch now cleared of the random items of clothing previously strewn on it.

"Jeez, you really are my mother," he muttered.

Holly looked over at him with sharp green eyes. "What happened with Savannah? Did she dump you?"

"No." He set his jaw. "I dumped her."

"Why would you do that?" Annabelle demanded.

"None of your business." He swiped his keys from the little basket on the table by the couch and jiggled them. "Do you want a ride or not?"

He could practically feel the curiosity radiating from them, but to his surprise, neither female pushed him for details. He chalked it up to the wedding they were heading to, knowing that if the two weren't occupied with something else right now, they'd be all over him, prying information from him like a dentist extracting teeth.

"We need to stop by Shelby's bakery," Holly said as she slid into the backseat of the SUV. "We stored all the food there."

Annabelle got into the passenger seat. She buckled her seatbelt and shot him a sideways glance. "Thanks for doing this. Ryan was going to lend me the Jeep but it's still in the shop."

Matt wrinkled his brow. "He wrecked it?"

"Jeez, were you in an alcohol-induced coma for the past three days? He called you the day before yesterday to tell you about it. A dog ran right in front of his car and he had to swerve to avoid hitting it. He crashed into a tree, remember?"

Matt had a vague recollection of Ryan's voice bitching in his ear about a dog or something. Fuck, how much had he drank in the last seventy-two hours?

"He's okay, though, right?"

She sighed. "He's fine."

Shoving his sunglasses onto his nose, he focused on driving to Shelby's bakery. The shower had helped clear his head, and the two beers he'd consumed this morning were starting to leave his bloodstream. He felt alert now. And pissed off.

Yup, still pissed off at Savannah for being so damn stubborn and so damn scared.

But what could he do about it? No way was he going to beg. He was way too proud for that. Besides, what would it achieve? Savannah wanted to live in her heartache-free world of first kisses and whirlwind thrills, and who was he to force her into a relationship?

Best thing to do was move on.

Put her out of his mind, find a new, cute chick to strike up a thing with, and fuck the love he still felt for Savannah right out of his body.

SAVANNAH EXAMINED HER REFLECTION IN THE MIRROR, WONDERING IF the low-cut violet dress she'd chosen was too sexy for a first date. The silky material fell down to her knees, so it wasn't too indecent, but her breasts practically poured out of the bodice. After a second, she shrugged and moved away from the mirror. Whatever. You could never go wrong with sexy.

Her arms ached in protest as she lifted them up to adjust the artfully messy twist of her hair. She was still sore from yesterday. She'd gotten up at six in the morning and spent seven hours getting the flowers ready for the wedding. She'd driven around town like a maniac, first to the Rose Room, the banquet hall where Jeannine and her husband-to-be Henry were holding their wedding reception. Along with bringing Chad, Savannah had hired a few temporary workers to help her set up all the tables, chairs and wall panels. She'd left half of the workers to finish up, then went with Chad and a couple of others to St. Augustine's Chapel to get the aisle and altar ready for the actual ceremony. She'd left Chad in charge, headed back to the banquet hall, then back to the chapel, back to the hall, and so on, until she was ready to collapse by the time noon rolled around.

During one of her trips to the Rose Room, she'd had a moment to chat with Annabelle and her business partner, Holly, who mentioned Matt had just left. Apparently he'd given them a ride and stayed to help unload supplies. Savannah had just missed him, and she hadn't been sure whether she was happy or sad about that.

His parting words had been buzzing through her head like angry wasps for three days now.

Hope you had fun.

He hadn't sounded cruel when he said them. Just sad and resigned. She almost wished he'd been cruel. At least then she could feel better about the way things ended. If she hated him, then she wouldn't have to miss him.

Unfortunately, she didn't hate him.

And she totally missed him.

Good thing she had a solution for that.

The wedding had gone off without a hitch, the flowers were a success, and Prestige Events wanted to work with her again. To celebrate, Savannah was going on a date with Tony, the tall, dark-haired hottie who'd waltzed into her shop yesterday evening to buy flowers for his newly engaged cousin. The two of them had flirted until finally he gave her a sexy smile and asked if she wanted to have dinner with him the following evening. She'd said yes immediately.

Tony was just the kind of guy she liked spending time with. Gorgeous, easygoing, and not looking for a relationship. He'd told her he worked long hours at a law firm where he was a junior partner, and didn't have time for anything serious.

Exactly the way she liked it.

A flicker of guilt went through her as she left the apartment. She felt kind of crappy, going out with someone else when the dust of her time with Matt had barely even settled. But hopefully Tony would be a nice distraction. A way to put Matt out of her mind for good.

Downstairs, she found a sleek black BMW waiting at the curb. The passenger window rolled down and Tony's cute grin greeted her. "Hop in."

Despite herself, she was a tad irked that he hadn't gotten out to open her door for her. Matt always did, even if they were just going for a quick cup of coffee. His Southern gentleman manners, as he always said.

Don't think about Matt, a sharp voice ordered.

She decided to heed the advice. She was going out with Tony. Tony, not Matt. So there was no reason to think about anyone other than Matt—shit, Tony, anyone other than *Tony*.

"Hey," she said as she got into the car.

Tony's dark eyes studied her appreciatively. "You look amazing."

"Thanks."

He moved the gearshift. "I made reservations at an Italian place a few blocks from here. Is that cool with you?"

"It's great."

They didn't say much more as he drove to the restaurant. Savannah normally excelled at first date chitchat. She had no problems asking questions or dropping a few flirtatious remarks, maybe even innocently brushing a guy's arm to make that first contact.

But she didn't do any of that tonight. And when they were seated at a secluded corner table with a red-and-white-checkered tablecloth, she actually felt nervous.

"So," Tony said, reaching for the menu, "how do you like being a florist?"

She fumbled for her own menu. "It's great."

"Cool. Did you always want to work with flowers?"

"Uh-huh. Flowers are…well, they're great."

She tried not to cringe. She'd uttered the word "great" like fifty times already and they were ten minutes into the stupid date. Drawing a breath, she pretended to study the menu, all the while gathering up confidence. Enough was enough. She was acting like a total loser. She was in her element, for Pete's sake. These first encounters, the exciting, flirty moments leading up to fun between the sheets—she lived off them, damn it.

Savannah picked up the water glass on the table and took a long swallow. "What about you?" she asked smoothly. "Have you always wanted to be a lawyer?"

With an enthusiastic nod, Tony began explaining how law was his passion, only to be interrupted by the arrival of their waiter, a twenty-something-year-old guy with spiky brown hair and hazel eyes.

"Are you ready to order?" he inquired.

Savannah noticed the waiter had glued his gaze to her cleavage. She suddenly wished she'd brought a cardigan or something. The way this kid checked her out was almost criminal.

"No, we need a few more minutes," Tony said.

The waiter turned to Savannah, but his eyes never reached her face. He just kept ogling her tits like a horny teenager. "Something to drink then?"

"A few more minutes," she echoed.

With one last lingering look, the waiter walked off, while Savannah rolled her eyes and said, "I hope he doesn't roofie my drink. I'm not in the mood to be sexually assaulted tonight."

Tony gave her a blank look. "What? Why would he put drugs in your drink?"

She grew flustered. "He wouldn't. He was just looking at my...I was making a...whatever."

Her date was looking at her in such confusion she almost laughed out loud. But then Tony's face brightened and he continued his recitation of all the reasons he'd chosen to become a lawyer.

Savannah tuned him out, still thinking about how he'd completely missed the sarcasm in her tone. Matt would have appreciated the sardonic remark. Like the day they'd been lying side by side on the bank floor and he'd laughed at her whispered barbs. They'd joked back and forth that day as if they'd done it for years. She still couldn't believe he liked—and got—her sense of humor.

Her mind drifted, the memory of his childhood anecdotes coming to the surface. She'd loved hearing those stories, mostly because it was fun picturing big, tough Matt O'Connor as a little kid fussed over by all the females in his family. She liked hearing his voice too. Deep and gruff, and so deliciously husky when he was turned on.

She smothered a groan. Why couldn't she stop thinking about him already? They'd had a few fun weeks together, and she'd gotten out just in time. He'd told her he was falling in love with her! How could she stick around after that and risk another painful breakup? She'd been through too many of those. Like when Kevin dumped her after she burned yet another dinner. He'd gone on and on about how much he valued marriage and how he didn't think she would make a good wife. Asshole. The words had stung back then, but eventually she'd accepted the truth to them. Men didn't want to settle down with someone like her. She was too forward when it came to sex, too sarcastic, and not at all domestic, unless you counted her affinity for flowers.

Matt might be a bit of a commitment-phobe too, but she suspected he secretly did want the kind of loving relationship his sisters had. He would want a wife someday, and like an asshole once told her, she wasn't wife material.

Or maybe it would have ended the way things did with Greg, her last serious boyfriend. The routine they'd fallen into had been so boring she'd wanted to tear her own hair out. So she'd broken up with Greg, hurting him deeply in the process. She didn't want to hurt Matt, which would no doubt happen if the chemistry between them decided to fizzle out.

The sharp clearing of a throat jerked her from her thoughts. She blinked, finding Tony watching her in concern. "Huh?" she said.

"I asked if you were ready to order. You've been staring at the menu for five minutes. And you ignored me the four times I asked you what you wanted."

Five minutes? She'd spaced out for that long? And she hadn't even noticed him talking to her. What was the matter with her?

A startling thought sliced into her consciousness.

She wasn't having a good time.

Here she was, on a first date with a seriously cute guy she'd normally be attracted to, but the thrill wasn't there.

She didn't want to feel Tony's lips on hers for the first time. Didn't want to undress him and find out what lay beneath his black trousers and navy-blue suit jacket.

She felt zero enthusiasm about starting a casual fling with this man.

Because she still wanted Matt O'Connor.

Because she'd *fallen* for Matt O'Connor.

Swallowing hard, she met her date's annoyed eyes and said, "How about we call it a night?"

"GOD, YOUR CHEST IS ROCK-HARD," THE BRUNETTE IN MATT'S ARMS purred. "No wonder you're so good at this game."

Matt decided not to point out that hard chests had nothing to do with a game of pool. Precision, maybe. A steady grip. But not a damned chest.

Smothering a weary sigh, he slowly ducked out of the woman's grip and reached for the cue he'd rested against the table. "Let's finish the game."

Her brown eyes flickered with irritation as he moved to the other side of the pool table and pretended to study the placement of the balls. Fuck, why had he bothered coming here tonight? The Sand Bar was always the place to go when you wanted to find someone to spend the night with, but for some reason, the mob of bodies and the scent of sweat and perfume made him nauseous. And the loud reggae music blasting from the speakers was giving him a headache.

He shouldn't have come. The idea of sex with a total stranger held absolutely no appeal for him right now.

"Actually," he said, setting down the pool cue again, "I think I'm going to head out. I feel like I'm coming down with something."

The brunette whose name he hadn't even asked for gazed at him in disappointment. Then, without another word, she sauntered off, her firm ass swaying at each step she took. Not even the sight of a nice ass could lift his spirits.

Finally releasing the sigh lodged in his chest, he maneuvered through the crowd. Two blondes with heavy makeup shot him come-hither smiles but he ignored them, intent on getting the hell out of there. He also ignored a throaty "What's the hurry, stud?" and a teasing "Hey, baby" from two other chicks.

When he stepped into the balmy night air, relief swam through him. Fuck. It was like a feeding frenzy in there. Hungry female piranhas after his body. Usually his ego would inflate from all the attention, but right now he just felt sleazy that he used to spend so much time in a place like that.

"Hey."

At the sound of yet another female voice, he clenched his fists, ready to shoot the chick down—and probably not in a gentle way.

But then he turned around and the irritated retort got stuck in his throat. Savannah stood by the entrance of the bar.

His eyes ate her up, taking in the short violet dress and open-toed silver sandals she wore. Her hair was tied up in a complicated-looking twist, and subtle makeup emphasized her beautiful features.

He cleared his throat, searching for his voice. "What are you doing here?"

"Looking for you," she said simply.

There were about ten feet separating them, but Matt didn't make a move to bridge the distance. What was she doing here? After the way they'd left things, he hadn't thought he'd ever see her again.

She took a step toward him, then stopped awkwardly. "I went by your apartment building, but you weren't there. Annabelle was on the balcony and told me you came here, so..." Her voice trailed off.

"Why are you all dressed up?" he asked guardedly.

"I was on a date."

Pure agony slammed into him. She'd been on a date? Though it didn't surprise him, it still elicited an unbearable wave of jealousy.

"Did you have a good time?" he muttered.

She took another step. "No."

He put on a neutral tone. "Sorry to hear that."

"Me too," she admitted.

Straightening her shoulders, she kept walking, this time making it all the way to him, pausing when their bodies were a foot apart. Her familiar scent floated into his nostrils. He forced himself not to inhale.

"I was really looking forward to having a good time tonight," she went on. "I got all dressed up, as you can see, and I wasn't even against the idea of going to bed with him. Don't usually do that on the first date, but you know, desperate times…"

Every muscle in his body ached. He felt like he was undergoing serious torture here. Along with the pain, anger collected in his gut, slowly spreading through his bloodstream. Was she purposely trying to hurt him? He knew she always spoke her mind, but this was borderline cruel.

"I have to go," he ground out.

Before he could move, a soft hand touched his arm. "I'm not finished," she said quietly.

"I don't want to hear the rest."

"Really? Because I was just getting to the apology part."

He eyed her dubiously. "Didn't fucking sound like it."

She sighed. "I had all these plans for tonight, Matt, but I couldn't go through with a damn thing. The date was awful. Not because of Tony. He was cute and nice and, sure, he didn't get my humor, but that hasn't stopped me from getting involved before. There was one problem, though."

"Yeah, what's that?" he said testily.

"He wasn't you."

Matt refused to react to the soft-spoken confession. "Sorry to hear that," he said again, shrugging her hand from his arm.

Savannah let her hands dangle at her sides. Something that resembled vulnerability entered her gray eyes. "I was wrong, Matt. I always thought it was better to have fun and focus on all those first thrills, but I don't want that anymore. When I was with Tony, the only time I felt anything remotely thrilling was when I thought about you."

He averted his gaze. Didn't want to listen to any of this. "Fuck, Savannah," he spat out. "Do you actually think I'm going to get back together just because you had a bad date with *some other guy*?"

"No, but I'm hoping you'll want to do it because I'm in love with you."

He didn't even blink. "Four days ago, I told you the same thing and you dumped me."

"I was an idiot." Her voice shook. "And you were right, I was scared. I've always believed I can't be in a successful relationship because all my past ones failed, so I avoided them. But I can't keep avoiding. You were right about something else too—when you meet the right person, it *can* work. And you're the right person, Superman."

His heart shifted at the familiar nickname. Feeling himself soften, he curled his fingers into fists again, determined not to give in to her. He'd told her he *loved* her, for chrissake. Put himself out there, only to get shot down like a fighter jet.

"You're the only man I've ever met who enjoys sex as much as I do," she continued, and though he wasn't looking at her, he could hear the smile in her voice. "You're the only man I've held more than ten minutes of conversation with, the only one I talked about my work with, the only one I went to bed smiling about. You're the only one, Matt."

Another squeeze of his heart. Shit, if she kept going like this, he was totally going to cave.

Reading the expression on his face, Savannah reached for him again, circling her fingers around his forearm. "Please give me another chance. I know I walked away from us, but I'm asking you not to do that. I promise you, I'll spend every second of every day proving to you that I mean everything I'm saying."

He slowly looked at her, and the sincerity shining on her face floored him. He might have brushed it off as a lie if it weren't for the naked shards of vulnerability in her eyes. Savannah Harte didn't do vulnerable. She didn't expose her emotions, same way he didn't like to expose his.

"You're serious," he said gruffly.

"As a heart attack," she whispered.

"You're in love with me."

"Yes." She bit her bottom lip. "And I hope you still feel the same way about me."

God help him, but he did. From the moment he'd met her, she'd gotten under his skin in a way no other woman ever had before. She'd made him laugh during a bank robbery. Her enthusiastic attitude toward sex had blown him away. After three weeks, he hadn't tired of her the way he always tired of the girls he hooked up with.

But she'd also broken his fucking heart, another thing no other woman had ever done.

Sensing his hesitation, Savannah reached into the small purple purse hanging off her shoulder. "I brought you something. I stopped by the shop to get it before I came here."

Matt fought his curiosity as she stuck her hand in the purse. He furrowed his brows when she held up a flower about three inches long with delicate white petals. "You brought me a flower?"

"It's a white violet."

Taking the fragile flower from her hands, Matt studied it for a moment, then smiled.

Savannah's mouth curved in an answering smile. "You know what it means, don't you?"

He nodded.

"Say it out loud," she murmured.

He spoke through the lump in his throat. "It means let's take a chance on happiness."

They both went silent, as Matt sifted through the emotions swimming inside him. He knew how difficult this was for her. She tried so damn hard to be fun and breezy, to keep everything surface-level, but she was laying everything on the line right now. She was giving him her heart.

"Okay," he said, his voice rough.

Her head shot up. "Okay?"

"Let's give it another try."

The joy that lit her eyes told him he'd made the right decision, especially since it mirrored the happiness that lightened his own heart. He'd met his match in Savannah. From day one, she'd intrigued and excited him. She'd made him laugh and turned him on and showed him that staying with one woman could be as exhilarating as any casual fling.

With a grin, he yanked her toward him and kissed her. The second their lips met, the sense of sheer *rightness* infused his body. He pushed his tongue through her parted lips and deepened the kiss, and they were both panting by the time they broke apart.

"What if you get bored of me?" he teased, brushing his lips along the sweet curve of her jaw.

"I won't." She tipped her head to meet his eyes. "What if you do?"

"Impossible." He nibbled on her earlobe, then bent closer and whispered, "Trust me. With us, darlin', nothing can *ever* be boring."

The End

About the Author

A *New York Times*, *USA Today* and *Wall Street Journal* bestselling author, Elle Kennedy grew up in the suburbs of Toronto, Ontario, and holds a BA in English from York University. From an early age, she knew she wanted to be a writer and actively began pursuing that dream when she was a teenager. She loves strong heroines and sexy alpha heroes, and just enough heat and danger to keep things interesting!

Elle loves to hear from her readers. Visit her website www.ellekennedy. com, and while you're there sign up for her newsletter to receive updates about upcoming books and exclusive excerpts. You can also find her on Facebook (ElleKennedyAuthor), Twitter (@ElleKennedy), or Instagram (@ElleKennedy33).

Are you ready to meet rookie Cash McCoy? Enjoy this excerpt from the first full-length novel in the Out of Uniform series, Feeling Hot...

SHE SLANTED HER HEAD. "WHAT LINE OF WORK ARE *YOU* IN?"

He hesitated for a beat, then said, "Security."

Fine, he was lying again, but he'd already escaped one navy groupie tonight and he wasn't looking for a repeat performance. Then again, this woman was so beautiful he might be willing to make an exception.

"Huh. I figured you'd say military. You give off a military vibe. I mean, look at that big, buff body of yours — it ought to be illegal."

He didn't miss the slight note of derision when she said the word *military.* "Got something against military men?" he asked lightly.

"Nope. I respect the hell out of them," she answered. "I just don't want to date them."

He frowned, a part of him wanting to admit he'd lied about his job, just to see how she'd react. But she kept talking before he could get a word in. "I bet you're good at security. Me, on the other hand? I suck at everything."

Cash smiled. "I don't believe that."

"It's true. That's why I always get fired. School was never my thing, so I didn't go to college. I have no interest in medicine like my mom, no distinguishable talents, no great passions. I like messing around with my camera and taking pictures, but that's just a hobby." Vulnerability flashed in her big blue eyes. "Do you think there's a certain age when you should have everything figured out? Because I just turned twenty-six, and I still have no idea what I want to do with my life."

He shrugged. "I think everyone figures stuff out at their own pace. Eventually you'll find yourself on the right path."

"I guess." Her shoulders sagged. "Maybe I should get into porn. According to some creepy producer who approached me on the street, I have the 'look' for it."

"You really got asked to do porn?" Well. Apparently he wasn't the only one who could totally picture this blue-eyed beauty in his own personal naked film.

"Yes, I really did," she said in a glum voice.

"Porn's an admirable profession," he said solemnly.

She pursed her lips in thought. "But my porn-star name sucks. You know how you're supposed to take the name of your first pet and pair it with the street you grew up on? Well, our dog's name was Boris and I grew up on Denton Street. Boris Denton. That sounds like a dictator."

"I'm not even going to ask why you'd name your dog Boris."

"That's my brother's doing." She fired him a curious look. "What would your porn name be?"

"I don't know. I never had any pets growing up." He shrugged again. "Besides, I've been told my real name sounds like a porn name anyway, so I guess I've already got one." He supplied his name before she could ask. "Cash McCoy."

She promptly shook her head. "That's not a porn name. That's cowboy all the way."

"Cowboy," he echoed dubiously.

"Hell yeah. Or maybe an actor." She clapped her hands together. "An actor who *plays* a cowboy. Can't you see it?" Her voice deepened to mimic the movie-man voice from the previews. "*One duel, one chance to avenge his pa's murder…Cash McCoy in…*High Noon Outlaw." She grinned at him. "Maybe that's what I should do—write the copy for movie trailers."

"I think you should stick to porn. *High Noon Outlaw* sounds like the worst movie on the planet."

As another peal of laughter left that Cupid's bow mouth of hers, lust slammed into his groin again. Damn, her lips were so damn sexy. Pink, ripe and utterly kissable. His mouth tingled, and he had to fight the urge to lean in and press his lips to hers. He was dying to know if she tasted as sweet as she looked. The kind of noises she'd make when their tongues touched.

"Why do you keep staring at my lips?"

Sheepish, he met her eyes, which were narrowed with distrust. "I can't help it. You have really nice lips."

"And let me guess, they'd look even nicer wrapped around your dick."

He choked out a laugh. "You said it, not me."

"But you were thinking it."

Yup, he sure was. And his cock seemed to enjoy the wicked thoughts running through Cash's mind — the big boy was harder than a baseball bat, pushing against his zipper and begging for some attention.

"So it's true, huh? Men really do think about sex like every other minute," she said in a wry voice.

"Afraid so," he confirmed.

Rolling her eyes, the blonde bombshell ran a hand through her hair, causing the scent of her shampoo to drift into his nose and wreak havoc on his senses. She smelled like cherries — man oh man, he loved cherries.

Make a move, McCoy.

His brain's order — or had that come from his cock? — called attention to the opportunity staring him square in the eye. Here he was, sitting in the dark with a beautiful woman and an erection — why the hell was he dilly-dallying?

"You know, I just had a thought," he drawled.

"Is that a new occurrence for you? Is your brain tingling?"

One of them is...

Cash fought a grin and slid across the couch, stopping when only a mere foot separated them. "See, you just got fired, which means you're upset. And I'm not the kind of man who walks away when he encounters a damsel in distress."

"Uh-huh. Go on."

"It's in my nature to want to ease that distress. Lucky for you, I know exactly how I can make you feel better."

"I'm sure you do." Her lips twitched as if she were holding back laughter. "So, pray tell, what will make me feel better?"

"A kiss."

"Ah." She paused. "I think I'll pass."

"You sure about that?"

He slid even closer, so that his thigh pressed into hers. The moment contact was made, a jolt of heat seared through his camo pants and scorched his skin. The blonde's eyes widened at his nearness, but she didn't scoot away. In fact, he was certain he glimpsed a flicker of desire in those baby-blues. And he'd definitely heard the hitch in her breath.

Oh, and look at that, the tip of her tongue was sweeping over her bottom lip.

Cash chuckled. "You totally want to kiss me."

Even in the darkness, he saw the blush staining her cheeks. "I do not."

"Yes you do. You licked your lips."

"So?"

"So that's a clear sign of anticipation." His voice took on a note of pure male arrogance. "You're dying for me to put my mouth on you. And don't think I forgot about your big, buff body comment. You're into me—don't bother denying it."

He expected her to deny it. He expected her to hop off the couch in indignation and tell him where to shove it.

What he *didn't* expect?

Getting mauled.

Before he could blink, two warm hands cupped his chin and yanked his head down, and then that sexy mouth collided with his in a hard, reckless kiss.

Oh yeah. *That's* what he was talkin' about.

Pick up your copy of *Feeling Hot* today!

CPSIA information can be obtained
at www.ICGtesting.com
Printed in the USA
LVHW012121070821
694771LV00010B/748